"I really, truly, want y

"Do you?" Angel looked up, straining to see his face in the shadowy light.

Jason did not answer. She put her hand on his chest, feeling the strong beat of his heart through the fine silk waistcoat. It sent the blood pulsing through her own body. Daringly, she leaned a little closer. With something like a groan, he lowered his head and kissed her. Not the chaste brush of the lips of previous occasions. This time his mouth crushed against hers, demanding a response. Angel's heart leaped as his arms came around her. He teased her lips apart and his tongue darted and danced against hers. Her bones turned to water. Hitherto unknown, unimagined sensations rippled through her and she clutched to his coat. She breathed in the scent of sandalwood from his skin. She felt lightheaded, almost faint, and there was an unfamiliar ache low in her body, a yearning for more. Much more.

She was about to slip her arms about his neck when he broke off the kiss.

"Enough now." His voice was ragged. He caught her hands and held them firm against his chest. "I shall be gone before you wake in the morning, but I wanted to kiss you goodbye. Something to remember while I am in London."

Remember? That kiss was burned into her heart.

Author Note

Celebrities today live their lives in the glare of publicity. It cannot have been that different for those members of the ton in Regency times. True, there were no cameras to capture their every move, but the newspapers and cartoons of the day never held back when lampooning the great and the good. Rumors and scandals also provided excellent entertainment in the salons and ballrooms of London society.

I wanted to create a duke, a private man who had been brought up with a strong sense of duty. As a widower, Jason must marry again. He has a daughter and stepdaughter who need a mother, houses that need a mistress. He also needs an heir. So who better than Angeline, his childhood friend? She is a young woman with no romantic illusions and a practical turn of mind. Angel is ready to take on all the challenges, because she believes the real Jason lies hidden beneath that cold and rather stern exterior. As his duchess, she does her best to draw him out, but her attempts seem to make everything worse, not better.

This story flew out of my head and onto the page, although it was not always easy helping Angel and Jason find their way through the maze of problems that beset their marriage.

I do hope you enjoy reading their journey as much as I enjoyed writing it.

WED IN HASTE TO THE DUKE

SARAH MALLORY

Recycling programs for this product may not exist in your area.

ISBN-13: 978-1-335-59618-5

Wed in Haste to the Duke

For questions and comments about the quality of this book, please contact us at CustomerService@Harlequin.com.

Harlequin Enterprises ULC
22 Adelaide St. West, 41st Floor
Toronto, Ontario M5H 4E3, Canada
www.Harlequin.com

Printed in U.S.A.

Sarah Mallory grew up in the West Country, England, telling stories. She moved to Yorkshire with her young family, but after nearly thirty years living in a farmhouse on the Pennines, she has now moved to live by the sea in Scotland. Sarah is an award-winning novelist with more than twenty books published by Harlequin Historical. She loves to hear from readers; you can reach her via her website at sarahmallory.com.

Books by Sarah Mallory

Harlequin Historical

Lairds of Ardvarrick

Forbidden to the Highland Laird
Rescued by Her Highland Soldier
The Laird's Runaway Wife

Saved from Disgrace

The Ton's Most Notorious Rake
Beauty and the Brooding Lord
The Highborn Housekeeper

The Duke's Secret Heir
Pursued for the Viscount's Vengeance
His Countess for a Week
The Mysterious Miss Fairchild
Cinderella and the Scarred Viscount
The Duke's Family for Christmas
The Night She Met the Duke
The Major and the Scandalous Widow
Snowbound with the Brooding Lord

Visit the Author Profile page
at Harlequin.com for more titles.

To the Quayistas,
writing buddies through thick and thin.

Chapter One

'What a glorious day for a wedding!'

Angeline Carlow gazed out of the window, little bubbles of excitement bursting within her.

'Aye, it is, miss, but you won't be ready for it if you don't hurry up and change,' retorted her maid.

'We have well over an hour before we need to leave,' replied Angeline. 'Besides, it is not important whether I am ready or not. No one will notice me. Everyone will be looking at the bride and groom.'

'But you will want to look your best, miss, so let's get on with it. Lady Tetchwick asked to see me before she leaves her room,' said Joan, dealing with the fastenings at the back of Angeline's new gown of shell-pink muslin. She added with a sniff, 'Her Ladyship might have her own very superior dresser now, but she isn't above asking her old maid to step in and help with the final touches.'

'Poor Alice, so anxious to show everyone here how fashionable she has become!' Angeline chuckled. 'How fortunate that Barnaby is marrying Meg, who lives in the same parish. It means our sister can show herself off to all her old neighbours. However, what *I* think is more important is that our own people from Goole Park will all be able to come to the church for the wedding. Many of you have watched us grow up. I am sure you all want to come and wish them well.'

'Well, of course we do, Miss Angeline, but there's a deal of work to do before any of us dare leave the house!'

Angeline knew it only too well. She had been up since dawn, smoothing the way. First she had pacified Mrs Penrith. The housekeeper had taken umbrage at the fact that Lord and Lady Tetchwick had brought their four children but only one nursemaid and expected one of the housemaids to fill the gap. Then there had been Cook to placate, Mama having changed her mind on the menu for the wedding breakfast so often that no one in the kitchens knew if they were coming or going. And in the preceding days she had taken on many of her mother's duties, since Mama had been so overwrought by all the preparations for her only son's wedding that she just could not cope with the usual day-to-day tasks.

'There.' Joan stood back at last and gave her mistress an appraising look. 'That's the best I can do for you, Miss Angeline. Pray do not go back into the nursery now, or those children will be creasing your gown or pulling at your hair, and *then* where shall we be?'

Angel laughed. 'We will be in the suds! Off you go now, Joan dear. I promised to look in on Mrs Penrith again before I leave, just to ensure all is in readiness for when the guests return here for the wedding breakfast.'

The maid went out and Angel stood for a moment, enjoying the solitude. Various sounds filtered through her door but nothing that signified alarm. She hoped now that she could relax and enjoy the wedding.

She set off down the grand staircase, but as she reached the landing she noticed a man in the sober garb of a personal servant carrying two portmanteaux and hurrying out of the hall. So their last and most important guest had arrived: Barnaby's groomsman, the Duke of Rotherton.

As Angel ascended the final stairs she saw him. He had already divested himself of his hat and, as he had his back to her, she was able to take in the raven-black hair and tall, athletic figure as he shrugged off his many-caped greatcoat and handed it to the waiting footman. Then he turned and saw her.

'Angel! Good day to you.'

Her heart gave a little skip of pleasure. She was inordinately pleased that he had not forgotten her pet name, only it sounded far more attractive when uttered in that deep, smooth voice. She went towards him, smiling and holding out her hand. 'I hope you had a good journey, Your Grace.'

'Excellent, thank you.' The Duke took her hand and saluted it. 'The roads were good and the weather fine.' He straightened. 'But you used to call me Jason.'

'When you were a grubby schoolboy!' She laughed, trying to ignore the sudden tingle of excitement that had rippled down her spine when his lips brushed her fingers. 'You are much changed.'

'Am I?' He subjected her to a compelling gaze from those slate-grey eyes. 'I recognised you instantly.'

Angel had been a skinny child, so it was hardly a compliment, but she let it go. Her eyes shifted to his severe coat and black neckcloth. He was in mourning for his beautiful wife, tragically killed when her phaeton had overturned, and she needed to say something.

'I know Papa wrote to you, but please allow me to offer my condolences.'

He put up a hand. 'Thank you, but that is not a subject for today.'

'Jason!'

The Duke raised his eyes and looked over her head as Barnaby's voice sounded from the stairs and the next minute her brother was beside them.

'What time do you call this, you rogue?'

'I thought I had made very good time.'

'You should have slept here last night, then I would have been sure of you.'

'As I wrote to tell you, I had business in the north.' Jason spread his hands, a faint smile touching his lips. 'But, as you see, I am here now and at your disposal.'

'You will barely have time to change before we set off for the church!'

'Nearly an hour,' he replied, glancing at the long-case clock. 'I am no dandy who takes all morning to tie his neckcloth! Adams will be laying out my clothes as we speak.'

'Then I will come with you to your room. We can talk while you dress,' said Barnaby, linking arms with him. As he led the Duke away he looked back. 'Make sure they have sent up hot water for His Grace, will you Angel? There's a good girl.'

She watched them walk off, her brother talking incessantly as they disappeared up the stairs, and a sudden sadness gripped her, much as it had twelve years ago. Jason Darvell had been just fifteen then and mourning his father and trying very hard to bear with his new situation as Duke. Her young heart had ached for him. She'd known how she would have felt if Papa had been taken from them so suddenly.

She had told Jason he had changed, but she thought it was not so much in appearance. He was taller now, of course, his face leaner, the rather hawkish features more pronounced, and his cheeks were dark with stubble. With his colouring, she guessed the shadow would remain, even when he was freshly shaved. But his near-black hair still fell forward over his brow as it had done when he was a boy. No, it was not in looks that he had changed, but the shyness she had noted in the boy had hardened into a cool reserve, she thought, setting off for the kitchens. It was as if he was determined to keep the world at a distance.

It was years since Jason had been at Goole Park, but it was just as it always had been, the faded grandeur of the old house, the cheerful bustle of servants who were efficient but not cowed into silence. Jason was relieved. His happiest memories were attached to this house.

Barnaby ushered him into a large apartment with a dressing room to one side, saying, 'Mama has given you the best guest chamber.' He waved towards the windows. 'You get the best views.'

'I am honoured, naturally, but I would have been very happy with my old bedchamber, near the schoolroom.'

'No chance of that,' Barnaby told him, grinning. 'Alice's brood are in residence up there.' He sobered and went on, 'I am very glad you could come, Jason. I mean, you are still in mourning. It is only six months since Lavinia died. I would have understood if—'

'Yes,' Jason said quickly, turning away from his friend. 'Do you think everyone will be scandalised?'

'No, no, you have buried yourself away from the world for too long. And it is not as if there will be dancing or anything like that while you are here. A quiet ceremony and a couple of days with the family will cause no comment at all.' Barnaby put a hand on his shoulder. 'But how are *you*, Jason? Truthfully, now.'

How was he? Jason considered. He had been stunned, when he'd first learned of the carriage accident that had killed his duchess. Saddened that such a gloriously beautiful and vivacious creature should come to a tragic end. But his main emotion? Relief that his nightmarish marriage was over.

He had loved Lavinia to distraction at first, and been wilfully blind to her greed and selfishness. Later, when it had become impossible to ignore her infidelities, he had chosen to look the other way. He had not been able to bring himself to put them both through the humiliation of a divorce. Everyone thought him a grieving widower and he had done nothing to disillusion them.

He gave a little shrug. 'I am well enough.'

'Aye.' For a moment Barnaby's fingers gripped his shoulder, then he smiled and nodded. 'Come along, then, let's get you changed. You ain't fit to be my groomsman in those dusty clothes! Where's that rascally man of yours?'

The little parish church was packed out with family, friends and neighbours of the bride and groom. When the service ended, everyone moved outside the church and Jason found himself standing next to Lord Goole.

'Never one for weddings,' the Viscount muttered, throwing him a conspiratorial glance. 'Always afraid someone is going to stand up and declare some just impediment, what? But there we are. My only son leg-shackled at last. And Meg's a fine gel…she'll make him a good wife.'

Jason saw the very moment the Viscount realised that he was talking to a recently widowed man, for he coughed nervously and quickly changed the subject.

'Well, well, it's very gratifying to see so many of our neighbours here. I suppose I must go and do the pretty, too, if you will excuse me, Your Grace…?'

He hurried off and Jason moved away from the crowd, content to stand and watch the proceedings. Everyone was now milling around the bride and groom and he was glad his rank precluded strangers approaching him. Since Lavinia's death he had concentrated on business matters, using his bereavement as an excuse to shut himself away. It felt disconcerting to be out in the world again.

At last the carriages appeared, and soon the Duke was travelling back to Goole Park with the rest of the guests invited to the wedding breakfast. Arriving at the house, he escorted an aged dowager duchess into the dining room and they were already seated by the time he spotted Angeline. She walked in, looking neat as a pin in a gown of shell-pink muslin, her dark hair pulled smoothly back and confined by a matching ribbon. She had given her arm to an elderly spinster and it occurred to him that almost everyone took precedence over an unmarried daughter. For all that, when he happened to catch her eye the cheerful smile she gave him seemed to fill the room with sunshine.

The wedding breakfast was finally over. Jason relaxed, knowing he had done his duty. When Barnaby and his bride disappeared to change into their travelling dress he moved out to the great hall with everyone else to wait for them, wondering how soon after their departure he could make his excuses and leave.

Lady Goole had invited him to remain at Goole Park for as long as he wished, but he had only committed himself to two nights. Now he thought even that was too long. Despite this happy occasion he found it difficult to make polite conversation with anyone. He had never been truly at ease with strangers and today was especially difficult. There were too many surreptitious glances and sly hints on the circumstances of his wife's death, a subject that had no place at a wedding.

The chatter in the hall suddenly increased. Jason looked

up to see Barnaby coming down the stairs with his new wife. Summoning a smile, he stepped forward to escort them out to the waiting carriage.

'So glad you could come,' Barnaby said again, as he helped his bride into the travelling chaise. 'And a thousand thanks for the use of your Brighton villa for our honeymoon. Meg is in raptures about it already.'

'I am indeed, Your Grace,' replied the lady, glancing shyly at Jason.

'I never use it now. I shall be glad to think it is occupied.'

Jason touched his hat to them both and closed the carriage door. As the driver whipped up the horses he glanced up at the clear blue sky. It was a fine April day. He had driven here in his curricle, and if he left now he could be back in London before dark.

'Well, thank heaven that is over!' exclaimed the Viscount, taking his arm. 'Come along inside, my boy. Such a long time since you were here…ten years at least! We've missed you, you know. My lady is eager to catch up. We think of you as part of our own family…'

Listening to the kindly words, it dawned on Jason that Lord and Lady Goole would be hurt beyond measure if he suddenly said he was going straight back to town. He could not do it. This went far deeper than duty. The Carlows had welcomed him into their home and shown him such care, such hospitality in the past, that it was impossible to cut his stay any shorter.

'And Brighton, eh?' The Viscount went on as he walked with Jason into the hall. 'Dashed good of you to lend them the house, my boy. Surprised you don't want it yourself, the place being such a fashionable haunt these days.'

'I never go there,' replied Jason. It had been a wedding

present for Lavinia, something she had set her heart on. 'In fact, I am thinking of selling it.'

'What?' The Viscount was scandalised. 'No, no, dear boy, you must not even think of it. It is early days, I know, but you will take another wife and she will no doubt want to enjoy the Brighton society. And don't forget your children. They need a mother.'

'The girls are very well cared for in Kent,' he said shortly. 'And I shall not take another wife.'

Even before he'd married Lavinia she had set up the establishment there for her own daughter, Rose, and when Nell had been still a baby she had persuaded Jason to agree to the child joining her stepsister. Not that he had needed much persuading. His own upbringing had been much lonelier, living at Rotherton with only the servants for company. His duchess had maintained that she could not live with children in the house and Jason, besotted with his new wife, had agreed.

He was glad now that they had never been witness to their mother's profligacy or her lovers.

He felt the bile rising at the thought of his disastrous marriage and suppressed a shudder. Once had been enough.

'Not take another wife?' The Viscount turned to stare at him. 'Now, that, my boy, is out of the question!'

He pulled Jason away into one corner, where they would not be overheard.

'Oh, I know it is early days yet, and you are still in mourning, but you need an heir, my boy. That must be faced, and I would be a poor friend to you if I didn't say so. Surely you do not want that good-for-nothing cousin of yours stepping into your shoes? I am sorry, Your Grace, but it just won't do! Tobias Knowsley is a spendthrift. He will run through your fortune before you are cold in your grave. Not that it is any business of mine,' he added hastily, after a glance at Jason's face. 'But I have known you since you were a boy, and I have only your best interests at heart. I cannot believe you would want Knowsley taking up residence at Rotherton!'

Lord Goole was right. The idea of Toby Knowsley inheriting Rotherton was not something Jason liked to contemplate, but neither did he want to discuss it. He wished he might retire to his room, but a moment's reflection told him that would cause just the sort of comment he most loathed. *Poor Rotherton, the grieving widower.* Or the cuckold. Confound it, he hated being pitied.

He forced himself not to frown and instead summoned up a tight smile. 'You are quite right, sir, and a fount of wisdom, as always.' He waved towards the drawing room. 'We should go in, I think.'

For the sake of his hosts Jason exerted himself to speak with everyone. He liked the Carlows. They were the nearest thing to a family he had ever known. His mother had died when he was a baby and the widowed Duke had little time for his only son. Once he was sent off to school Jason saw even less of his father. The old Duke was rarely at Rotherton for the holidays, and Jason was allowed to spend time at Goole Park with his new friend Barnaby and his happy, loving family.

One protracted circuit of the room was more society than the Duke had experienced for the past six months. He needed a respite. Noting that the long windows leading out onto a terrace had been thrown open, to make the most of the warm spring day, Jason made his way towards them with a nod here, a few words there, until finally he could escape.

There were several people on the terrace and a few more strolling around the flower gardens, but he avoided them all, running lightly down the shallow steps to the lawn and away from the house. No one approached him, but that was no surprise. After all, everyone knew he was still in mourning. What was more natural than that he should wish to spend some time alone?

He was familiar with the gardens and walked on past the rose garden and through an avenue of yews, which led to the shrubbery. It was just as he remembered, surrounded by high hedges and with a well-tended path winding its way between the bushes and with the occasional bench where one might rest. It was quiet, too, which he wanted.

He was just thinking it unlikely any of the guests would venture this far from the house when he heard someone singing. It was a female voice, soft and melodic, crooning a lullaby. Jason had no idea who it might be and, intrigued, he walked around the next curve of the path and came upon Angeline.

She was sitting on a wooden bench and rocking a sleeping baby in her arms. Her head was bent over the child and one glossy dark curl had escaped from its pins and was hanging down over her shoulder. She looked up and he stopped.

'Excuse me.' He felt like an intruder. 'I did not know it was you, I have never heard you sing before.'

She chuckled. 'I rarely do so in company! My little nephew was fractious and Alice needed someone to take him away, because the poor nursemaid was trying to get the others to sleep.'

Her response was so natural that the years fell away. He was a schoolboy again, talking with his friend's little sister.

He sat down beside her. 'Why could Alice not do it?'

'She is required in the drawing room.'

'And you are not?' He frowned. 'Do you *like* children?'

'You sound surprised.' She giggled. 'I like them well enough, and I am content to be out here with the baby, away from all the crowds and chatter. This is quite relaxing after such a busy day.'

'I think you are a very good aunt.'

'I am useful—which makes me of some consequence here, I hope.' That sounded a trifle dispirited, but the next moment she was smiling. 'And how are your daughters, Your Grace?'

His daughters! Jason felt a stab of conscience. His occasional visits to the children were stilted, uncomfortable. His own fault, of course. He had no idea what to do when he saw them.

'I hope you left them well,' Angel said now.

'Yes, they were very well when I last saw them.'

'I am sure they have been a great solace to you this past year.'

He nodded. The girls reminded him too much of their mother, when all he wanted to do was forget.

'Mama and Papa are so happy you came,' she went on. 'It has been such a long time since you visited Goole Park. Why, it must be all of twelve years!'

Jason was well aware of it. After his marriage he had only seen Barnaby in town or at various house parties. He had never brought his wife to Goole Park. Looking back, he knew now he had been afraid of spoiling his happy childhood memories by sharing the place with Lavinia.

He said, 'Well, I am here now.'

'Yes, for a mere two days!' She shook her head at him and he grinned.

'I know, Angel. Hardly long enough to discover everything you have done since we last met.'

'Oh, *I* have done very little,' she replied, 'Save my come-out.'

'Ah, I missed that,' he said apologetically.

'Yes, you and the Duchess were in Paris, I think.'

'That's right. For the short-lived peace.' He did not want to think about that time, when he had watched his wife flirting with every officer in sight. 'How did you enjoy it, all those gowns and parties?'

There was the faintest hesitation before she replied.

'Well enough, but I was a sad disappointment to Mama. I ended the season without one offer of marriage.'

'What? Not one?' He sat back, his brows raised in surprise. 'You did not fall in love with anyone?'

She flushed. 'I did not say that.'

Her arms tightened around the sleeping baby, and there was such a look of sadness in her countenance that he was tempted to ask what had happened.

But before he could speak she had shaken it off and said cheerfully, 'Suffice to say that it cured me of romantic love for ever! I did not go to town again, but I was not sorry for it. It was Lettie's turn the next year, you see, and Alice was increasing.'

He frowned. 'I do not understand...how should that affect you?'

'Because Mama could not be in two places at once. She took Lettie to town while I went off to Shropshire, to stay with Alice. It was not the happiest time. My brother-in-law is very good-natured, but has not an ounce of sense! He fretted so when the baby was born that I wished he had gone off to the races or something with his friends, instead of fussing around Alice and insisting that his own doctor should be present at the birth.' She laughed at the memory. 'I spent most of my time smoothing the midwife's ruffled feathers. She was perfectly competent, but took exception to having her every action questioned.'

'What a horrid situation for you,' he said.

'It was, but I should have disliked London a great deal

more!' There was an engaging twinkle in her brown eyes. 'Lettie was a hit, you see. She received no less than *two* very respectable offers before Marland came along, and would have taken great pleasure in crowing over her achievements if I had been there. You must remember what a little beast she could be, always trying to belittle others.'

He shook his head. 'I remember very little about her, or Alice. To me they were only Barnaby's disapproving sisters. In fact, you are the only one I recall with any clarity.'

'I am?' She blushed, but went on cheerfully, 'I expect that's because I was a nuisance. Quite a little hoyden, Barnaby says. I am sorry if you found me tiresome, but I always enjoyed your visits. It still gives me a great deal of pleasure to look back on them whenever I am in low spirits.'

How could she have enjoyed being teased and scolded for being in the way?

She rose. 'The sun is setting. I must get little Henry back to the nursery.'

'And then will you return to the drawing room?'

'Alas, no. I promised the housekeeper I would help with preparations for supper. One of the kitchen maids has broken her arm and they cannot manage without someone to help carry the food upstairs.' She gave him a little nod. 'Goodnight, Your Grace.'

'Jason,' he reminded her.

For a moment she regarded him, her brown eyes serious and dark as sable now. Then she gave another little nod and walked away.

He watched her, noting the sway of her hips, the way the thin muslin clung to her shapely limbs. He'd been wrong when he'd said she hadn't changed. She was still petite, and she looked younger than her twenty-four years, but there was definitely a womanly figure beneath that pink gown.

When Jason had first visited Goole Park, Angel had been too young to join in their games, but she was clever and quick-witted and hung around them like a shadow, despite their teasing. How old had she been when he last saw her? Twelve? Thirteen? He folded his arms, smiling. By then she was a fearless rider, had a talent for billiards, and she'd also proved a useful extra when they played cricket.

Another memory returned: his last visit to Goole Park. He had just buried his father, and his guardian, an uncle he barely knew, informed him that he would not be going back to school but would finish his education at Rotherton, under the aegis of a tutor. He was the Duke now, his uncle reminded him, and must learn to act like one.

He had been granted one final holiday: a few precious weeks with Barnaby and his family.

When the time came to leave, Jason recalled being assailed by the enormity of the changes to his life. On his way to the drawing room before that final dinner he'd stopped. He'd wanted to turn and run. To hide from everyone and everything. His grief, the sympathy of this kind family, but mostly from the responsibilities that lay ahead for him. He remembered it so vividly now. He was standing outside the door, trying to screw up the courage to re-join the family, when little Angel appeared. She had tucked her hand into his and gone with him into the room.

That was the last time they had met. He had been swept away to take up his new life and never saw her again. Rarely thought of her. Until today.

When Jason finally returned to the drawing room, the wedding guests had departed and only the family were left. This comprised the Viscount and his lady, plus their eldest daughter Alice and her husband Sir Humphrey Tetchwick, who had travelled with their children from their estate in Shropshire for the wedding. The final couple was the Carlows' youngest child, Lettie, and her husband Lord Marland, who lived but two miles away.

Angel had not reappeared. She and Barnaby had been his constant companions on previous visits and he was painfully aware of their absence. His instinct was to withdraw again, but he fought it down and strolled across to take a seat beside Lady Goole.

'We are so pleased to see you here again, Your Grace,' remarked Lady Goole. 'You have been away from Hertfordshire for far too long. I hope you mean to remedy that now.'

'Thank you, ma'am, I shall try to do so.'

'And when you do come again we will hold a little party for you,' declared Lady Marland. 'Nothing too grand. I am sure you must have your fill of ceremony when you are in town! No, this will be a cosy affair, just friends and neighbours.'

'And perhaps a little dancing,' added Alice. 'If you can promise me dancing, Lettie, then we will most definitely come. And I shall bring Sir Humphrey's sisters with me, too. They are both diamonds, in their own way. Young ladies always add lustre to such parties, do you not agree, Your Grace?'

Jason inclined his head but did not reply. He could see the calculation going on behind the lady's smile. She was hoping to provide him with his next bride. When it was clear he was not to be drawn on the subject, the conversation moved on. They began to discuss their plans for the following day.

'I suggest a ride,' said Marland, helping himself to a pinch of snuff from a silver box. 'The fine weather looks set to hold for another day.'

'Oh, what a splendid idea, my love!' exclaimed Lettie. 'I should so enjoy that, but can we mount everyone?'

'Alice and Sir Humphrey can have our hacks,' declared Lady Goole. 'Your father and I plan a very quiet day at home tomorrow, after the rigours of the wedding.'

Alice sighed. 'I would dearly love to ride out with you, but alas little Henry is proving very difficult. Nurse says he is teething, which makes him fractious, and she cannot manage all four children. I told Sir Humphrey we should bring the second nurserymaid but he would not be moved.'

'If my wife had her way we would have hired another coach to accommodate everyone,' replied her loving spouse, laughing.

'Well, I wish we had,' retorted Alice. 'I have not had a moment to myself. Why, I spent a good half-hour in the nursery with the children yesterday, while everyone else was enjoying themselves!'

'Angel can help Nurse while you are gone,' put in Lettie.

'Oh, yes. What a good idea, Sister,' said Alice, much struck. 'The children mind her so much better than I.'

Unable to stop himself, Jason said, 'But surely Miss Carlow will want to ride out too.'

'Oh, no,' replied Lettie, who was, in Jason's opinion, a very managing female. 'Angel is going to distribute the wedding cake to our neighbours. That and helping with the children will fill her day very nicely.'

'There you are, then, it is all settled.' Lord Marland gave his wife an approving smile before turning to Jason. 'You will be joining us I hope, Your Grace? I have a very good second hunter who will be up to your weight. He will give you a good day's sport, I am sure.'

'Thank you, but I have other plans. It is such a long time since I was at Goole Park. I want to reacquaint myself with the grounds here. On foot,' he added firmly, when he saw Lady Marland was about to speak.

'I have had several more paths opened up in the park since you were last here, Duke,' said Lord Goole. 'You will find the vistas from the hill are well worth the walk.'

'Thank you. I shall make sure I go there.'

Soon after that the Marlands' carriage was called and Jason took the opportunity to bid everyone goodnight and escape to his room. He had had enough company for one day, and he was still irritated by Lady Tetchwick's clumsy attempts at matchmaking.

By the time he climbed into his bed, the sheets comfortably warmed beforehand, Jason's ill temper had abated. He lay on his back, hands behind his head, and considered his situation. As a duke without an heir he knew the world would expect him to marry again, but Lavinia had only been dead six months. He had hoped everyone would give him at least a year before they began to throw prospective brides in his way. But it was not only Alice scheming to marry him off. He had already received hints in letters from various members of his family.

He could not deny that he had made a mull of it the first time, marrying for love and against their wishes. And afterwards he had been too proud to admit his mistake in taking for his duchess a widow eight years his senior, a woman with a voracious appetite for lovers.

If Lavinia had provided him with a son, an heir, then perhaps he might have been able to avoid a second marriage, but no more than Viscount Goole did he want to see Toby Knowsley take his place. And if Knowsley predeceased him—which, given his dissolute lifestyle, Jason thought highly likely—then those next in line were no better.

A sigh escaped him. Much as he disliked the idea, it was his duty to marry. He would have to take a bride. But this time it would be purely for convenience. Love would have no place in his next marriage.

Having resolved that issue, Jason thought sleep would come easily, but another source of disquiet intruded. He could not forget the sisters' casual disposal of Angel's time. Not just Alice and Lettie, but Barnaby, too, he thought, recalling how his friend had ordered Angel to make sure hot water was fetched up for their guest. He had barely seen Angel since his arrival, she was always busy with some household task or running errands for her family.

Irritably he turned over and closed his eyes. It was no wonder she looked back so fondly to her childhood. They had turned the poor girl into a drudge.

Chapter Two

Fortune smiled on Goole Park's guests the following day. The sun was shining, although a fresh spring breeze had replaced yesterday's unseasonal heat. The Tetchwicks were in high spirits at breakfast as they discussed their forthcoming outing.

'What time do you expect to return?' asked Angel.

'Oh, Lord, I have no idea,' Alice replied. 'We are riding over to Marland Hall to meet up with Lettie and her husband, and we shall doubtless stop at the Crown for refreshments before we return. Do not expect to see us before dinner.'

'Well, I hope you all enjoy yourselves,' declared the Viscount, as his daughter and son-in-law hurried away. He rose, preparing to take himself off to his study to read his newspaper, but first he turned to the Duke. 'And you, my boy. You said you would be walking the grounds today, did you not? I shall not stand on ceremony with you, Jason. You may come and go as you choose. But if you wish for company I am at your disposal.'

'Thank you, my lord, I am quite happy to explore alone. Unless Miss Angeline would like to come with me?'

Angel felt a rush of pleasure at the unexpected invitation and it was with real regret that she declined, citing her busy day.

Her mother had risen, and was about to follow the Viscount from the room, but now she stopped.

'My dear, I am sure we can do without you for a few hours, if His Grace wishes you to go with him.'

'His Grace is very kind,' replied Angel. 'However, I have other commitments today.'

Her mother gave a soft tut but she did not stay to argue, and Angeline was left alone at the breakfast table with the Duke. She felt a little disappointed that Mama had not insisted she accompany Jason. Everything could have been rearranged with a little effort. But it was clear that the Viscountess saw the invitation as mere courtesy. Which it was, of course.

'It is chastening to think I am of less importance than cake...'

Angeline started. 'Your Grace?'

'I understand you are distributing the bride cake today.'

'Oh...that.' She saw the smile lurking in his rather hard grey eyes and relaxed, knowing he was not really offended. 'Yes, but also I am helping Nurse with the children, and I cannot leave her to cope with four of them alone.'

'No, of course not.' He nodded and put down his napkin. 'I shall leave you to your domestic duties, then.'

With a final nod he left the room and Angel smothered a sigh. The Duke's invitation had come as a surprise, and she would dearly like to have gone with him. However, a moment's reflection convinced her that he had only offered out of kindness. They had nothing in common now. She had no doubt that he would be bored within a half-hour of setting out.

Perhaps an hour, she amended. After all, she was reasonably well educated. Yet there was no escaping the fact that she was a spinster of four-and-twenty, living quietly in Hertfordshire. She cringed inwardly at the thought of the worldly-wise Duke of Rotherton exerting himself to make idle conversation with her. That was something neither of them would enjoy, she decided, and was therefore best avoided.

Jason left the house a short time later, but before heading off on his walk he went to the stables. The head groom there remembered him from his schooldays and was only too delighted to show him the changes, pointing out with some pride the matched pair Lord Goole had recently purchased for his curricle.

'Of course, my lord and lady's hacks are out today, but you'd be pleased with their quality, too, Your Grace.'

'I am sure I would,' said Jason. He walked up to the loose box where a glossy chestnut gelding was looking out, watching him with an intelligent eye.

'And who rides this handsome fellow?' he asked.

'That's Apollo, Your Grace. Miss Angel's horse.'

'She does still ride, then?' He posed the question casually as he scratched the horse's head.

'Oh, aye, that she does. Whenever she can. Your Grace can't have forgotten what a clipping rider she was.'

'No, I haven't forgotten.'

With a final word to the groom Jason set off on his walk, remembering the wild gallops he had enjoyed with Barnaby and Angel, riding across this very park. Such happy, carefree times they had been, before he had become Duke. After that his life had become one of duty and restraint, hiding all emotion.

It was hunger that sent Jason back to the house some hours later. In the past he would have gone to the kitchens and cajoled Cook into finding him something to eat, to keep him going until dinner time. Now, as Duke, he need do no more than lift a finger and his slightest request would be carried out, but he was not inclined to lift that finger. He really wanted to make his way around to the kitchen door and take pot luck there, but he had visions of the kitchen staff being overwhelmed by His Grace the Duke of Rotherton invading their domain. No, that would make them too uncomfortable. He would enter the house the same way he had come out—through the garden door.

He stepped into the inner hall just as Angel was coming down the stone staircase. She smiled when she saw him.

'Did you enjoy your walk, Your Grace?'

'Very much. Have you finished delivering all the cake?'

'Why, yes. I took the gig out this morning for that purpose, and since then I have been in the nursery with my niece and nephews. We did not expect to see you for another hour at least.'

'I was driven back by the need for food.' He grinned as his stomach rumbled. 'I do not believe I can last until dinner time.'

'I should think not.' She indicated the tray she was carrying. 'I am on my way to the kitchens now. I will have something sent up—'

'No.' He put up his hands. 'You do not need to wait upon me. I can easily deal with the matter.'

'But why send another servant running up and down when I am already on my way?'

Jason hesitated. 'Your logic is irrefutable, but by that reasoning I could just as easily go myself.'

'You could indeed,' she agreed cordially. 'If you are that hungry then I suggest you follow me now and we will have you fed in a trice!' She had descended the final few steps and now stood in front of him, smiling. 'We used to raid the kitchens quite often when we were children, so will you come?'

The walk in the sunshine had raised his spirits and her words made him laugh with genuine pleasure, something he had not done for a long time.

'How can I refuse?'

He followed Angel into the nether regions of the house, where she stopped at the servants' hall.

'You had best sit down in there while I take these dishes to the scullery. Poor Cook will go off in a fit of apoplexy if she finds you in the kitchen.'

'Yes, I had thought as much.'

He went into the empty hall and sat down at the scrubbed table while Angel disappeared with her tray. She returned in a very short time with a jug and two tankards, and was followed by a kitchen maid carrying a second, larger tray of dishes.

'Thank you, Maria. Do put the tray down before you try to curtsy to His Grace, there's a good girl.' Angel waited until the maid had left her tray and departed before she set down her own burden. 'I thought you might prefer small beer to quench your thirst after your exertions.'

'And you are going to join me?'

'I really cannot leave you here on your own,' she explained, twinkling at him. 'You would have everyone from the boot boy to the laundrymaid coming to gawp at you and I did not think you would like that. You saw the effect you had on Maria.'

'I was afraid the poor girl was going to faint off.'

Angel laughed. 'She will regale all her friends with the story of how she waited on a duke!' She set the food out before him while he poured the ale. 'There is some of last night's game pie, and a little bread and butter, and cheese with pickles. Simple fare, but you were used to enjoy it.'

'Yes! I remember coming in here with you and Barnaby,

famished from playing out of doors all morning.' He raised his tankard to her. 'Those were good times, Angel.'

'They were, weren't they?' She reached over and stole a morsel of cheese from his plate.

'There is plenty for two,' he said.

'Thank you, but no. I had luncheon with the children, and I am not really hungry, but I could not resist.'

This was the Angel he remembered, her brown eyes shining with mischief and her hair escaping from its pins. They were totally at ease together and conversation flowed, although Jason could never afterwards recall what they talked about. However, he did remember the feeling of disappointment when he had eaten his fill and Angel told him it was time to go.

'It cannot be time to change for dinner just yet.'

'No, but the flowers in the morning room need replacing, and I want to see what pots we have in bloom in the orangery.'

'Surely someone else can do that,' he said, following her out of the room.

'They could, of course, but I *like* to choose the plants.'

'You do too much.'

'I enjoy being busy.'

When they arrived back at the inner hall he stopped her. 'Tell me honestly. Would you not rather be out riding today?'

Jason watched her carefully. He noted the slight hesitation before she shook her head.

'I was needed here.'

'That is not what I asked.'

Angel was subjected to a fierce scrutiny from those rather hard grey eyes and, seeing the stubborn set to his mouth, she knew Jason would take nothing less than the truth. She chose her next words with care.

'I admit I should have liked to be given the choice. But that does not mean I am unhappy—you must never think that.' He did not look convinced and she went on. 'I enjoyed sitting below stairs with you, Your Grace. It was just like we used to do, when you and Barnaby were here for the holidays.'

'Aye. It is a pity we had to grow up.'

There was a wealth of sadness behind his words. Angel wanted to ask him what he meant by it, but the moment passed in a heartbeat and he waved her away.

'I have taken up far too much of your time. Go and choose your plants, Angeline. We will meet again at dinner.'

Jason went up to his room where he found Adams already preparing a bath for him.

'How the devil did you know I was back?' he demanded.

'One of the servants informed me that you were below stairs,' replied the valet.

Jason scowled. He did not need to ask who had sent the lackey, or who had ordered the water to be heated. Angel. From what he had seen so far, she practically ran the household at Goole Park.

If only Rotherton had such a mistress.

The thought caught Jason unawares. He looked about, as if the voice had come from somewhere in the room, rather than inside his own head. Angel considered everyone's comfort before her own, but how would it be if she had her own establishment? If she could please herself over more than the choice of flowers…

'Well, Your Grace, will you bathe now, before the water grows cold?'

'What? Oh, yes. Yes.'

* * *

An hour later he was dressed in his evening coat and pantaloons and making his way to the drawing room when he met Lady Goole, coming up the stairs and looking flustered.

'Oh, Your Grace, I am most sorry to tell you, but Alice and Sir Humphrey have only now returned from their riding expedition. I have just sent word to the kitchen to put dinner back an hour.'

She looked so upset that Jason quickly reassured her he was not inconvenienced in the slightest.

'I can easily amuse myself for an hour,' he told her, and she hurried on, still murmuring disjointed apologies.

'There is already a good fire in the drawing room, if you wish to sit in there.' Angel was standing at the foot of the stairs. 'It is surprising how chill the house can become of an evening.'

'I was thinking I might go to the library and find a book.' He carried on down the stairs, glancing at the apron she wore over her gown. 'What are you going to do?'

'The gardener has brought in several flowering pots for the morning room and I have yet to arrange them.' She waved him away, very much as he had done to her, earlier. 'Go and find your book, but do take it to the drawing room to read. You will be far more comfortable there, and no one will disturb you.'

With a smile she left him, and Jason went off on his quest. But although the Viscount's library was well stocked he could find nothing to distract him from an idea that had been growing within him all morning. It was his duty as Duke of Rotherton to marry again, but the idea of returning to Society's Marriage Mart was abhorrent. Eligible females would be paraded before him and he would be obliged to choose one, but they would be strangers. There was no guarantee of lasting happiness.

How much better, then, to marry Angel, his childhood friend? They understood one another, and neither of them had any illusions of romance. It would be the ideal solution for both of them. What could possibly go wrong?

Angeline was alone in the morning room and surveying a row of Delft pots on a side table. She looked around as he came in.

'I decided upon hyacinths. What do you think?'

'Yes, very pretty. Angel—'

'They are not very showy, but they look well against the blue and white of the pots.'

'Angel, forget about the flowers a moment. I want to talk to you.'

'Yes, of course.' She turned to him, her brows raised. 'Is something wrong?'

'No, nothing like that.' He began to pace the room, trying to order his thoughts. At last he came to stand before her. 'Angeline, will you marry me?'

Her cheeks paled, making her dark eyes look even larger. She said slowly, 'You should ask Papa first.'

'I do not want to marry your father.' He winced at the frivolity of his response, but he saw the slight flicker of her eyelids, a lessoning of tension in her slight frame. He said, 'You are a woman with a mind of your own, Angel. It is what *you* want that matters. I thought…' He searched for the right words. 'I have seen how much you do here for everyone. Too much. You should have a house of your own, rather than running your parents' establishment.'

Silence. Angel had turned away from him and was studying the flowers.

'That is a very kind offer, Your Grace, but…' She straightened one of the pots, moving it barely an inch. 'I do not understand why you should be asking me this. You have pointed out the advantages to *me*, but what about you? What has prompted you to make this offer?'

She turned and fixed Jason with her disconcertingly frank gaze. He remembered as a child she had always been honest and forthright. Nothing missish in her behaviour. He was relieved they could discuss the matter so sensibly.

He smiled. 'You must not think I am doing this purely for your sake. Quite the contrary, in fact. I am being very selfish. I must marry again. I need an heir.' She blushed violently and he said quickly, 'Not immediately, of course. You may be sure I shall not rush you on that! We have always been good friends, Angel, so let me be perfectly honest with you. As long as I have no wife everyone, my family, friends and even complete strangers, will be trying to find one for me. Indeed, it has started already,' he added, thinking of his very first evening at Goole Park. He stepped closer and took her hands. 'I need a wife and I can think of no one I would prefer to have at my side. I believe we would deal very well together, you and I. What do you say? Will you be my duchess?'

'Your Grace does me great honour,' she said, gently pulling her hands free. 'But I regret I must refuse.'

'Refuse! May I ask why?'

'You have been widowed for less than a year. You cannot know what you want yet. You may meet someone else and fall in love again. Someone beautiful and worldly, like your first wife.'

Never! I shall not make that mistake again.

He shook his head. 'No. You have already said you are done with love; I, too, have no wish to suffer from it ever again. Love is a foolish emotion, only designed to cause pain to the unwary. But I am sincerely fond of you, Angel. This would be a marriage of convenience for both of us. You have always been a very practical person. What could be more sensible, more comfortable, than two friends making their life together? I think, no, I am *sure* we can be happy.'

'Are you, Jason?'

It was the first time since he had arrived that she had used his name and he was encouraged by it.

He said, 'I am. Most sincerely. As my duchess you would have my houses to oversee, and the gardens too, if that is your interest. You can be as busy as you want to be, but it will not be all work. You will be able to ride out whenever you please and have your own carriage too, as well as enough pin money to spend as you wish.' He stopped and took a deep breath. 'You would be your own mistress, Angel. You could live the life that *you* want.'

He waited, hoping he had done enough to reassure her.

Angel's mind and her emotions were in turmoil. It was an effort to think, to speak calmly. They had not seen each other since they were children. She knew so little about him.

In your heart you know him very well!

She quickly squashed that rebellious thought. This was far too important for such childish fantasies. Her own happiness and Jason's were at stake. She was thankful he had not made any pretence about loving her. The hero worship she had felt for Jason as a child was no basis for marriage.

'No,' she said again. 'It would not work, Your Grace.'

'But why? Why do you say that?'

He raked his fingers through his hair, pushing it back from his brow in frustration. It was a gesture she knew well, a reminder of the boy she had known. But Jason Darvell was not a child any longer. He was a man. A duke, no less, with all the responsibilities and obligations the title carried.

'I am very fond of you, Angel,' he said now. 'I always have been. And I think—I hope—you feel the same for me?'

'We were happy enough together as children,' she admitted.

'Exactly! And we can be happy together now. I would not be saying any of this if I was not sure of it. I am offering you independence, Angel. A home of your own. Money, servants, a secure place in society where you will not be the last in consequence. We can travel, if you wish, and there are all the diversions of London to enjoy: lectures, art exhibitions, the theatre. Everything your heart desires.'

Except your love.

Angel was surprised and shocked at her silent *cri de coeur.* Surely she couldn't be in love with Jason Darvell? At least, not in a meaningful way. She was in love with a memory… the boy he had been.

She gave her head a little shake and with a sigh he turned away from her.

'I have seen the way you are treated here,' he said, walking over to the window. 'You are taken for granted. Your sisters want you to be an aunt to their children, your mother wants a companion. Even Barnaby treats you like a servant! I want you to be yourself, Angel. To live as *you* wish and not to be at everyone's beck and call. Rotherton needs a mistress. There would be duties, of course, but you would be in charge. You would have free rein to order things as you wish. The same applies to my other properties. Naturally we would discuss any major changes to ensure we are in agreement, but as my duchess your opinion will be valued. *You* will be valued.' He turned to face her again. 'I shall do everything in my power to make you happy, Angeline, if you will do me the honour of becoming my wife.'

With his back to the light she could not see his expression, but there was no mistaking his sincerity. She felt shaken, unnerved.

Her eyes shifted to the hyacinths. 'I came in here to arrange the flowerpots.'

'Would you not rather be arranging your own flowers, in your own morning room?'

She watched him come back across the room towards her. He was dressed with severe simplicity, his shirt and white waistcoat in stark contrast to the black coat and pantaloons. His black hair was slightly dishevelled now, but she preferred it that way. It suited him. She knew some people found him intimidating. He had a commanding presence and a forthright way of speaking, plus those rather harsh, aquiline features, but she recognised the man behind that rather forbidding exterior. She had seen the smile lurking in those hooded eyes and the slight lift at the corners of his mouth when he was amused.

Something shifted inside her. He would be a kind, considerate husband. They were friends already, and wasn't it possible that might turn to love in time?

'Do you truly believe we can be happy, Jason?'

'I do.' He took her hands again. 'Say yes, Angel. Say you will marry me.'

She swallowed, gripping his fingers to steady herself as the ground seemed to sway beneath her feet.

'Very well.' It was a struggle to speak. Her voice seemed to be coming from a long way away. 'Yes, I will marry you.'

And with that, the darkness closed in.

Jason caught Angel as she collapsed. Going over to the sofa, he gently put her down and sat beside her, chafing her hands until she stirred.

'I beg your pardon.' She struggled to sit up. 'I do not know what came over me.'

'Easy now,' he murmured, pushing her back against the cushions. 'Lie still for a moment. You fainted, that is all.' A rueful smile tugged at the corners of his mouth. 'Not quite the reaction I had hoped for. Do you remember my asking you to marry me?'

'Yes.' She looked up at him shyly. 'Were…were you teasing me?'

'No! How can you think I would jest about something like that? I was in earnest. And you agreed.' He stopped rubbing her hands and held them together between his own. 'But you must be sure, Angel. Did you mean it when you said yes?'

She nodded. 'I did.'

Relief flooded through Jason. Relief and a surprising jolt of happiness. He had thought she would not hesitate to accept him, and her refusal had thrown him completely off-balance. He had then made every effort to persuade her to change her mind—not because she had dented his pride, but because at that moment it had been borne in upon him how much he wanted this marriage. He felt as if the barrier he had built up around himself had cracked a little.

He squeezed her fingers and lifted her hands, one after the other, to his lips.

'You have made me the happiest of men.' He berated himself for not finding a more original response, but at this moment it was all he could think of. 'Shall I fetch you a glass of water, or some wine?'

'No, nothing, thank you, Your Grace.'

'Jason.'

'Jason.' She gave him a little smile. 'You do not need to sit with me. I shall be very well again in a moment. In fact, I should like to be alone, I think.'

'If you are sure… Would you like me to call your maid?'

'No, thank you. I shall be perfectly well if I sit quietly for a little while.'

'Then, with your permission, I will go and find your father, to tell him the good news.' He hesitated. 'Would you object if we announced it immediately?'

'N-no, not at all.'

She was looking a little dazed, but smiling still. He leaned in to kiss her cheek and went off to find the Viscount.

Angeline did not move after Jason had left her. Everything was silent, still. Like the quiet after a storm. She no longer felt faint, but the hope and certainty she had felt when she had accepted his offer had quite disappeared.

She lifted one hand to her cheek. The skin still burned where Jason had kissed it.

'Oh. What have I done?' she whispered to the empty room. 'What have I done?'

Chapter Three

Duchess! I am a duchess.

The words echoed in Angel's head as the carriage hurtled through the Surrey countryside, bowling along lanes where the hedgerows were white with May blossom. She was the Duchess of Rotherton. How was that possible?

It was barely one month since Jason had asked her to marry him. After the initial shock and surprise of their betrothal, her family had risen nobly to the challenge of a second wedding. The Duke had suggested they marry quickly, a quiet ceremony with few guests, but Jason had told Angel they could delay and plan something far more grand if she wished it.

But Angel had not wished it. If Jason wanted a quick, quiet wedding she would be quite content. She had also been happy to go to Rotherton directly after the service. It was, after all, little more than seven months since his first wife had died, and Angel was not ready to be subjected to the gossip and speculation of London.

They had been married that very morning, in the same parish church where her brother had been wed. She was even wearing the same shell-pink gown, although this time her hair was adorned with pink rosebuds and she wore the diamond and pearl necklace that Jason had given her. However, there had been none of the celebrations that had accompanied Barnaby's nuptials, and they had left for Rotherton directly after the service.

The ceremony itself had gone off without a hitch, although Angel half expected someone to stand up and declare that the marriage could not go ahead. Barnaby, perhaps.

Her brother had cut short his honeymoon in order to repay the favour and be the Duke's groomsman. Angel had been very happy to see him and Meg, but her pleasure at the forthcoming ceremony had been dimmed when, the day before the wedding, she'd come out of the library and heard Barnaby and Jason talking.

They were out of sight, on the other side of the grand staircase, and she'd continued towards the stairs, unconcerned, until her brother's voice floated across the hall to her with disastrous clarity.

'Are you sure you want to do this, Jason? Oh, I know Angel is a great gel, and all that, but after Lavinia… Well.' He broke off, then said in a rush, 'My sister is hardly a beauty.'

Angel stopped and drew back, folding her arms across her stomach.

Hardly a beauty! The words hit her like a body blow. There was a console table at one side of the stairs, with a large mirror fixed above it, and she only had to move a couple of paces to see her reflection. Her dark hair was lustrous enough, but she wore it pulled back, smooth and neat. Sensible, if not the height of fashion. Her brown eyes were fringed with dark lashes and her skin was clear. Everything about her was good enough, she thought, but not exceptional. Nothing to set man's pulse racing.

Jason spoke, his tone reproachful.

'That is unkind, Barnaby. And beauty is not always what it seems, my friend.'

Angel would not skulk here any longer, she despised eavesdroppers. Putting up her chin, she walked around the staircase just as Jason laughed.

'Enough of this folly! Angel and I will rub along together very well. There is no more to be said.'

She stepped into sight just as he finished speaking and both men saw her immediately. Barnaby's face was a picture of guilt and confusion.

'Angel! Where the devil did you come from?' He'd glanced up at the grand staircase, knowing as well as she that anyone descending must have heard every word.

'From the kitchens.' She waved a hand back towards the narrow stone staircase the servants used, smiling as if she had not a care in the world. 'Why? Were you looking for me?'

'Oh, no. No. I was, er…'

'But I was,' said Jason, coming forward. 'I thought we might take a little stroll together before dinner.' He pulled her hand onto his sleeve, saying as he walked her out of the house, 'You do not need a wrap, it is a warm day and we shall not be very long.'

They had walked only a few yards across the lawn when he said, 'You heard your brother's remarks, I suppose.'

Angel bit her lip. 'Yes.'

'He is a fool not to appreciate your worth, my dear.'

'But he is right. I am not beautiful.'

'True beauty is not always visible, Angel. It is easy to be misled by a pretty face.'

'Or a handsome one!'

The words were out before she could stop them.

'Ah. The reason you have…er…foresworn romantic love?' he asked lightly. 'Would you like to tell me about that?'

'I would not wish to bore you.'

'I should like to know, all the same.'

He spoke almost casually, but Angel heard the kindness in his voice. She had not even told her family about this, but her conscience argued that if Jason was to be her husband, there should be no secrets between them.

'It was a silly thing, really. A gentleman I met during my come-out. He was handsome, charming… I suppose you would say he swept me off my feet. But I was fortunate. His shallow nature was revealed to me before any harm had been done. He stole a kiss. Nothing more.'

'Not true!' He stopped and pulled her round to face him. 'He hurt you, Angel. That is unforgiveable.'

She gave a little shrug. 'It would have been so much worse if I had married him.'

'And his loss is my gain,' said Jason, bending to kiss her cheek.

It was the merest touch, but it struck her like a lightning bolt, shaking her to the core. She'd put one hand against his waistcoat. 'Oh, Jason, are you quite sure you want to marry me? I have *nothing* to offer you. I am a country mouse. I have been to London but once in my life and know so little of society.'

'Then it will be my privilege to introduce you! Not that we shall spend all our time in society. Rotherton will be our main residence and I am eager to show it to you.' He covered her hand, holding it against his heart. 'Believe me, Angel, you are all I want in a wife. You are honest and practical, infinitely kind, and sensible, too.'

Yes. Sensible Angeline. That thought was enough to steady her racing pulse. Neither of them wanted to suffer more heartbreak, so it was far better that they marry as friends.

Even so, as they strolled on Angel could not forget her brother's words any more than she could forget that Jason had not suggested taking her to the villa at Brighton, the one he had loaned to Barnaby for his honeymoon.

Again, she tried to be sensible. His first marriage had been a love match. To see another woman in the villa might bring back unwelcome memories for the Duke.

As the carriage rattled on, she could only hope the same would not be true at Rotherton, since that was to be their home.

The coach slowed to negotiate an imposing entrance.

'Look, Angel, that is Rotherton, set out below us. What think you of your new home?'

The Duke's question brought an end to her daydreams and she turned obediently to look out of the window.

The drive wound downwards in a wide arc, affording her a good view of the house. It was a palatial building, created in the baroque style. The creamy stone façade of the east front boasted at least a dozen long windows between embedded columns stretching out on either side of the main entrance with its grand portico. She already knew that this huge stately pile had been the seat of the Darvell family for three centuries. In that time it had been much altered and enlarged, and now looked dauntingly grand, even for the daughter of a viscount.

The Duke was watching her, smiling faintly. 'Well, Duchess?'

'It is considerably larger than Goole Park.'

He laughed. 'It is, but you will very soon be at home in it.'

She thought that doubtful, but said nothing.

The carriage rattled on through the elegant park and came to a halt at the shallow steps of the portico. A liveried servant was waiting on the drive to open the door and the Duke jumped out, acknowledging the man's bow with a nod before turning to offer his hand to Angel. When she had alighted he did not release her fingers, but pulled them onto the sleeve of his coat.

'And here is my butler, on his way to greet us,' he remarked, as a soberly dressed figure came down the steps towards them. 'Good day to you, Langshaw.'

'Welcome home, Your Grace. To you and the new Duchess.'

Angel nodded, and hoped a smile would suffice. She felt so nervous she was not sure her voice would work.

'Langshaw has been butler at Rotherton since my father's time,' said Jason cheerfully. 'Anything you need to know, just ask him—isn't that right, Langshaw?'

'I will endeavour to answer any questions Her Grace may have,' replied the butler, allowing himself a little smile that made him suddenly look far less intimidating. 'However, I am sure Her Grace will find Mrs Wenlock a much better informant on domestic matters, having been here even longer than I.'

'Ah, yes.' Jason nodded. 'Our excellent housekeeper, who runs Rotherton with a rod of iron! Where is she?'

'In the Marble Hall, Your Grace, where the staff are gathered to greet their new mistress.'

Jason nodded, and ushered Angel inside. The formidable Mrs Wenlock was indeed waiting for them—only the housekeeper was not at all formidable. She greeted the Duke with the same warm affection Angel had noted in the butler, and was at pains to put the new Duchess at her ease, while an army of servants looked on. A few were brought to Angel's attention, but there was no attempt to introduce every one of them. The housekeeper remarked shrewdly that no one could be expected to remember all their names in one go, and they were quickly despatched about their duties.

'The baggage coach arrived some time ago and all your

luggage has already gone up,' the housekeeper informed them. 'I will have hot water taken upstairs shortly, but in the meantime I have had refreshments carried into the Yellow Salon.'

The Duke was in the act of removing the cloak from Angel's shoulders and she felt him pause. Glancing up, she saw he was frowning. It was gone in an instant, and when he replied to the housekeeper his tone was perfectly calm.

'Thank you, Mrs Wenlock. There will be plenty of time for Her Grace to see the rest of the house tomorrow, but I suppose we might as well start with the Yellow Salon.'

He shrugged off his greatcoat and handed it to a waiting footman before leading Angel across the hall. At the salon door Jason hesitated, then gestured for her to precede him.

Angel walked in and stopped to look about her. Tall windows overlooked the drive and the parkland beyond, and the room was as large as the drawing room at Goole Park. However, unlike the worn and slightly faded glory of Angel's old home, everything here was startlingly new and decorated in every shade of yellow, from the creamy walls to the straw-coloured silk on the chairs and sofas and the butter-yellow damask curtains.

'What a...a cheerful room,' she managed at last.

Jason poured two glasses of wine and handed one to her.

'Aye.' His lip curled in sardonic amusement. 'Very *yellow*, ain't it?'

'Possibly because all the furnishings are so new.' She sat down cautiously on one of the sofas and ran a hand over the rich fabric.

'True. This room has hardly been used since it was refurbished. It was my first wife's decision to decorate it thus, to match her portrait.'

He waved towards a large canvas hanging on one side

of the chimneypiece and Angel obediently looked at it. She had seen the painting the moment she had come in. It would have been impossible not to do so.

Encased in a richly carved and gilded frame, the life-size depiction of the Duke's first wife dominated the room. A statuesque and golden-haired goddess, gowned simply in flowing white muslin, her blue eyes stared out of the painting as if she were gazing at the park, visible through the windows opposite. She was standing on a carpet of wild spring flowers, predominantly white and yellow blooms, and cradling an armful of daffodils.

Angel swallowed before saying in a hollow voice, 'She is very beautiful.'

She glanced at the Duke, but he was not looking at her. His eyes were fixed on the painting.

'I commissioned it soon after our wedding.'

He fell silent, and after a few moments she tried again. 'The setting is Rotherton, I think. Is that not the house in the background?'

'It is—although the wild flowers are never so abundant as that in the park. The deer see to that!' Another silence, then he said bitterly, 'She is depicted as Persephone, the goddess of spring. And, ironically, of the dead.'

He raised his glass and took a sip while Angel remained silent and still. She did not want to interrupt his thoughts, whatever they were. A moment later he shook off his contemplative mood and turned to her.

'If you have finished your wine I will escort you up to your room. Your maid should have everything ready for you by now. On the way I will show you the drawing and dining rooms, so that you will know where to find them.'

'Thank you, that is very thoughtful.' She rose and put her

fingers on his proffered arm. 'I think it would be very easy to get lost in this house!'

He covered her fingers where they rested on his arm.

'You will soon grow accustomed.'

His words and the gesture were reassuring, but as he escorted her out of the room Angeline looked back at the beautiful woman staring out from the portrait. She felt an icy finger running down her spine. How could dark hair and a petite figure ever match the golden beauty of Jason's first wife?

Having given his new bride into the care of her maid, Jason went to his own room, his brow furrowed. Adams was waiting for him, but after one look at his master's face he did not speak, merely went on preparing the bath for the Duke to wash off the dirt of travelling.

Jason barely noticed his man's silence. His thoughts were dark and not altogether happy. The day had passed off as well as he could have hoped, but now he was here at Rotherton with Angeline, doubts were setting in. He could not forget Lady Goole's look of concern as he took his leave of her.

'Take care of Angel, Your Grace,' she had begged him. 'I thought she might never recover from the disappointment she suffered at her come-out, but I am glad she has. She deserves to be happy.'

Why on earth had he been in such a hurry to marry again? He should have courted Angel properly, not proposed within days of her brother's wedding. But he had been so incensed at the thought of leaving her at Goole Park, little more than a servant for her family, that he had determined to carry her off at once and give her a new life of ease and comfort.

He should not have rushed her into marriage, and such a small, private affair at that. He had convinced himself he was doing it for her benefit. Now he realised it had been an act of pure self-interest on his part.

He had not seen Angel for years, but almost as soon as they'd met again it had been as if they had never been apart. She challenged him, teased him. She made him feel more relaxed and at ease than he had done for years. But that was no reason to marry without giving her time to consider. What if she came to regret tying herself to a man she did not love?

He recalled his short visit to London before the wedding, and a visit to his club, where he'd announced to his acquaintances that he was getting married. They had been surprised, but he remembered one of them saying, with a laugh, 'Well, good luck to you, Your Grace. If you do change your mind I suppose you can always get an annulment!'

He had laughed at that, along with everyone else, but was it such a nonsensical idea? He had no qualms about consummating the marriage, but what of Angel?

Jason took in a sharp breath as Adams tipped the final jug of hot water over his head, but it did not distract him from the unpleasant truth. Confound it, there were plenty of women ready to marry him and give him an heir, but by marrying Angeline he risked losing her friendship, and only now did he realise just how precious that was to him.

'I should never have done it!'

'Your Grace?'

His man was standing by the bath, holding up Jason's robe and regarding him with a questioning eye.

'Talking to myself,' he muttered, pushing himself up out of the tub.

He slipped his arms into the robe and took the proffered cloth to wipe his hair, but even as he dried his body confusion continued to rage in his mind. Finally, as his man tenderly eased him into his new blue coat and settled it across his shoulders, the question that was bothering him the most burst out.

'Damn it, Adams, was I a selfish brute to marry her out of hand?'

His valet was the soul of discretion, and Jason expected him to maintain a dignified silence. He was more than a little surprised when Adams responded.

'It is not my place to comment, Your Grace. But, since you ask, from what I have seen and heard of the lady, I think she will suit you very well.'

Jason stared. Adams had been with him ever since he'd become Duke at the tender age of fifteen, and he had never before heard the valet express an opinion on anything other than the cut of his coat or his choice of footwear.

'Confound it, 'tis not about whether she will suit me,' said Jason. 'Will I make her happy?'

'As to that, I cannot say, Your Grace. But I think it very likely.'

Adams gathered up the discarded towels and carried them away, leaving his master to digest those words as best he could.

The evening sun was pouring in through the drawing room windows when Jason walked in. Angeline was already there, inspecting the paintings. She was wearing a cherry-red silk gown with a fine cream shawl arranged about her shoulders. Her dark hair was pinned up and confined by a red ribbon, and when she turned towards him he saw she was wearing the demi-parure of pearls and diamonds he had given her as a wedding gift. She was a picture of simple elegance, and Jason thought he had rarely seen anything more beautiful.

'You have some fine works of art here,' she commented.

It took him a while to realise she was speaking. He had to give himself a mental shake before he could answer.

'Yes, my grandfather brought most of the landscapes back from his Grand Tour.'

'The portraits, too, are very good.'

'They should be. The Dukes of Rotherton only ever commissioned work from the finest artists of their day.'

He watched her move around to stand before a large painting of a family group on the right of the chimney breast.

'Is this your grandfather?'

'Yes. The Fifth Duke and his duchess with their three children.'

'The boy, then, is your father.'

'That's right.'

'And this is he as Duke?' She moved across to the far side, gesturing to the couple staring out from the gilded frame on the left of the fireplace.

'Yes.'

'You are very like him.'

'Am I?' He studied the bewigged figure dressed in velvet and lace, staring out so haughtily. 'I hardly knew him.' He saw that Angel was regarding him, her brows raised, and he shrugged. 'My mother died soon after I was born and my father rarely visited Rotherton. I lived in the nursery wing here until I went off to school at eight years old.'

'Oh, how sad!'

He looked at her in surprise. 'I never thought so. At least, not until I met Barnaby and spent my holidays with him at Goole Park.'

'Our family must have come as a shock to you!' She laughed. Then she asked, 'When will I meet the children?'

'The children?'

'Your daughters. Will they be coming down to join us before dinner?'

'They are in Kent.'

'Oh, are they visiting family?'

'No, they live there. I beg your pardon, I thought you knew.'

Angel looked shocked. 'I assumed they lived here, at Rotherton.'

'No. You are frowning. Is there aught amiss with that? The nursery here has been woefully neglected. Their present accommodation is much more suitable for two young girls.'

'Oh. I should have thought…' Her voice trailed off, then she said brightly, 'It is no matter. If we mean to make this our home we can refurbish the nursery and bring them to live with us.'

'Why? They are perfectly happy with Mrs Watson.'

'But they are your daughters, Jason.'

He flushed and found himself repeating the argument Lavinia had used. 'You would find it a dashed nuisance, I am sure, having them in the house.' He added, 'I thought you would like to settle in here before anything else.'

Under her steady, thoughtful gaze he felt uneasy, but at that moment the butler came in to announce that dinner was ready, and Jason gave a rueful smile.

'I am proving a very poor host! We were so busy discussing the artwork I omitted to serve you with a glass of wine. Would you like Langshaw to send word to the kitchens to delay our meal?'

'Oh, there is there is no need for that,' she said quickly. 'I am perfectly ready to go in to dinner.'

He detected an odd note in her voice and he said, as Langshaw withdrew, 'Is something wrong, Angel? Are you unwell?'

'No, no,' she assured him. 'I am a little tired, I think, that is all.'

'Yes, of course.' He was relieved. 'It has been a long day. A good meal will revive you, I hope.'

'Yes, I am sure it will,' she agreed, laying her fingers on his arm and going with him to the dining room.

Crossing the hall with Jason, Angel knew it was not exhaustion that was weighing down her spirits. It was the thought that Jason did not care about his family. She was sure that was not his true nature. He had been very young when he'd first married, and had scandalised society by marrying a widow so much older than himself.

Angel remembered Barnaby telling their parents all about it, quite forgetting that his fifteen-year-old sister was in the room. Jason had stood firm against the wishes of his family, and even his guardian, and insisted that he would marry the love of his life, who was already carrying his child. Angel also remembered her mother's disapproval when the society pages had reported that the Duchess had returned to London very quickly.

'The fact that the baby was born just four months after the wedding is neither here nor there,' Lady Goole had explained to her husband. 'These things happen. But to leave her baby with only the wet nurse and servants so soon after her confinement—it would not do for me, I can tell you!'

It was not unusual to put children to a wet nurse, Angel knew that. She could understand why the Duke, only eighteen himself, would have had little interest in a baby, or in his eight-year-old stepdaughter.

But surely now the children would be a comfort, thought Angel. They would be a link with the wife he had loved so much. The wife she was very much afraid still held his heart.

They reached the dining room and Angel put these thoughts aside as a liveried servant jumped forward to open the door. It was her first dinner at Rotherton with Jason and she would not spoil it with vexing questions.

'Good heavens!'

She could not help exclaiming when she saw that one place had been set at each end of the long dining table and the space between covered with a vast amount of silverware.

Jason, coming to a halt beside her, gave her a questioning glance.

'It, it is very impressive, Your Grace, but.' She hesitated. 'Do we really have to dine like this, when there are only the two of us?'

He raised his quizzing glass and surveyed the table.

'It is rather daunting, isn't it?' he replied, the trace of a laugh in his voice.

She said slowly, 'Do you always dine like this when you are here?'

'Er...no. The little parlour downstairs suits my purposes very well when I am alone. There are, in fact, several rooms set aside for use by the family, although the rest of them have not been used since my parents' time.' He looked back to address the butler, who had followed them into the room. 'I shall sit at Her Grace's right hand tonight, Langshaw. Pray have everything moved there for me. And in future, when we are dining alone, the Duchess and I will use the small dining parlour.'

'Very well, Your Grace.'

'I think they are eager to impress their new mistress,' Jason told her, escorting her over to one side of the room while they waited for everything to be rearranged. 'Ain't that so, Langshaw?'

'It is, Your Grace. We were all anxious that Her Grace should not find anything wanting at Rotherton.'

'Everyone has been to such a lot of trouble to make me welcome and I am most obliged to you all for your efforts,' Angel addressed the butler, smiling. 'This is a very elegant room, and everything looks most impressive, but His Grace and I will not put you to the trouble of all this when we are dining *à deux*.'

'Very well, Your Grace.'

'I do hope I have not offended,' she murmured, as the butler made his stately exit.

'Not at all, you were very gracious. You are mistress here now, and must order everything as you wish.'

'As long as you will be happy dining in the small parlour?'

'Aye, it will be much cosier. And it is closer to the kitchens, too, so it will suit everyone better.'

Dinner progressed slowly, for Cook also wanted to impress the new Duchess. There was such a multitude of dishes on the table that it was almost impossible to try every single one. Angel did her best, taking minute quantities from each until finally she could put down her knife and fork and sit back in her chair.

'I am replete,' she declared. 'That is the finest meal I have ever enjoyed!'

She knew her words would find their way back to the tyrant who ruled the kitchens, and she hoped it would ease her path as she took charge of the household.

The covers were removed. Sweetmeats and dishes of nuts and sugared almonds were brought to the table, and Langshaw placed decanters of wine at the Duke's elbow before following the other servants out of the room. At last they were alone.

Jason picked up one of the decanters. 'Madeira?'

'Yes, thank you.'

'Did you really enjoy your dinner?' he asked, filling her glass and serving himself with port.

'Very much. I am looking forward to spending the morning with Mrs Wenlock. I have a great deal to learn about Rotherton and I know it will take time. I hope she will bear with me.'

'I have no doubt she will, but she will also remind you that you are mistress here now. I want you to be comfortable at Rotherton.'

She chuckled. 'We will not be very comfortable if I upset all your servants!'

'Oh, I doubt you will do that. But there must be changes you wish to make.'

Angel thought about suggesting once again that they invite his children to Rotherton, but decided now was not the time.

She said instead, 'Certainly, but not yet. I shall not rush into anything.'

'Not even redecorating the Yellow Salon?'

'Certainly not that. It would be the height of extravagance to change the furnishings in that room upon a whim.'

'You are free to order things at Rotherton just as you wish, Angel. Even *"upon a whim"*.'

'Thank you, but spending money for the sake of it is not my way,' she replied firmly. 'I do not intend to make any changes at all until I am more familiar with the house.'

'So I shall not come back to Rotherton in a month's time to find you have remodelled the whole?'

She did not notice the teasing note in his voice.

'You are going away?'

'I am.'

He was no longer looking at her, but intently studying the glass held between his long fingers.

'I spoke with my steward Simon Merrick earlier. There are a number of business matters concerning my estates that require attention. It will involve talks in town with my lawyer, and with Telford, my man of business, then I must also go north to one or more of my other properties before returning to London. My going now to deal with these matters will give you time to settle in and become acquainted with Rotherton. And you will be busy with morning calls.' He grimaced. 'The ladies of the neighbourhood will call and you will visit them in return, but you do not need me for that. In fact, I should be very much in the way!'

'Oh.' She tried to digest this news. 'When do you propose to leave?'

'Tomorrow.'

'Tomorrow?'

'I am sorry. I should have told you before.'

'Yes, you should!' She set down her glass with a snap. 'You are in a tearing hurry to be gone from me, sir.'

'No, Angel, you misunderstand me.'

'Do I?' She stared at him. 'We were married *this morning*, and you propose to leave me after just one night…' Something about his manner, the way he kept his eyes averted, made her uneasy. She even felt a little sick. 'Or are we not even to have that?'

She and Jason had exchanged nothing more than a chaste kiss so far, but Angel knew what was expected of a bride and had been preparing herself to do her duty in the bedroom.

He looked uncomfortable. 'I said I would not rush you. I want to give you time to grow accustomed to your new position.'

'Alone?'

From everything she had learned or observed from her sisters, Angel did not anticipate much pleasure in the experience, but to suddenly discover the Duke had no intention of taking her to his bed was a cruel blow.

Jason saw the suspicion of tears in her eyes and cursed himself for a fool. There had been so little opportunity for reflection in the past month that he had thought she would welcome some time alone. For his part, there was indeed business to be dealt with, but it could have been avoided if he had really wished to do so. He was using the excuse to get away from Rotherton…to give them both a little time to consider their situation.

He was haunted by the Viscount's final words to him, declaring how relieved he and Lady Goole were to have Angeline so comfortably settled at last. Jason wanted to be sure she had not been coerced into this marriage.

'Angel—' He reached across to touch her hand where it rested on the table, but she snatched it away.

'Am I *that* repulsive that you c-cannot even bring yourself to c-consummate our marriage?'

'No, that's not it at all!' He jumped up and caught her arm as she left her seat. 'Angel, please. Let me explain.'

She resisted for a moment, then sank back down onto the chair.

'Well, Your Grace?' Her tone was arctic. 'What is it you want to explain?'

Jason resumed his own seat. He had to make her understand, but he must be careful. He could not afford to get this wrong.

'Everything happened so quickly,' he said at last. 'It was only when we left the church, man and wife, that I realised how much I had rushed you into this. I know, too, that your parents were eager for the match, and that must have weighed with you. There was no time to reflect upon whether we were doing the right thing.'

She maintained a stony silence and Jason forced himself to go on.

'All this...' he waved a hand '...this *grandeur* can be daunting. I thought you might be regretting your decision to marry me. If that is the case, then it is not too late. The marriage can be annulled.'

Angel was very pale, her dark eyes troubled.

'Is that what you want, Your Grace? Do you *regret* marrying me?'

'No, not at all. But I have been wed before. I know what marriage entails. You are an innocent. A maid. It would be no wonder if you were a little frightened of...what lay ahead.'

Her cheeks flamed. 'If you are referring to the...the marriage bed, I have two married sisters, sir. I know something of what is required of a wife.'

'But I fear you may not know what is required of a *duchess*, Angel. I have duties, obligations, and so does my wife. My houses and estates require a mistress.'

He stopped, recalling Lavinia's reaction when he had said something similar to her.

'I cannot live my life at Rotherton, darling Jason. It would destroy me. I will not be a prisoner in that cold barrack. Or in any of your houses!'

He shook his head, trying to block out that disdainful voice.

'There is the townhouse, of course, but the other properties cannot be ignored. We cannot live in London all year.'

'You think that is what I want?' She leaned towards him. 'I enjoy living in the country, Jason. I am prepared for my life to be different, for it to be hard work. I am not daunted by any of it.'

She was gazing at him so earnestly that he felt a constriction around his heart. It would be so easy to take her to his bed, to bind her to him, but the doubts persisted. He must be honest with her.

'If that were the only thing! You do not know me well enough yet, Angel.' He shrugged. 'I am not at ease in society. I dislike fuss and grandeur. I have been told I am cold-hearted. Morose, even. And I can be overbearing. I have a temper.'

'Is that all?' she replied with a faint glimmer of a smile. 'You are not cold-hearted, Jason. And I have a temper myself—as you witnessed when we were children. I do not believe it will be a barrier to our happiness.'

He was grateful for her attempts to alleviate the gloom, but he would not trap her into a marriage she might later regret. He knew only too well what hell that could be.

'No, Angel, we cannot make light of this. I shall leave at dawn. You will have time to become familiar with Rotherton, time to reflect upon everything this marriage entails. When I return, if you are of the same mind, then we shall begin our married life.'

'And you will be gone for a month?'

'At least. Perhaps a little longer.'

He waited. Some of the colour had returned to her face and he hoped now that she understood he was doing this for her sake.

'Very well.' She pushed aside her half-filled glass. 'Then I shall bid you goodnight, Your Grace.'

'Allow me to escort you to your room.'

He expected her to refuse, but she nodded and he pushed back his chair, holding out his hand to help her up.

Angel was silent as Jason escorted her from the dining room. This was not how she had imagined her wedding night.

She did not doubt Jason believed he was being kind, giving her the chance to reconsider her decision. However, his proposal had been too persuasive. He had pointed out to her the disadvantages of her life at Goole Park and shown her a vision of something far better. A future she had never dreamed could be hers. She would not change *her* mind, but despite the Duke's protestations she suspected he was having second thoughts.

Her heart sank at the idea, but if that was the case then it was better to delay consummating the marriage. Far more sensible.

And that was what he had called her, was it not? *Sensible.*

'Here we are.' Jason's voice interrupted her thoughts. 'There is a connecting door between our rooms, but it is locked at present. The key is on your side, so you need have no fear that I shall impose myself upon you.'

'Oh.' This was a wretched start to their marriage. She stifled a sigh and said quietly, 'Thank you…you are very kind.'

'I hope you will sleep well, Angel. And you must feel free to do what you will with Rotherton while I am away. I know I can trust you not to dispose of all the family treasures!'

She could not bring herself to respond to his attempts at a jest, and after a moment he went on.

'Order the household as you wish. I really, truly, want you to be happy here.'

'Do you?' She looked up, straining to see his face in the shadowy light.

He did not answer.

She put her hand on his chest, feeling the strong beat of his heart through the fine silk waistcoat. It sent the blood pulsing through her own body. Daringly, she leaned a little closer. He hesitated only a moment, then lowered his head and kissed her.

It was not a chaste brush of the lips, as on previous occasions, the kind of kiss she had been expecting. This time his mouth crushed against hers, demanding a response, and Angel's heart pounded against her ribs. His arms came around her and he teased her lips apart, his tongue darting and dancing, making her bones melt. Hitherto unknown and unimagined sensations rippled through her and she clutched his coat. She breathed in the musky scent from his skin. She felt light-headed, almost faint, and there was an unfamiliar ache low in her body, a yearning for more. Much more.

She was about to slip her arms about his neck when he broke off the kiss.

'Enough now.' His voice was ragged. He caught her hands and held them firm against his chest. 'I shall be gone before you wake in the morning, but I wanted to kiss you goodbye. Something to remember while I am in London.'

Remember? That kiss was burned into her heart. She would never forget it.

He squeezed her fingers before turning to open the door of her bedchamber. 'Goodnight, Angel.'

She could not move, shocked to the core by the feelings he had aroused. Silently she watched him walk away, heard the faint scrape as he opened his door. When he looked back at her, his face was no more than a pale smudge against the darkness, then he was gone.

It had been a long and exhausting day, but Angel was so on edge she knew she would not sleep easily. She was glad Mama had said she might bring Joan with her as her dresser—one familiar face in a house full of strangers. The maid helped her into her nightgown and tucked her between the warmed sheets, but after tossing and turning for several long minutes Angel slipped out of the luxurious feather bed.

She padded across to the windows in the south wall and threw back the heavy curtains.

A pale half-moon shone down on a blue-grey landscape. She stared at it for a moment, before the chill night air drove her back to her bed. The wedding and the drive to Rotherton had taken its toll, but Jason's hard, searing kiss and the exhilaration she had felt for those few precious moments after his lips met hers, threatened to keep her awake all night.

Chapter Four

The sun was just rising as Jason's travelling carriage bowled away from Rotherton. He yawned and leaned back against the silk squabs, looking out at the familiar landscape. He had barely slept, conscious that only a wooden door separated him from Angel. He had told her this was a marriage of convenience, but he knew now it was anything but that. If he was honest, he had known it when she had swooned and he had caught her up. How good she had felt in his arms. How *right*. Light as a feather, her warm body resting against his chest, she had aroused his protective instincts, but also something much more primal. That goodbye kiss last night had confirmed it, and it had taken every ounce of his willpower not to carry her off to bed there and then.

More than once during the long night he had been tempted to go to her, but he had fought it. He had endured one disastrous marriage and was determined not to bind Angel into life with a man she did not love.

Angel woke to a chorus of birdsong coming in through the open window. She sat up and looked towards the connecting door. Before returning to her bed last night she had unlocked it, hoping Jason might change his mind and come to her, but he had not. She reached for her wrap. It was very early. If he had not yet left then she must speak to him. It was important to tell him she had no regrets about this marriage. That she would never change her mind.

Even as she scrambled out of bed she heard the sound of a carriage. She ran over to the windows that overlooked the drive and was in time to see the carriage pulling away, the coat of arms on the door glinting in the early-morning sunshine.

She stood watching until the carriage disappeared amongst the trees. Jason had said his trip was for business, but she thought of him in London, amongst his friends, in the company of beautiful ladies. Perhaps he had a mistress. Many men did.

Angel shrugged and turned away from the window. The idea of Jason with another woman provoked a stab of jealousy like a physical pain, but there was nothing to be done about that now. Or, at least, she amended, not at present. She was his wife, his duchess, and she had no wish to change her mind.

She could only pray that Jason would not change his.

Determined not to mope, Angel did not return to her bed but rang for her maid. She was mistress of Rotherton now, and there was much to learn about her new domain. The Duke had told her she might order everything as she wished, but she would defer to Mrs Wenlock until she was more familiar with this house and its ways.

She set to work directly after breakfast, joining the housekeeper for a tour of the house. This took some time, because once Mrs Wenlock realised that her new mistress was interested in the whole house she became expansive. She detailed everything she knew of the history of Rotherton and its traditions, and Angel drank it all in.

They began in the attics and the topmost rooms, which were set aside for servants and children, then the smaller bedrooms that Mrs Wenlock explained could accommodate single gentlemen if all the other guest rooms were in use.

Angel listened closely, taking in as much as was possible. Upon her arrival she had experienced the grandeur of the drawing and dining rooms, but even that did not prepare her for the magnificence of the public rooms on the first floor—especially the two state bedchambers, renamed after a royal visit forty years ago. They were lavishly appointed, with gilded furniture and elaborately plastered ceilings, and the state beds were curtained with magnificently embroidered silk hangings.

'The late Duchess commissioned them to replace the originals,' explained the housekeeper. 'They are perfect replicas in every detail.'

Angel shook her head and sighed. 'It seems a pity to go to all that trouble when no one ever uses these rooms.'

'Oh, they have been used, ma'am. When—' The housekeeper broke off, her cheeks flushing scarlet, then went on in a rush, 'But I shouldn't be rattling on like this when we have so much more of the house to see. If you'll come with me, Your Grace?'

Angel was tempted to ask Mrs Wenlock what she had been about to say, but the housekeeper was already hurrying away, and she was obliged to follow her down the stairs.

There were several rooms on the ground floor that were set aside for the family, all very elegant but with none of the opulence of the public rooms. These included the small dining parlour Jason had mentioned, which had double doors leading to a family drawing room. Also a sunny morning room and a small, booklined room that Mrs Wenlock told Angel was the Duke's study.

'And is there a duchess's sitting room?' Angel enquired as she followed the housekeeper across the hall. 'Somewhere I might sew, or read, or write my letters?'

'Why, yes, Your Grace, this one.'

She threw open a door and Angel found herself in the Yellow Salon, where Jason had brought her on their arrival yesterday.

The housekeeper gave a little cough, her glance straying to the portrait of the last Duchess. 'I am sure His Grace would not object if you wished to make a few changes.'

'No. no. I do not think we should do that,' Angel disclaimed quickly. 'This is a most elegant room and…and quite perfect for welcoming guests. However, I should be comfortable with something a little less…grand.'

'There *is* a smaller room, ma'am, but it is presently unfurnished.'

'May I see it?'

Angel followed the housekeeper to a door tucked away beyond the dining parlour.

'Here we are, Your Grace.'

Angel stepped into the room. It was small, but windows on two sides made it very light. The walls and oak panelling were all painted in the palest cream, and it reminded Angel of a blank canvas, waiting to be used.

'This was the cabinet room in the old Duke's day, ma'am. Full of papers and maps. They were all moved to the library early last year, when the late Duchess decided to decorate. Sadly, it was not to be.'

Angel walked around the room. It was on the northwest corner of the house, with a view of the drive and the park from one window, and from the other she could see out over the formal flower garden to lawns that swept down to a lake.

'It will suit my purpose admirably.' She turned back, smiling. 'Mrs Wenlock, I noticed a great deal of furniture in the attics… May I see what we have to furnish my new sitting room?'

* * *

Within days the Duchess's sitting room was complete. Not only had Angel found sofas and chairs in the attics, but also a pretty little writing desk and a bookcase. It was all furniture that the housekeeper informed her had been set aside when the Yellow Salon had been decorated. Mrs Wenlock also showed her a trunk, in which they found suitable window curtains, and a further search unearthed a rug that would fit perfectly in the room.

Angel had helped to clean the furniture, brushing the dust from the padded chairs and sofa and polishing the wood until it gleamed. She'd enjoyed the effort, and now she gazed at the result with no little satisfaction. The flowered fabrics were a little worn, and the colours faded over the years to soft greens, pinks and whites, but the effect was charming. The little writing desk had been placed beneath the window, so she could look up from writing her letters to gaze out at the lake, and the bookcase was already home to the selection of favourite books she had brought with her from Goole Park.

She only wished Jason could be there to see it.

Setting up her own room had encouraged Angel to make more changes. When Mrs Wenlock had taken her to the nursery wing Angel had been surprised to discover it was not in such poor condition as she'd expected. As well as bedchambers for children and their attendants, there was a schoolroom, a dining room and a small suite of rooms for a governess or tutor. She took it upon herself to have them all cleaned, but gave instructions that the battered cupboards and worn but comfortable chairs in the nursery should not be removed. It was just the sort of room where children could enjoy themselves without worrying about damaging anything precious.

Not her children, of course. At least, not yet. But there was the Duke's daughter, Lady Elinor, and his stepdaughter Rose Haringey to consider. She did not think it right that they should be living in a separate establishment if their father was going to make his home at Rotherton, and she was formulating a plan to remedy that. It was a rather daring one, and she was not sure she should do anything until she had spoken to Jason.

However, the arrival of an express shortly after dinner gave her thoughts another direction altogether. With a trembling hand she took the letter from the butler, fearing something had happened to Jason. Then she saw that it had come from Hertfordshire, from her sister, and she tore it open, expecting bad news about her parents.

'Oh, dear!'

She put a hand to her mouth as she scanned Lettie's hasty scrawl. Taking a deep breath, she looked up at the waiting butler.

'Langshaw, will you send Mrs Wenlock to me, if you please?' She added, as cheerfully as she could, 'Visitors will be arriving tomorrow evening. We must prepare!'

Her sisters descended upon Rotherton, declaring that they had set out as soon as they heard she was alone. Angel was relieved to find that their husbands had not accompanied them, apparently preferring to visit when the Duke was present.

'We can only stay for four nights,' Lettie told Angel. 'Marland is taking me to Brighton later this month, but Alice and I just had to come and keep you company.'

Angel had ordered refreshments to be served in the Yellow Salon. She thought it far less comfortable than her own little sitting room, but she knew her sisters would be impressed. As she'd expected, they exclaimed in delight at the bright magnificence of the room.

'But what on earth is Rotherton about, Angeline, leaving you here while he goes off to London?' demanded Alice, helping herself to one of the little fancy cakes.

'He has business in the north, too,' replied Angel. 'It means a great deal of travelling.'

'But surely you could have arranged to meet up with him in town?' said Lettie.

'I did not think of it.'

'But the Duke should have thought of it. Is he ashamed of you?'

'Ashamed!' Angel blushed. 'No, not at all. You will recall it was agreed, before we left Goole, that we will be going to town for the winter.'

'One has to admit you are not quite ready for society,' said Alice, casting a disparaging glance at the apricot muslin day dress her sister was wearing. 'You will need *dozens* of new gowns. Everything must be worthy of a duchess.'

'Precisely. Which is why I could not accompany the Duke at such short notice. Mama is ordering pattern books for me to take to Madame Sophie. She is the local seamstress in Middlewych, and highly recommended by my neighbours. They say she is very good.'

'Yes, but is she good *enough*?' countered Lettie.

Angel frowned. It had not occurred to her that Jason might be ashamed of her.

'Did you know the late Duchess?' she asked, glancing up at the painting beside the chimneypiece.

'We saw her in town, of course,' said Lettie, 'but we were not acquainted.'

'And does this portrait do her justice?'

It was Alice who replied, saying airily, 'It is a good likeness, but nothing can compare with the original. She was a glorious creature—there is no denying it. Men could not keep their eyes off her.' She laughed gaily. 'Even Humphrey was captivated. Said she was the handsomest woman he had ever seen. And always so gay, so vivacious!'

Angel thought of her staid, rather pompous brother-in-law and her heart sank a little. Lavinia must indeed have been quite dazzling.

'No one ever refused an invitation to one of her parties,' Alice went on. 'She was famed for her entertainments. Everyone was shocked when she died in that carriage accident.'

'You told me most of the ladies breathed a sigh of relief,' Lettie remarked, smirking. 'Especially the married ones.'

Alice threw her a frowning look before turning back to Angel.

'Let us not talk of the past. Instead I shall say what a treat it is to be here with you, Angeline. How soon may we look over the house? If it is all as impressive as this room, then it must be magnificent!'

'The state rooms are indeed splendid,' agreed Angel. 'However, the family rooms on this floor are far more comfortable. We will be dining in the small dining parlour tonight.' Angel ignored their murmurs of disappointment and went on, 'However, I have put you in the state bedchambers.'

The change in both her sisters at this news almost overset Angel. Their looks of dissatisfaction were replaced by such beaming smiles that she almost giggled.

'Can you imagine what Marland will say when I tell him I have slept in a royal bed?' declared Lettie, clapping her hands. 'I should not care if it was hard as a board!'

Angel laughed 'I hope it will be more comfortable than that. The rooms were very recently refurbished. On the orders of the late Duchess,' she added, determined to be scrupulously fair to Jason's first wife.

Lettie snorted. 'In readiness for the Prince of Wales to call, no doubt— Now what have I said?' She raised her brows at Alice, who was frowning at her across the table. 'You told me yourself everyone save Rotherton knew that she and Prinny—'

Alice broke in quickly. 'No, no, you must have misunderstood me.'

The atmosphere in the Yellow Salon had grown very tense.

Angel looked from one sister to the other. 'Are you saying the Prince of Wales stayed here?' she said slowly. 'That she was his *mistress*?'

That would certainly account for Mrs Wenlock not wishing to disclose who had used the state bedchambers. Now it seemed only too obvious.

'Goodness, Angel, how you do take one up!' declared Alice, much flustered. 'I have no idea if Prinny ever visited Rotherton. There was never anything more than rumours. Let us talk of something else.'

'But I should like to know.'

'Of course you would,' agreed Lettie. 'One forgets that you have been incarcerated at Goole Park all these years, and I doubt Mama or Papa would talk of it.'

'They never listen to tittle-tattle,' retorted Angel, sitting up very straight, 'And they brought us up to think unfounded gossip quite reprehensible.'

'Yes, of course,' said Alice hurriedly. 'And the poor lady is dead now, so it can have no relevance.'

'Perhaps not.' Angel's hands were resting in her lap, and she had to work hard not to clasp them tightly together. 'However, I will be sure to hear of it when I go to London. Tell me what they were saying, if you please.'

'I know nothing, only hearsay,' Lettie declared. 'Marland and I spend far less time in town than Alice.'

'And Sir Humphrey and I were never part of the Duchess's closest circle,' said Alice, looking a little uncomfortable. 'It was clear the Prince of Wales was very taken with the lovely Lavinia, but there is always gossip and speculation about persons of high rank, Angel. Especially princes.'

'And dukes,' giggled Lettie. 'Once you are in town, Angel, you will discover that for yourself. Just the fact that Rotherton chose the incomparable Mrs Haringey at his duchess was enough to cause a scandal. Although you were still in the schoolroom then, and will not remember.'

Angel said nothing. She *did* remember, and had thought it highly romantic that Jason should fly in the face of his family's opposition to marry the woman he loved.

'If it was a love match then it did not last long,' said Alice, as if reading her thoughts. 'After the first few years they were rarely seen together. The Duchess held court in London, and invitations to her lavish entertainments at Darvell House were much sought after.' She leaned forward to say in hushed tones, 'She was notorious for her...*flirtations*. Her name was linked to any number of gentlemen.'

'And what of Jason?' Angel forced herself to ask. 'Did he have any number of mistresses?'

'My dear, if he did you must not blame him,' said Lettie, giving her a condescending smile. 'It is the way of the world.'

Yes. Angel was well aware of that. A man like Jason, titled, rich and handsome, would be impossibly attractive.

'But you must not let that upset you, Angeline,' said Alice, determined to be practical. 'Jason has made you his duchess. That puts you in a very strong position.'

It would, if we were truly married.

Angel swallowed the thought. It would not do to let this conversation unsettle her. Jason had married her and entrusted Rotherton to her care. That must be enough. For the present.

'You need to assert yourself, Angel,' Alice went on, glancing up at the portrait of Lavinia. 'You should start by removing that painting.'

But this Angel would not allow. 'The room was decorated to match it and its absence would be noticed.'

Her sisters argued but Angel stood firm, saying finally, if not quite truthfully, 'A likeness of the late Duchess does not trouble me.'

'Well, it should.' Alice was blunt. 'She was a beauty. Which you are not.'

Angel shrugged. 'She is dead, which I am not.'

She knew this calm response would irritate her sister. But she was as yet unsure how Jason felt about his late wife, and until she knew that she would not make any changes to the Yellow Salon.

Alice huffed. 'I still say you would be well advised to remove it, if you do not wish the Duke to make the obvious comparisons.'

Angel inclined her head, acknowledging the point, then turned the conversation.

The little party broke up shortly after. It was clear that Lettie and Alice were eager to see their bedchambers, and Angel rang for the housekeeper.

'Mrs Wenlock will show you to your rooms,' she said, excusing herself from this duty. 'She will be able to answer any questions better than I. We shall meet again at dinner.'

'Oh, I almost forgot!' exclaimed Lettie, as she was leaving the salon. 'Papa asked us to bring your horse. He is in the stables.'

That news brought a genuine smile to Angel's face.

'Oh, thank you, Lettie! I shall write to Papa and thank him for his thoughtfulness in sending Apollo so quickly.'

Her sisters went off with the housekeeper, leaving Angel alone with her thoughts. However, she did not want to dwell on what they had said, and turned her mind to planning some diversions for their stay.

With an hour or so before she needed to change for dinner, she decided to visit the stables. She had not yet done so, and not only could she see her beloved hack, she could also find out what vehicles were at her disposal. The weather looked settled for the moment, and she thought her sisters might enjoy a drive through the park or the surrounding countryside.

Stopping only to change her shoes, Angel walked briskly to the stables, where she sought out Thomas Crick, the elderly groom who was in charge. When she explained her mission he was happy to show her where Apollo was being housed, and after Angel had made sufficient fuss of the horse Thomas accompanied her around the rest of the stables.

'Are there any other horses suitable for a lady?' she asked him, thinking that perhaps her sisters would like to ride.

'Alas, ma'am, no. Her Grace's mounts were sold off when she died,' he told her. 'Every last one of them.'

'Oh! How many did she have?'

'Well, there was the grey…' Thomas began to tick them off on his fingers. 'That was her favourite. Then there was the black mare—part Arab, she was. Then the chestnut mare. And a hunter, which she never rode.' He coughed. 'They was all of them bought for their looks, ma'am, if you'll excuse my saying so. Having seen that gelding of Your Grace's, I doubt they would have suited you. Showy creatures, they was, like the pair she bought for her phaeton. His Grace was quick to sell 'em all off after Her Grace's accident. He did keep the carriage horses, though.'

'Oh? Did the late Duchess have her own carriage?'

'Aye, ma'am. Would you like to see it?'

'Yes, please!'

Angel hoped it would be an open carriage that she and her sisters might use to drive around the countryside when the weather was fine, but when they reached the carriage house Thomas led her over to an elegant travelling chariot.

He opened the door and Angel looked inside. The padded seats and squabs were covered in blue and yellow silk, with matching blinds at the windows. However, there was only one bench seat.

'It was a wedding present from His Grace,' Thomas explained. 'The very latest design. Her Grace used it a lot. Always gadding around the country, she was. Mostly without the Duke.' She heard a note of disapproval in the old man's voice. 'The last few years we saw very little of Her Grace here at Rotherton.'

Angel stepped away from the chaise, saying, 'Sadly it will only hold two people, so it is not what I require. I was hoping to take my sisters out to see the countryside, if the weather holds.'

The old man grinned at her. 'In that case, Your Grace, you'll be wanting the landau.'

The four days passed swiftly, despite Angel's misgivings. She was glad of her sisters' company when her neighbours made their morning calls, and they were loud in their praise of her new home, but when Lettie or Alice pressed her to make changes she held firm.

There was some respite from their attempts to interfere when they spent a whole day driving out in the landau. Its luxury and elegance, and the ducal crest emblazoned on the sides, were everything that Lettie and Alice desired. They thoroughly enjoyed themselves.

The visit had gone better than expected, but Angel felt only relief as she waved them off. She had not allowed her sisters to bully her and, heartened by this small success, she turned her mind to the matter that had been niggling away at her since her arrival at Rotherton.

The very next day she went in search of the Duke's steward. He was surprised when she entered his office, and he quickly rose from his desk to welcome her.

'Your Grace! Is there anything amiss? How may I help you?'

He pulled out a chair and invited her to sit down.

'No there is nothing amiss, Mr Merrick. I simply wish to make contact with the children.'

'Children?'

'Yes.' She nodded. 'The Duke's daughters. I believe they have their own establishment in Kent?'

'That is correct, Your Grace. Near Ashford. They are in the care of Mrs Watson. A widow, and a most genteel and capable person. His Grace and I have both called there, and I can assure you that they are most comfortably settled.'

'I do not doubt it, Mr Merrick, and I should like to write to Mrs Watson. Today.'

'I see…'

She did not miss the slight hesitation.

'Perhaps it might be better to wait until His Grace has returned,' he said.

'Alas, we do not know quite when that will be. Unless you have heard from him?'

She looked hopefully at Simon Merrick, but he shook his

head. 'The Duke's plans were extensive, Your Grace. His last letter said he was on his way to London, but I believe it will take another three weeks at least for him to conclude all his business.'

That would be a full six weeks since he had left Rotherton. Angel's heart sank a little, but she refused to be downhearted and summoned up a smile.

'His Grace left so suddenly that we did not have time to discuss everything.' She paused. 'He told you I have his blessing to do as I wish, did he not?'

'Yes. Yes, he did, ma'am. But…'

'Excellent!' She beamed at him. 'Then if you will furnish me with Mrs Watson's direction, I shall leave you in peace!'

Chapter Five

It was midnight when Jason arrived back in London and he fell into bed, exhausted. After his initial visit to the capital he had spent most of the past three weeks visiting his estates in Hereford, Nottingham and Yorkshire. Abandoning his chaise in town, he had elected to travel by horse for speed, and made the most of each day, concluding his business as quickly as possible and hurrying back to London for a final meeting with his lawyer.

For the first time in years he was eager to return to Rotherton. He couldn't help wondering how Angel was faring without him.

When Adams came in with his morning cup of coffee, Jason opened a bleary eye and reached out for his pocket watch.

He sat up. 'Ten o'clock! By heavens, Adams, why did you not wake me earlier?'

'I thought it best to let you sleep, sir, after your jauntering all around the country.'

Jason heard the minatory tone in the valet's voice and felt a smile growing. 'You are in high dudgeon because I would not take you with me?'

'In no way, Your Grace. You explained at the outset that you did not require my services during your travels.'

'Quite. I had a lot of miles to cover and no time to wait for a baggage coach to catch up with me.' He grinned. 'And you would have been damnably uncomfortable riding everywhere, Adams. Just think of the affront to your dignity!'

His valet afforded this with no more than a look and went back to laying out his master's clothes.

'I suggest the new Bath Superfine, Your Grace. With the dove-grey waistcoat, if you intend to visit the city this morning.'

'Aye, that will do.' Jason sipped his coffee and leaned back against the pillows. 'Although I might put off seeing Telford until tomorrow.'

He yawned. Perhaps his business could wait another day. The rest would be very welcome after all the miles he had ridden recently.

He took his time dressing and went down to break his fast in the dining room, where he found a small pile of letters awaiting him on the table. That, too, could wait. At least until he had consumed a sustaining meal of eggs, ham and cold beef.

Having satisfied his appetite, Jason began to look through the assortment of invitations, calling cards and letters, which he tossed aside. The familiar handwriting on one letter, however, caught his attention.

'Now, what would Simon be writing to me about?' he murmured, breaking the seal and unfolding the crisp paper.

He scanned the short note, his brow contracting. Then, with an oath, he stormed out of the breakfast room, barking orders as he went.

Three days later Jason was back at Rotherton. He jumped out of the carriage almost before it came to a stand on the sweeping drive and ran up the steps into the house. Langshaw was crossing the hall, but stopped at the sight of his master, startled for once out of his stately demeanour.

'Y-Your Grace!'

'Where is she?' Jason tossed his hat and gloves onto a bench. 'The Duchess,' he barked, seeing his butler's blank face. 'Where will I find her?'

'I believe Her Grace is on the north lawn, sir.' Langshaw had recovered himself a little now. 'Shall I send—?'

'No,' said Jason, grimly. 'I will go myself.'

He strode off through the house, cutting through the rooms to take the most direct route and going out via a garden door in the north front. A terrace ran the length of the house, with shallow steps to a small flower garden, and beyond that the lawns leading down to the lake.

A carriage rug was spread out on the grass and there were signs of a picnic, although no one was in sight. Then he heard voices and laughter coming from beyond the willows that screened some of the water from view. Quickening his pace, he moved on past the trees and soon discovered the reason for the merriment.

Angel and the girls were on the lake in a small boat.

He stopped, a chill running down his spine when he saw Rose, his stepdaughter, plying the oars with her young sister facing her. Angel was sitting in the bow, giving commands between peals of laughter.

'What the devil do you think you are doing!'

His voice thundered across the water. The laughter stopped immediately and the two girls looked up in alarm. Angel, sitting with her back to him, twisted around quickly.

'Oh! Y-Your Grace! I didn't think you would be back yet.'

'No! Don't stand up—'

His warning came too late. The little boat rocked alarmingly, Angel lost her balance and tumbled headlong into the water.

Jason swore, but even as he ran along the small wooden jetty she emerged from the water, coughing and laughing at the same time.

'No, no, I do not need rescuing,' she called to him as he unbuttoned his coat, ready to dive in. 'You see, it is not too deep here. I can walk to the bank. Although… Rose, dear, I think perhaps you had best row back to the jetty now.'

'You had indeed,' barked Jason.

'Pray do not be cross with them, Jason,' Angel begged him. 'It was my idea.'

He bit back a cutting retort and turned his attention to securing the boat and helping the girls to alight. They were both looking very frightened, and since Angel was in no immediate danger he took a moment to reassure them that he was in no way angry with them.

'Where did you learn to row?' he asked Rose, all the time keeping one eye on Angel, who was wading through the water.

'The Duchess has been teaching me.'

'She was going to teach me, too,' Elinor piped up, her face crumpling with disappointment.

'Another day, Nell,' Jason told her.

He could see Angel moving steadily towards the jetty. It was too high for her to climb out of the water and he knew he must help her, even though part of him—a very ignoble part—wanted to leave her to struggle.

'You two had best go back to the house.'

Rose hesitated. 'But what about the Duchess?'

'I will deal with the Duchess.' He hoped his calm tone was reassuring, even if he could not quite manage a smile. 'Off you go now. Take your sister indoors.'

He waited until they were running off to the house before turning back to the lake. Angel was at the jetty by this time, and he reached down to lift her out of the water.

'Thank you.'

'Damned foolishness! You don't deserve that I should rescue you.'

'If you had not bellowed at us I should not have fallen in!'

She was glaring at him, trying to look dignified and failing miserably. She was wet through, her dark hair hanging in tangles about her shoulders. As for her summer gown… the thin muslin clung like a second skin. Jason could see every contour, the soft swell of her breasts, the tiny waist and long, shapely legs.

Suddenly, the blood was thundering through his body. All he could think of was stripping off her wet clothes and running his hands over every inch of that dainty body…

With a growl of frustration he grabbed her hand. 'Come along, let's get you back to the house.'

He set off quickly, trying desperately to ignore the heat inside him…the strong desire to pull her down onto that carriage rug and kiss her senseless. Confound it, this was no time to lose his head over his own wife!

Angel stumbled and Jason slowed his pace. She was shivering, her bare arms resembling goose-skin.

'We need to get you warm.' He scooped up the rug. 'Here, put this around you.'

Her teeth were chattering now, and once he had wrapped her in the rug he swept her up into his arms.

'No, don't fight me,' he said, ignoring her protests. 'We will be much quicker this way.'

She stopped struggling, and after they had gone a few more yards she put her arms around his neck.

'I beg your pardon, Jason,' she murmured, resting her head against his shoulder.

'So you should. You are a dashed nuisance.'

'The gardener told me the lake is quite shallow at this end. I thought it would be safe enough.'

'Safe enough for you, perhaps. What if little Nell had fallen in?'

'I would have rescued her. I can swim, you know.'

This information did not lessen his irritation one bit. He said savagely, 'If there is any justice you will contract a severe chill and perish horribly!'

This retort elicited nothing more than a small chuckle, and he glanced down at her.

'You should be quaking in your wet little shoes, madam!'

'No, I shouldn't. You used to say just such things to me when we were children. Your bluff and bluster has never frightened me.' She raised her head. 'But it might make Rose or Nell anxious. They do not know you.'

That put an end to his softening mood.

He said, defensively, 'Yes, they do. I make regular visits to Kent to see them.'

'Once a month at most, they have told me. It is not enough, Jason.'

He was about to say it was none of her concern, but they had reached the house and Mrs Wenlock was at the door.

'Oh, good heavens, Your Grace! Bring the poor mistress in, sir. Miss Rose told us what had happened. I have had hot water taken up to Her Grace's room and hot bricks put in the bed. Peter and Samuel are here, and ready to carry her up the stairs.'

Jason glanced at the hovering footmen and his arms tightened. He would not allow anyone to relieve him of his burden, even if she *was* the most annoying female he had ever encountered.

'No! I will do it.'

Angel breathed a little sigh. There was something tremendously comforting about being in the Duke's arms. He had lifted her from the water as if she weighed no more than a feather, and although he had been furious with her she had never doubted that his anger was borne of concern. Wrapped in the rug, and with his arms holding her firm, she found the trembling had soon subsided. She was still cold, but not dangerously so. She felt quite well enough to make her own way to her rooms and would have done so, rather than have the servants convey her to her room. However, she was content for Jason to carry her. He was holding her against him, his arms strong and secure around her, and a little thrill went through her. A frisson of happy anticipation for what might happen next.

She kept her arms about Jason's neck and her cheek against his shoulder as he followed the housekeeper up the stairs. He was still in his travelling clothes, and she could smell the dust of the road on his coat, but there was also a faint trace of musk and sandalwood that made her feel lightheaded. His hair brushed against her hands, soft as silk. He wore it slightly longer than was fashionable and she closed her eyes, imagining what it would be like to run her fingers through those raven locks while he kissed her until she was dizzy…

'Here we are, Your Grace.'

Mrs Wenlock's voice dispelled Angel's pleasant daydream. The housekeeper opened the door and Jason carried Angel into her bedchamber. It was bustling with maids and warm from the hastily kindled fire. A hipbath had been placed before the hearth and the rising steam was scented with roses.

'There.' He put Angel on her feet, but retained his hold for a moment. 'Can you stand?'

Oh, she was so tempted to say no! What on earth was wrong with her? She was always so independent—why would she now want to behave like some poor weak creature?

'Yes, thank you, Your Grace.'

'You should remain in your room for the rest of the day.'

'I am very well now,' she assured him, risking a smile. 'I shall join you in the drawing room before dinner.'

'I shall look forward to it,' he said coolly.

Angel's giddy excitement faded when she glanced up at his hooded eyes. There was no warm glint in their slate-grey depths. They were hard and dark as stone.

He had not forgiven her for bringing the girls to Rotherton.

Jason left his wife to the ministrations of the maidservants and went off to change out of his own travel-dusty clothes, wondering what the devil had been going on at Rotherton in his absence. An earlier letter from his steward had warned him that Angel intended to write to Mrs Watson, but Merrick's subsequent letter had come as a severe shock. He had not expected Angel to bring the girls to Rotherton without consulting him. Now he asked himself what other mischief she had been about in his absence.

Well, he had only himself to blame, he thought wryly. After all, he had given her free rein.

But if that was not enough, she had frightened him half out of his wits by falling into the water. She had then completed his downfall by standing before him like some water sprite, ready to drive him to distraction. He cursed silently. It was years since he had felt so out of control!

'I must fight this.' He stopped at the door to his own bed-chamber and closed his eyes. 'I lost my head over one woman. I am not about to let that happen again!'

He went in to find his valet waiting for him, apologising for the lack of hot water.

'I have managed to procure you half a pail, Your Grace, but the water in your bathtub is barely lukewarm. All the rest has been diverted.'

'I am well aware of that,' Jason snapped, throwing off his clothes. 'It doesn't matter, a cold bath will suit me very well.'

Refreshed and rested, Angel made her way downstairs to the family drawing room at the appointed time. The Duke was already there, staring out of the window. She stopped in the doorway, wishing that this room did not overlook the lake. It would remind him of her folly.

He turned and came towards her, fixing her with a frowning gaze.

Trying not to feel daunted, she smiled at him and carefully closed the door upon them.

'Mrs Watson and the girls have been joining me here each evening, but I thought tonight it would be better if they took their dinner in the nursery.'

'They will take their dinner in the nursery every night for the rest of their visit,' he snapped. 'You will see to it, madam.'

She lowered her eyes. 'As you wish, Your Grace.'

'I do wish it!'

She heard his sigh of exasperation.

He said, 'You showed some good sense, at least, in bringing Mrs Watson with the children. How long have they been here?'

'Only four days.' She sat down and folded her hands in her lap. 'After calling upon Mrs Watson, I invited them all here for a short visit. A few weeks, nothing more.'

'I am glad to hear it. Their home is in Kent.'

'Their home should be here, with us.'

'*Us?* I did not think the matter of our marriage was quite settled yet!'

Angel did her best to hide her dismay at his icy tone.

'I have already told you, Jason, I made my decision when I married you.' She glanced down at the plain gold band upon her finger. 'If, however, *you* have changed your mind then pray tell me.'

'Of course not! I beg your pardon, Angel, it's just that I was taken by surprise, seeing you and the girls together.' He looked at her, a reluctant smile tugging at his mouth. 'Not quite such a shock as I gave you, it seems.'

'I did not expect you to return for at least a se'ennight.'

His scowl returned. 'You should have written, madam, to inform me of your intentions.'

'Asking your permission? You would have refused.'

His eyes narrowed but he did not contradict her.

She went on, 'I did not mean to surprise you, Jason. I know Mr Merrick corresponds with you regularly and thought he would tell you.'

'Simon informed me that you were *writing* to Mrs Watson. Then he sent an express saying the children had arrived. *That* was enough to have me concluding my affairs in London!'

'Are you very angry with me?'

'Only for trying to drown yourself.'

'I would not have drowned. I told you—I can swim.'

'I did not know that at the time!' He frowned at her. 'When

did you learn? I cannot recall that Barnaby and I were ever that lost to all sense of propriety.'

'No, no.' She blushed. 'I discovered our governess could swim and persuaded Mama to allow her to teach us. Alice, Lettie and me, that is. We used the sheltered end of the lake at Goole Park. I thought it most unfair that Barnaby should be the only one to learn.'

Jason nodded. 'And you can row, too.'

'Of course. *You* taught me that, do you not remember?'

'I remember having some tiresome brat pestering me.' The frown lifted. He threw himself down upon the sofa beside her. 'How long ago that seems now.'

'A lifetime,' she agreed. Angel waited a moment, then said quietly, 'You were very patient with that tiresome brat, Jason. I am sure you could do as well by your own children.'

Immediately he stiffened. 'Rose Haringey is *not* my daughter.'

'But she is your stepdaughter. And she is not really a child, either. She is seventeen, old enough to go into Society.'

'Mrs Watson will see to that.'

'Her mother was your duchess, Jason. I also understand that Rose is not penniless.'

'No. She will inherit a substantial sum from her father's estate when she is five-and-twenty.'

'Even more reason for us to bring her out.'

'No.'

'Why not?'

'Because.' He stopped. 'Because it would be too much of a burden for you. As my new wife, you will have enough to do once we reach town.'

'I am aware of that, Jason, and I am prepared for it. I shall need to buy new gowns in London, gowns more suited to a duchess. We could buy some for Rose at the same time. What is to prevent us taking both the girls with us to London? Mrs Watson, too, of course,' she added quickly. 'Then it would not be nearly so much work for me.' She paused, and when Jason remained silent she went on cheerfully, 'I should enjoy taking the girls to the museums and the parks, and Rose could be introduced to Society under your aegis. She will be eighteen in December, is there any reason why we should *not* bring her out?'

'No.'

'There, you see,' declared Angel. 'We could even take them to Astley's Amphitheatre. Or *I* could,' she added, teasing him, 'if you think it beneath your dignity.'

'I mean no, it will not do. I will not take Rose to London.'

'But—'

'Enough, madam!' He jumped up. 'We will talk no more about it, if you please. Neither will we discuss bringing the children here to live. Once they have finished their holiday Mrs Watson will take them back to Kent. That is the end of the matter.'

'The end of the matter.' Angel rose slowly to her feet. 'Is this how it is to be? Your word in this house is law?'

'In this instance, yes!'

'But you told me I could order things as I wish. That I have...how did you phrase it?...free rein.'

'In the running of my household, yes!'

'*Your* household?' She drew herself up, although she still had to look up at him. 'Is that all I am to you, Duke, some sort of *housekeeper*?'

'No! Of course I don't mean— Confound it, madam, do not take me up so!'

For a long moment they glared at one another. Angel thought of several choice ripostes. She was also tempted to storm out, slamming the door behind her, but that would achieve nothing. Instead she merely nodded.

'Very well, Your Grace. It shall be as you wish.' She resumed her seat and after a moment she said, 'Pray come and sit down, Jason. You have not yet told me what you have been doing while you were away.' She waited until he had joined her on the sofa then went on chattily, 'I trust your trip to town was successful, and you achieved everything you wished to do?'

'Angel…' There was a note of warning in his tone but she ignored it.

'You visited your other estates too, I believe. Mr Merrick told me about them. I particularly liked his description of the hunting lodge in Nottingham. I hope you do not mean to keep it all for yourself. And the house in Hereford. Darvell Hall, is it? I believe that dates back to Tudor times.'

'Angel, stop!'

'Is anything wrong, sir?'

He frowned at her. 'I am not going to change my mind about this, madam!'

'About what?' she asked innocently.

'Stop it, Angel, *now*!'

She turned to look at him, her eyes wide.

'You used to do this when you were a child. If Barnaby and I refused to let you join in with our games, you pretended to accept the situation.'

'I was *obliged* to accept it. You were both older than I. Stronger, too.'

He regarded her for a moment, then his frown disappeared and he leaned into the corner of the sofa, stretching one arm along the back.

'And you were a minx!' he told her. 'Instead of having a tantrum or bursting into tears you would chip away at us, little by little. Wheedling and cajoling.'

'Surely not!' She saw his lips twitch and tried not to smile.

'Wheedling and cajoling,' he repeated. 'Until we gave in.'

Angel laughed. 'No, no, I was never so devious.'

'Oh, you were, my sweet torment.' There was a gleam of cynical amusement in his grey eyes now. 'And you still are. I know your game, Angel, and your wiles will no longer work on me!'

His hand brushed her neck and a little thrill ran though her. She had dressed her hair loosely, because it was still damp from her soaking, and now she felt his fingers playing with a stray lock. She was filled with unfamiliar sensations that excited and frightened her in equal measure.

Angel sat very still. The air in the room seemed to press in upon her…heavy, expectant.

'My *wiles*, sir?' She attempted to speak lightly. 'I do not understand.'

'No? I could almost believe you fell into the water deliberately.'

He was curling the lock of hair around his fingers and Angel's spine tingled. She felt she might melt with pure longing!

'Why…' She swallowed, folding her hands together in her lap to stop them shaking. 'Why would I do such a thing?'

'Because you knew that when I pulled you out your body would shine through that gossamer-thin muslin.'

'No!'

'Yes. You looked like Venus, rising from the sea.'

His words flowed over her, warm and soft as velvet.

'Oh!' Angel felt herself blushing with pleasure. Now she was too shy to look at him at all! She stared down at her clasped hands. 'I had no idea. What, what a lovely thing to say to me!'

He had moved closer. His fingers were no longer playing with her hair. They were on her back, holding her close.

He caught her chin and gently turned her face up to his. 'I missed you damnably while I was away.'

Her heart leapt at his words, at the heat in his look. She dared to tell him the truth.

'I missed you, too, Jason. I hope you won't leave me again. At least not yet.'

There was a flash of fire in his eyes that set her heart pounding, then his mouth descended on hers and set her body alight.

His kiss was hard, savage and thrilling. Tiny arrows of fire darted through her body, from her head to her toes, sending the blood fizzing through her veins, and she clung to Jason as he dragged her onto his lap. He continued to kiss her until she was almost swooning with desire. She drove her hands through his hair, revelling in the silky feel of it against her fingers. Every sense was enhanced. She was acutely aware of his hard body pressed against hers, the soft wool of his coat, the cool linen at his neck. The smell of his skin was intoxicating, the faint woody scent mixed with something very masculine, very arousing.

Finally, he raised his head.

'We should stop.' His voice was rough, ragged, as if he was labouring under a great strain.

Angel sighed and clung to him. 'I do not want to stop.'

She wanted him to scoop her up into his arms and carry her upstairs. Her body was crying out for him to continue the pleasurable caresses, to bring this to its inevitable conclusion, and her disappointment was severe when he eased her from his lap and onto the sofa beside him.

'Ah, Angel, you are too sweet, too innocent. I cannot take such advantage of you.'

He was slipping away from her. She grasped his hands, wanting him so badly it hurt.

'You are *not* taking advantage! I am your *wife*, Jason, I want this as much as you.'

She spoke calmly, but inside she was begging for him to kiss her again.

'No.' He shook his head. 'We will do nothing we might regret later.'

He was rejecting her. Again. The recent heat in her body was replaced by an icy chill, as if she was back in the lake. Only this time it was much, much worse, because he had pushed her.

'That *you* might regret,' she retorted. 'I have already told you I consider our marriage vows binding.'

'They will be, once the marriage is consummated.' He freed his hands from her grasp and rose to his feet. 'Then there is no going back. Think, Angel! We would be bound together for the rest of our lives, however unhappy. We could end up hating one another. Believe me, I know it!'

He had walked away to the window and Angel stared at his back. There was tension in every line of him, the broad shoulders tense and unyielding. An old saying came to her: *Marry in haste, repent at leisure*. He had married her because he was lonely. And perhaps out of pity for little Angeline Carlow, who had been fading into an old maid. Of course he regretted it.

Tears stung her eyes and she fought them back. She was a duchess now. Duchesses did not weep. They made the best of their situation.

She rose and shook out her skirts. 'We married too soon. You need more time to grieve for your dead wife.'

'No. Angel, I—'

'You have no need to explain.' She cut him off. He might be in control of himself, but she was not. She needed to get away before she collapsed in a puddle of tears and frustration. 'We will forget this ever happened and carry on as we have been. As we agreed.'

Only she had *not* agreed to this sham marriage!

She looked around her, suddenly feeling a little lost.

'Perhaps you will excuse me if I do not dine with you tonight. I, I have a headache.'

Jason heard the soft swish of skirts as she moved across the room and the gentle click of the door closing behind her. He rubbed a hand across his eyes. What a mull he had made of that! Angel was right. He did need more time. But not to mourn Lavinia.

He had expected marriage to his childhood friend to be one of convenience. Finding himself suddenly lusting after his own wife was something he had not foreseen, and it was mightily *inconvenient*!

Chapter Six

Angel went downstairs the next morning in some trepidation. Despite telling Jason they would go on as before, she was not sure if she could do so after that kiss. She had found it too intense, too searingly wonderful to forget it. However, it *must* be forgotten. She needed to act naturally, especially while the children were at Rotherton.

Everyone else was at the breakfast table and she hesitated in the doorway, unsure how to proceed.

Jason rose to greet her. 'Good morning, my dear.'

His smile was reassuring, but she suddenly felt quite shy, although she could not think why a mere smile from him should cause her any embarrassment. He held the chair while she sat down, and when his hand rested briefly on her shoulder it was as if a net full of butterflies had been unleashed inside her.

He was trying to be kind, to put her at her ease. Angel appreciated the gesture, but it only made her even more sorry that he had not taken her to his bed. She had spent the night tossing and turning, imagining how that would be. But there was still hope. She just needed to be patient.

There was surprising little constraint at breakfast. Rose and Nell chattered away to the Duke, who was at pains to draw them out.

Watching them, Angel wondered again why he should be so against having them to live at Rotherton. Mrs Watson was an admirable governess and companion for the girls, but Angel knew from her own childhood that there was no substitute for living in a home with kind and loving parents.

'And what are your plans for the day, Angeline?'

Jason's enquiry interrupted her thoughts.

'I was going to visit Madame Sophie, today, to choose a new gown and possibly do a little shopping. I thought Rose might like to come with me.' She smiled at the girl.

'I should like that, very much,' said Rose.

'But Papa is taking us out on the lake today,' Nell announced. 'He is going to teach me to row.'

'I thought since I…er…interrupted your lesson yesterday, it was the least I could do,' said Jason. He met Angel's eyes across the table. 'There is room for four in the boat. I thought we might all go.'

It was clearly an olive branch, but having mentioned the dressmaker to Rose, Angel could not disappoint her.

She said, 'It shall be Rose's decision. If she would like to go boating then we shall drive into Middlewych tomorrow.'

But it was clear the lure of a dressmaker and shopping appealed to Rose far more than spending another day on the water. They split into two parties and Angel went off to order the carriage.

Jason enjoyed the time with Nell far more than he had expected. His suggestion that he teach her to row had been made on the spur of the moment and he had instantly regretted it. He knew nothing about children—especially girls. As an only child he had grown up very much alone, except for his visits to Goole Park, where he had seen little of the older sisters. It was only Angel, the youngest, who had followed him and Barnaby around, making a nuisance of herself.

No, he corrected himself. She had not been a nuisance. She had been happy to fetch and carry for the boys and eager to learn. He remembered that in the later holidays she had also been good enough at cricket and battledore to join in, despite being four years their junior.

It was not until they were on the lake that he realised Nell was too young and too small to row proficiently, but when he pointed this out her disappointment tugged at his heart. He helped her with the oars, praising her efforts, and when she grew tired he took over and rowed her around the lake. He pointed out to her the hidden nests amongst the rushes, rowed towards the shallows to search for wading birds, and showed her the best places to look for dragonflies.

In spite of his initial doubts the hours flew by, and the afternoon was well advanced when he carried a tired Nell back to the house and handed her over to Mrs Watson, who was waiting for them in the schoolroom.

'Well, Your Grace, it was very good of you to give up your day like that.'

'It was a pleasure,' Jason replied, surprised to discover he really meant it. 'We will do it again, if the weather holds.'

'Oh, yes, please, Papa!'

Nell's obvious delight was gratifying, and he went back down the stairs, still smiling.

It was not yet time to change for dinner and Jason went off in search of Angel. He wanted to share with her the amusing things Nell had said, to describe the girl's attempts to handle the oars and the unexpected pride he had felt at her brave efforts.

When he was informed that the Duchess had not yet returned his disappointment was stronger than he had anticipated, but he put it aside and went off to see Simon Merrick and distract himself with estate business.

'I beg your pardon. I hope I did not keep you waiting.'

Angel entered the family drawing room a good twenty minutes after the appointed hour, the apology tripping off her lips.

'Not at all,' said Jason, politely and inaccurately. He had been impatient to see her. He threw aside the *Gentleman's Magazine*. 'Are the girls not coming downstairs?'

He went over to the side table to pour wine for them both.

'They have dined with Mrs Watson, as you decreed.'

Decreed! Jason stopped, the decanter in mid-air. 'I am glad to see my wishes still carry *some* weight in this house, madam.'

She smiled, not a whit perturbed by his acid tone.

'Pray do not be so tiresome, Jason. I would not deliberately flout your orders.' She sat down on the sofa and arranged her skirts before looking up at him again, her lips curving into a mischievous smile. 'Well? Are you going to stare at me all night or shall we take wine together?'

The anger that had been building vanished and Jason gave a crack of laughter. He filled the glasses and carried one over to her.

'How was your shopping trip?'

'Oh, we had a splendid time! Madame Sophie is an excellent seamstress. She showed me several garments that she is working on at the moment, and I have ordered a new morning gown and a walking out dress. But perhaps I should spare you the details.'

'Please do!'

He handed her a glass and she took it, glancing up at him.

'I also ordered a new gown for Rose. I hope you do not mind, sir?'

'Not at all,' he replied. 'Will it be finished in time for me to see her wearing it, or will we have to send it on to her in Kent?'

Angel took a sip of wine before replying. 'Their visit could always be extended.'

'No, it could not. The children need to get back to their routine.'

'Rose is hardly a child any more, Jason.' She had clearly observed the crease furrowing his brow and smiled. 'But let us not quarrel. Tell me about your day. I visited the schoolroom before coming downstairs and Nell can talk of nothing but the lake. There is no doubt that *she* enjoyed herself!'

'I am very glad about that. I did my best, but you know I have no experience of children.'

'She said that with your help she rowed across the lake. She is so proud. Before today, I believe she was more than a little in awe of you.'

'I cannot think why that should be.'

'Can you not? Rose told me that before coming to Rotherton she and Nell had never spent more than an hour or two in your company.'

Her tone was even enough, but it did not prevent Jason experiencing a small flare of guilt. Had he been wrong to leave the children in Kent? Surely they were safer there. Happy and secure. He did not want their vision of their mother tarnished by gossip. He wanted to protect them from the truth. At least until they were older.

'They want for nothing. Mrs Watson is an excellent guardian. They do not need me.'

Her shoulders lifted a fraction.

'You disagree?' he challenged her, on the alert for her next assault.

She hesitated, as if weighing her words carefully.

'You are their father, or stepfather, in Rose's case,' she amended. 'How are they to learn by what standards to measure a gentleman if you are never there to set the example?'

He wanted to believe her, but he had shirked his responsibilities towards the girls for too long. It was too late to change now.

He shook his head. 'Very flattering, ma'am, but you will not persuade me to change my mind. The children will return to Kent and there's an end to it.'

The entry of Langshaw at that moment prevented any further conversation. Jason escorted his wife to the dining room and the subject was not mentioned again, but he was not fooled. He knew Angel too well to think it really was the end of the matter.

Angel had certainly not forgotten Rose and Nell. The Duke was a kind man at heart, she knew that, but his upbringing had been very different from her own. He had been reared by servants and clearly saw no reason why his children should be treated any differently. Angel thought it might not be too difficult to persuade him that Nell should live with them, but his stepdaughter was another matter. Judging by the portrait of Lavinia in the Yellow Salon, Rose looked very like her mother. The idea that this reminder of his dead wife was too disturbing for Jason sent a chill through Angel that was hard to dispel.

Last night's kiss, which had set her body tingling, had clearly not affected the Duke the same way. That strengthened her suspicion that he was still in love with his first wife, and she could understand that to have Lavinia's daughter living at Rotherton would be a constant, painful reminder of what he had lost. But that would not stop her trying to change his mind.

When they sat down to dinner Angel engaged Jason in light-hearted conversation on a number of unexceptional subjects. That and the excellent food did much to restore the easy camaraderie between them, and after the meal Angel was pleased and surprised when Jason said he would take his brandy with her, rather than keeping solitary state at the table.

'And I believe you have a new sitting room,' he added, as they went through to the drawing room.

'Yes. Oh, dear, I beg your pardon, Jason. I should have told you.'

He shook his head at her. 'There is no need to look so guilty. We have been distracted by our visitors.'

'I suppose we have.' She hesitated. 'Would you like to see it now?'

She led the way into the little corner room she had taken for her own. It was glowing with the evening sunshine and she was pleased that he was seeing it at its best.

'I hope you do not object? The room was empty and Mrs Wenlock said there were no plans for it. She helped me to find all the furniture and the curtains from what was stored in the attics—'

'Hush, hush!' he interrupted her, laughing. 'You do not need to justify anything to me, Angel. I gave you carte blanche to do what you wished at Rotherton and you have turned this into a snug little lair for yourself. My only criticism is that it has cost me nothing. I recognise everything here, the faded chairs, for example, and that old writing desk.'

'But I do not need anything new,' she assured him. 'This is a room in which I can be comfortable.'

'I believe you can.' A heartbeat of hesitation, then he said, 'And will you allow me to join you, sometimes?'

'Of course, whenever you wish.' A little rush of happiness bubbled up and she added, 'We might sit here now, if you like. I could ring for Langshaw to bring in your brandy, and a glass of wine for me.'

When the wine had been served they sat together and talked. Angel asked him about his visit to London and the country estates before entertaining him with a description of her sisters' visit.

Jason sipped his brandy and watched her, observing how her hair gleamed like polished mahogany in the evening sunlight.

A feeling of quiet contentment stole over him. He remembered sitting on this very sofa years ago. It was still comfortable, despite the covers being a trifle worn. He could not recall when he had last felt so at home in his own house.

The sun had finally disappeared below the horizon and the shadows were lengthening when the butler came in with a lighted taper.

Jason put down his glass and jumped up. 'Thank you, Langshaw, I'll do that.'

He took the taper and made his way around the room, taking no small satisfaction in replacing the evening gloom with the soft glow of the candles.

'You know,' he remarked, 'Rotherton feels very different from how it was when I went away.'

'I have made only small changes, and done nothing without consulting Mrs Wenlock or Langshaw.'

'No, no, I am not complaining, I like it. The house is more...comfortable, somehow. More like Goole Park.'

'Mayhap that is because of the children. I did not wish them to be confined to the nursery wing.'

He chuckled. 'Aye, that would be it. They leave their

mark wherever they go…cushions disturbed, furniture out of place.'

'But they do no harm, Jason.'

'No, I know that.'

'Then why not allow them to make their home here?'

He paused before lighting the last candle.

Because I want you to myself. Selfish, I know, but I don't want to share you!

'No.' He blew out the taper and sat down beside her, searching for more excuses not to have the children there. 'It would be too much work for you. They would consume all your time and energy.'

She laughed. 'With so many servants they consume very little of either. And Mrs Watson would most likely come and live here with them. How can that be too much work for me?'

'It will be. Trust me on that.'

Jason tried to convince himself he was right. What did either of them know of raising a family? Lavinia had been a mother: she had made it plain to him that children were better off in their own establishment. He could still hear her explaining it to him, shortly after Nell was born.

'Believe me, Jason, children demand far too much of a mother's time. She has no leisure to think of her husband's needs…'

Something twisted inside. It was ironic that shortly after she had told him this he'd discovered how rarely she thought of her husband or his needs.

He turned to Angel, sitting beside him. She was gazing at him, a shy smile in her eyes, and he ran a finger down her cheek. The dark lashes fluttered and her lips parted a little, inviting him to kiss her. It set his pulse racing, but he knew it would not stop at one kiss. She filled his senses. It was difficult to think of anything except taking her to his bed and exploring every inch of that creamy, soft skin.

She touched his arm. 'It would take very little to refurbish the nursery wing, Jason.'

'No!' He caught her hand. 'Stop this now, madam.'

He saw her flinch, as if he had slapped her. The hurt in her eyes caused a sudden constriction in his chest.

She said quietly, 'Can we not even *talk* about it?'

His breath hitched as those dark eyes searched his face. Was she really so innocent that she did not know the effect she was having on him?

He said brusquely, 'We *have* talked, and I have given you my final word. I will not countenance it.' He pushed himself to his feet. 'It is growing late. I will escort you to your room.'

He braced himself for a scene. Tears had been Lavinia's weapon. Her blue eyes would glisten like sapphires and she would look more adorable than ever. The boy he had been had succumbed, time and again, giving way to her on every point. It had taken him years to realise it was all a sham… that she had never truly loved him.

It was a lesson he had learned well, he thought as he held out one hand to Angel. 'Well, madam, are you ready?'

He hardened his heart, steeling himself as he waited for her to weep or rail against him. Or to sulk.

Instead she took the proffered hand and allowed him to pull her to her feet.

'I am perfectly ready, Your Grace.'

Angel accompanied the Duke silently up the stairs. He had withdrawn from her as soon as she had mentioned bringing the children here, yet moments earlier he himself had spoken about them quite comfortably. They stopped at the door of her bedchamber.

'Are you still at odds with me?' she asked, noting his frown.

He started, as if his thoughts had been far away. 'No, no. I…er… I was thinking of something. Business I need to finish.'

It seemed a poor excuse and she did not really believe him. She searched his face for some sign of warmth, but his eyes were shuttered. Hard and indifferent, as if they were strangers. She wanted him to talk to her—about the children, about his dead wife—but she knew that was not his way. Not yet, at least.

She gave a little smile, a slight lift of her shoulders, and eased her hand from his arm. So be it.

He opened her door and stepped back for her to enter. 'Goodnight, madam.'

With a quiet 'goodnight' Angel walked past him into the room. It would take time and patience to bring out the kind, loving man she was sure lurked behind his cold exterior,

Having said he must work, Jason went back to his study and sat down at his desk, but it was impossible to concentrate on the ledgers spread out before him. He could not forget the way Angel had looked when he had left her. The enigmatic glance…the cool way she had wished him goodnight.

She confused him. No tears, no tantrums. The thought that she did not care for him occurred, only to be rejected. Angel was not like Lavinia. She was too sweet, too innocent to use her feminine allure to get her own way. At least not deliberately.

Jason shifted restlessly on his chair, recalling how good it had felt to hold her, to kiss her. He had been lost the moment he'd taken her in his arms. After Lavinia, he had not believed he could feel such an all-consuming passion for another woman, but it seemed he was wrong, and it disturbed him.

Two hours and a few glasses of brandy later, Jason slipped into his own bed, but sleep would not come. He tossed and turned, his mind wandering constantly to the woman in the next room. Was Angel asleep, or was she, too, lying awake, her body aching for his touch? He almost groaned at the thought, but he would not give in. He had promised himself he would be strong for both of them. His marriage to Lavinia had turned into a living hell because he had rushed into it. He was not about to make the same mistake again.

Shortly after dawn Jason gave up trying to sleep. He threw on his clothes and went out to the stables for an early-morning ride. The exercise and fresh air helped him to clear his head, and a couple of hours later he was able to join everyone for breakfast with at least the semblance of calm.

Angel was the first thing he noticed when he entered the room. She was very pale, as if she, too, had not slept well. She was talking calmly enough with Mrs Watson, and joking with Rose, but when he addressed a remark to her she avoided his eyes as she made her reply.

He knew then, without any doubt, that his coldness last night had upset her. His conscience smote him, he could not bear to see Angel unhappy. He needed to talk to her. Alone.

At the first break in the conversation he said, 'It is such a lovely day, Duchess, I thought we might go riding together. The ground is firm, but not too hard. Perfect for a gallop.'

'Oh…' A gratifying blush suffused her cheeks. 'But you have already been riding today.'

'Which is how I know it is the perfect morning for going out.'

She gave a tiny shake of her head. 'That is very kind of

you, Your Grace, but Rose and I are going into Rotherton to collect her new gown. Perhaps another day.'

Mrs Watson earned Jason's eternal gratitude by saying, 'If that is all, ma'am, I would be happy to go with Rose in your stead.'

'An excellent idea!' He turned back to Angel. 'Well, Duchess, what do you say? I have yet to see you put that handsome chestnut gelding of yours through its paces.'

Still she demurred. 'I would not want to take up your time. I know Mr Merrick has business matters to discuss with you.'

'There are always business matters to discuss, but they will wait.' He waved away her arguments. 'I will see Simon later. It would be a pity not to take advantage of this good weather.'

She was going to refuse. He saw it in her face and he waited to hear what excuse she would come up with next. Then help came from an unexpected source.

'Do go, Angel,' Rose urged her. 'I am sure Mrs Watson would enjoy a visit to Madame Sophie. And Nell has not yet been to Middlewych,' she added. 'She could come with us, too.'

'Well, if you are sure…'

'Good. I shall send word to the stables immediately,' declared Jason, before Angel could come up with any more excuses. 'Mrs Watson will take the girls into Middlewych.' He turned to smile at the widow. 'You must stop at the Rotherton Arms, ma'am. It is on the high street, and when you have finished your shopping they will provide you with a luncheon!'

'There appears to be nothing more to be said on the matter,' murmured Angel.

She was looking a little bemused, but she was at least smiling.

Jason grinned at her. 'Exactly. I shall tell Thomas to have our horses ready in, say, half an hour. Will that suit you?'

'Yes, thank you. If you will excuse me? I will go and change.'

Angel quickly donned her riding habit of tawny wool with its matching curly brimmed hat. It was not new, but it fitted her like a glove, making the most of her slender figure. Half an hour later she was holding up the voluminous skirts and hurrying down the stairs again.

The Duke was waiting for her in the hall and he smiled as she approached. 'Shall we go?'

They stepped out into the warm sunshine and made their way to the stables, where their horses were ready and waiting. Apollo was a little restive at first. However, by the time he had settled down any awkwardness she'd felt at being alone with Jason had evaporated.

'You did not ride that mare earlier this morning, I presume?' she remarked, nodding towards the rangy black hunter he was riding.

'No, I took out Major. He's an old boy now, but still enjoys a gallop.'

'I am surprised you wished to ride out again so soon.'

'As I said, it is a shame to waste such a day as this.' He glanced across at her. 'And I wanted to have you to myself for a while.'

His words and the glinting smile that accompanied them caught her off guard. She felt herself blushing, but Jason had already ridden ahead and she urged Apollo into a canter. The ground was not unfamiliar—a groom had accompanied her for a few gentle rides while the Duke had been absent from Rotherton—but this was different. Riding out with Jason, pushing Apollo to keep up with him. she felt like a child again, eager to prove she was his equal in the saddle. And when they eventually drew rein and he complimented her, she felt the same flush of unalloyed joy that she had done all those years ago.

'I am not offering you Spanish coin, Angel,' he told her. 'You are an excellent horsewoman. It was neck or nothing over those hedges.'

'That was all Apollo,' she said, leaning forward to pat the gelding's ruddy neck. 'Papa thought he might be too strong for me, but Barnaby persuaded him otherwise.'

'Yes, because he knows how well you ride. Do you remember how you used to steal off on his horse and go careering across the countryside? Without a lady's saddle, too!'

'Stop, stop!' she cried, laughing. 'I am ashamed to think I was such a sad romp!'

'Don't be,' he told her. 'I have always admired your spirit.'

His words took her by surprise. They pleased her, too, for it was a compliment of no mean order, although Jason appeared unaware of it. He was already looking to the far hills.

'There is a good viewpoint beyond the woods. If we push on we should be able to reach it before we need to turn for home. What do you say?'

Angel readily agreed and they set off again, cantering across the open ground and slowing only as they rode through a small area of woodland that covered the lower slopes of the hill.

When they reached the viewpoint, Jason came to a halt. 'Well, what do you think?'

'It's beautiful.'

While Angel gazed at the patchwork of fields and woodland spread out below them Jason took the opportunity to study her, thinking how well she looked on horseback. Her back straight, hands lightly holding the reins, she looked completely at home. Her figure showed to advantage, too, in that habit. It was the rich yellow-brown of autumn leaves and contrasted well with the glossy mahogany of her hair, peeping out beneath that fetching little hat. The mannish jacket fitted perfectly, accentuating a waist so small he thought his hands might well be able to encircle it. In fact, his fingers itched to try.

'Do we have time to walk for a little while?'

Her warm brown eyes were fixed on him, and it took a few moments for Jason to register what she had said and answer her.

'As much time as you wish!'

Having tethered the horses to a bush, Jason lifted her down, holding her for a fraction longer than was necessary.

'What is the joke, sir? Why are you smiling like that?'

She was looking up at him, her brows raised, and he felt the smile deepen inside like a warm glow.

'I had been wondering if I could span your waist with my hands. Now I know.'

She blushed adorably, and with a laugh he pulled her hand onto his sleeve.

'Come along, let us walk!' He led her to the edge of the escarpment, where the land fell away steeply. 'You can see Rotherton from here,' he said, pointing. 'Look for Middlewych first, over there. Then follow the river. Do you see? The house is just visible on the rise beyond the woods.'

'Yes, yes, I see it. I had not realised we had come so far.'

'Was it worth the ride?'

'Oh, yes, very much so.' She turned to him, her eyes glowing with pleasure. '*Thank* you, Jason, for suggesting it.'

'You are very welcome.' Something shifted inside him as he gazed down at her smiling, heart-shaped face. 'But I had my reasons for wanting to ride out with you. I needed to talk to you alone. To atone for my boorish behaviour yesterday.'

Her smile faded. She looked away from him and stared out across the landscape.

'You were angry with me. For suggesting Rose and Nell should live at Rotherton.'

'Yes, I was angry, and it was wrong of me. I should have explained why I will not have them at the house. It is for purely logical, practical reasons.'

They were the reasons Lavinia had given him, but that did not make them any less true. At least, that was what he had always told himself.

He went on. 'Children are noisy and disruptive. It is their nature. And they are forever getting under one's feet. If they lived with us then before long we would resent having them in the house. These are early days in our marriage. Their presence would cause arguments and possibly ill feeling between us.'

Angel turned to stare at him, a crease furrowing her brow. 'Who has told you this, Jason?'

'You have visited the establishment in Kent,' he said, ignoring her question. 'You cannot deny that Rose and Nell are very happy with Mrs Watson. Why move them?'

Angel did not reply but she looked down, hiding her thoughts from him.

He gave a hiss of exasperation. 'Why is it so important to you that they should live at Rotherton?'

'Why is it so important to you that they should not?' she countered.

'I have told you. They would destroy our comfort. Neither of us is experienced in rearing a family.'

'But we could learn, Jason. Will you not even consider it?'

'I *have* considered, and decided it will not do.'

'Not even for their come-out?'

He hesitated. 'Nell, perhaps, can be presented in London. But not Rose.'

She looked troubled at that, and he frowned.

'What? What is it, Angel? Out with it!'

'I wondered.' She stopped and Jason noted how tightly she was gripping her riding crop. 'Rose looks so very like her mother. I thought…the memories, your loss. I thought seeing her might be too painful for you.'

She was right, it *was* painful, Jason admitted to himself. But not for the reason she thought.

A shadow crossed her countenance. She said gently, 'It is true, then. She reminds you too much of your lost love.'

Jason knew he should tell her the truth. He wanted to tell her that it was not love he felt for Lavinia but rage and disgust. He was also fearful. If Rose turned out like her mother she would be a determined flirt. Then again, she was an innocent, and such a beautiful young woman would be the target of every rake in London. He was afraid he would not be able to protect her. He wanted to say all this, but it was as if the words were locked somewhere inside and he did not have the key.

He scowled in frustration. 'That is nonsense.' He waved one hand dismissively. 'Rose is a very pretty girl. Beautiful, even, but that is not why I am against her living at Rotherton.'

Angel did not look as if she quite believed that, but there was no judgement in her dark eyes. She merely wanted to understand him, and she deserved that he should at least try to explain.

He turned away and walked a few paces along the ridge, fighting against his reticence, the defensive wall he had built around himself. He must say something.

'If you want the truth,' *Well, part of it, at least…* 'I am afraid of not living up to their expectations. I.' *Deep breath, man. Tell her!* 'I do not know how to go on, how to behave, with children.'

'You managed very well with Nell,' Angel reminded him. 'She loved her time on the lake with you. It is now *Papa this*, and *Papa that* at every turn.' She chuckled. 'You have become quite a favourite.'

'I am glad. I do not want her to be afraid of me.' He looked back. 'But that does not mean I will allow the girls to be uprooted from Kent!'

'If it is because you feel ill at ease with them, that will change once you are better acquainted.' She came closer and touched his sleeve. 'You should give them a chance to get to know you.'

He shook her off. 'Dammit, Angel, why will you not let it be? We all went on very well before you started interfering!'

She said gently, 'We both know that is not true.'

He gave a sigh and stared out towards the horizon. 'You are quite right. It isn't true.'

He could feel his defences crumbling. 'Perhaps we could extend their visit,' he said at last. 'See how we all go on together.'

'That is a good idea.' She slipped one hand into the crook of his arm. 'Rotherton is a very large house, Jason. The girls need not trouble you.'

'No, well… We shall see.' He glanced at the sun. 'It grows late. We should be heading back.'

They walked to the horses in silence and he threw her up into the saddle, holding on to the bridle until she had Apollo under control.

'Thank you.' She smiled down at him and he shook his head.

'I make no promises about the girls,' he warned her as

he sprang up onto the hunter. 'You will say nothing to them about making their home with us!'

'But of course not, Your Grace. The decision to have Nell and Rose live with us at Rotherton must be yours and yours alone.'

Her meek tone made him frown suspiciously, but she met his gaze with such wide-eyed innocence that he did not challenge her further.

And yet, as they made their way down the hill, he had the feeling that he had already lost that battle.

Chapter Seven

By dinner the following day Mrs Watson and her charges had been invited to remain for another month. The Duke had also given instructions that they should dine together *en famille* in the little dining room.

Angel was surprised at this sudden change of heart and said as much, although she waited until Mrs Watson had taken Rose and Nell up to bed before broaching the subject.

'How kind of you to suggest they should all stay a little longer.'

They were alone in the drawing room and Jason was pouring them both a glass of wine.

'I could hardly do anything else after your cajoling yesterday.'

She saw the glint of amusement in his eyes and laughed. 'Perhaps not, but I had not expected you to act quite so soon.'

'It seemed…expedient.' He sat down beside her. 'I put the idea to Mrs Watson this morning and she thought it would be especially beneficial for Rose. Before they left Ashford she had been attracting a great deal of attention from the local beaux.'

'That does not surprise me. Rose is exceptionally pretty.' She slanted a glance at him. 'As I told you, she is no longer a child.'

'She is only seventeen.'

'But not too young to go into society a little.'

'Perhaps not.'

Angel waited a moment, then she said slowly, 'There is an assembly at the Rotherton Arms on Thursday next.'

'Surely you are not suggesting we take her?'

'Why not? I am sure it is perfectly respectable.'

'I would not know. I have not attended a dance there for years. You know I was never one for such occasions, Angel.'

She turned slightly to look at him. 'Did you never take your duchess to an assembly there?'

'At first, yes. But in later years…' His jaw tightened. 'We were rarely at Rotherton together.'

Angel hid her surprise. She recalled her conversation with her sisters and the rumours concerning Lavinia and the Prince of Wales. Could it be Lavinia had played the Duke false? Perhaps they had both looked elsewhere for their pleasures.

She quickly pushed the thought aside.

'Well, I shall make enquiries,' she told him. 'If reports are favourable then I shall take Rose to the assembly. It will give her a chance to show off her new gown. There will be no need for you to trouble yourself, Your Grace. Mrs Watson will come with us.'

But this Jason would not allow. 'If you go, then I must go with you.'

'But why? You have just said you dislike going into company. And after London I am sure you will find a provincial dance deadly dull.'

She could not keep a slight edge from her voice and he heard it.

'I was in London for business, madam. I did not attend

any balls,' he retorted. 'However, it would be my duty to accompany you to your first assembly at Rotherton.'

Ah, yes, duty. Her spirits dipped.

'Also,' he went on, 'I need to show the young bucks of Rotherton that Rose is under my protection and not to be trifled with.'

'Then we shall be very glad of your company,' replied Angel, rising. 'Now, if you will excuse me, I shall go to bed. No, don't get up, sir. You have not yet finished your wine and I am quite capable of finding my way to my room.'

With that she went out, closing the door gently behind her. This was definite progress. Even if he had only agreed out of a sense of duty, Jason had relented on extending Rose and Nell's visit and he had also declared he would accompany them to the assembly.

As she went up the stairs Angel's heart gave a little skip at the thought that he might even be persuaded to dance with her.

Alone in the silent room, Jason sat back and exhaled, long and slow. Why the devil had he said he would go to the Rotherton Arms? It was bound to be a tedious evening. He did not like assemblies. It was bad enough being obliged to stand up with a succession of elderly matrons or simpering debutantes. Even worse would be the stares and sly glances. The rumours shared in quiet corners.

He rubbed his chin. There really was no need for him to go for Rose's sake. The mere fact that she was his stepdaughter would ensure no one tried to take advantage of her. And he was confident that Mrs Watson would not allow her charge to indulge in anything but the mildest of flirtations.

But what about Angel? Who would protect her from the

whispers and the gossip? Or indeed from any roguish fellows bent on mischief?

'By heaven, I will go!' he exclaimed to the empty room. 'And I will stand up with her myself for every dance if necessary!'

He was startled by his sudden outburst, but amused too. Angel would never countenance such behaviour. He could almost hear her chiding him if he refused to dance with any other lady. Most unbecoming of a duke to snub his neighbours like that!

He finished his wine and set off for his bedchamber, but at Angel's door he stopped. Should he go in? Would she welcome him?

He reached out but stopped short of grasping the handle. She had made it perfectly plain she did not want him to accompany her. And their conversation had been all about the children.

His hand fell and he walked on.

Angel had no interest in him at all.

On Thursday evening Angeline left her room at the appointed time, arrayed in an evening gown of cerulean blue silk net embroidered with gold thread. She had ordered it from Madame Sophie at the same time as choosing new dresses for Rose, and she hoped that Jason would approve.

She made her way down the grand staircase to find the Duke was already in the hall and looking very handsome in his black evening dress. He was conversing with Mrs Watson, but broke off when Angel appeared and came towards her.

'Ah, there you are at last.'

He was smiling, and she was tempted to ask what he thought of the gown, but decided against it.

'I hope I have not kept you waiting?'

'No, no. The carriage is at the door, but the horses will take no harm for a few more minutes.' He took the silk cloak from her and began to arrange it around her shoulders. 'Rose has not appeared yet.'

'I am sure she will be here soon,' said Angel. 'I sent Joan along to dress her hair.'

At that moment Rose came down the stairs, wearing her new gown of white muslin.

'And I am here now.'

Angel looked up as Jason's hands gripped her shoulders. His eyes were fixed on Rose. He was very pale, and a muscle twitched in his cheek. He looked as if he had seen a ghost.

Angel's spirits plummeted, but the next moment he had released her and moved forward, smiling and holding out his hands to his stepdaughter.

'You look charming, my dear. You will be the belle of the ball tonight, I am sure.'

Rose blushed and disclaimed. 'Th-thank you, Your Grace. Do you not think Angel looks very well in her new silk gown?'

'I do. I think she looks beautiful.'

Angel had looked away and was busy tying the strings of her cloak.

'Pray, do not go on,' she said, forcing a little laugh. 'You will put me to the blush. Now, if we are ready, shall we go?'

Even to her own ears her cheerfulness sounded strained. Jason was looking keenly at her, but she avoided his eyes and hurried out to the waiting carriage.

The assembly rooms at the Rotherton Arms were already crowded when Jason escorted his party to the ballroom, although the dancing had not yet commenced. It was a warm evening and the ladies' fans were in play. A happy buzz of voices was filling the room, but the chatter sank to near silence when they walked in. The noise quickly swelled again and Mr Burchill, the master of ceremonies, hurried across to the newcomers, exclaiming at the honour His Grace was bestowing upon their humble gathering.

Angel had been very quiet in the carriage, but Jason was relieved to see she had quite recovered her spirits. As he exchanged a few words with the master of ceremonies he watched her responding to the Squire and his lady, who had come up to greet them. She was quite at ease and he relaxed a little. A country mouse she might be, but she knew how to go on in company.

The musicians struck up for the first dance and Jason prepared himself for the coming ordeal. He was naturally reserved, but he knew what was expected of him.

Burchill presented him to a dowager viscountess for the first dance, and then he stood up with the Squire's wife. His next partner was Lady Kennet, a rather alarming widow who still lived in the family home and tyrannised her son and daughter-in-law. She had known the Duke since he was a boy and took great pleasure in reminding him of the fact.

'So you have married again,' she remarked as the music ended. 'I met your new duchess at the little party Lady Whalton gave to welcome her to Rotherton. You were away at the time.'

Jason did not miss the faint note of censure in her last words. He said mildly, 'Yes, I had business that could not wait.' He gave her his arm to escort her off the floor. 'But I am here now, and mean to remain for some time.'

'I am glad to hear it. Everyone at Rotherton was surprised to find you had wed again so soon, but your new duchess is a charming gel. She will do very well for you.'

He inclined his head and said drily, 'I'm glad you approve, ma'am.'

'I do,' she replied. 'I also like the look of your stepdaughter. Very pretty manners. She is bidding fair to be a beauty, too. Like her mother.' She released his arm. 'Let us hope that is the only thing she has inherited from the late Duchess!'

On this parting shot she walked away, and Jason took himself off to the refreshments table to recover his composure. He had known coming here tonight would be a trial, but he had hoped no one would mention Lavinia to his face. Now he could not wait for the evening to end!

He was standing by the punchbowl when Angel came up to him.

'You are taking a second cup?' she asked, smiling. 'Oh, dear, is it as bad as that?'

The laugh in her voice instantly soothed his ill temper.

'I am rewarding myself for spending the first half of the evening doing the pretty on the dance floor with my neighbours.'

He filled a fresh cup and handed it to her. 'It really wasn't that bad. I am just out of practice at exchanging niceties with my dance partners.'

'Then dance with me next. You do not need to be polite to me.'

She was sipping at her punch and gazing away into the distance, as if his answer did not really matter to her.

He frowned. 'Have we ever danced together? I cannot remember it.'

'I was still in the schoolroom the last time you came to Goole Park,' she reminded him. 'You were fifteen and despised dancing. We never stood up together.'

Jason grinned. 'Then it is high time we rectified the matter!'

'Yes, isn't it?' Her eyes twinkled in response. 'Although

I believe it is highly unfashionable to dance with one's husband.'

'Do you care about that?'

The twinkled deepened. 'Not in the least.'

'Very well then.' He put down his cup. 'The next set is forming. Shall we join them?'

They danced two country dances together, then the Duke persuaded her to dance a reel, after which she begged to be allowed to sit down and he accompanied her to a couple of empty chairs.

Angel sat back with a sigh and closed her eyes. 'That is better. I am so hot I can scarce breathe!'

Taking her fan, he opened it and waved it to and fro, making the tiny curls around her face dance.

'There, is that better?'

'Yes, thank you.' Angel smiled. 'How pleasant it would be to sit here with you for the rest of the evening, but it cannot be.'

'Why not? We are Duke and Duchess. We can do as we wish.'

She chuckled. 'You know that is not so. Your neighbours all wish to speak with you, and you will want to look out for Rose, too.'

'Will I?'

'I thought you had come to make sure no young men became too familiar with her.'

'It was clear to me from the start that Mrs Watson is more than capable of looking after Rose.' He glanced around the room. 'At present my stepdaughter appears to be part of a large group of young people. She has made friends very quickly.'

'I took her to visit some of the families in the area as

soon as she arrived, so she is already acquainted with several of them.'

'You are very good to her.'

'Why should I not be?' She looked at him, surprised. 'I am very fond of Rose. And Nell, too.'

'Many new wives would resent their stepdaughters. And some new husbands might resent their bride giving so much attention to anyone but themselves. Not that that applies to me!' he added hastily, remembering his earlier selfish thoughts.

'No. Of course.'

Was that a note of disappointment in her voice? Did she *want* to spend more time with him?

Jason was about to ask but Angel was looking past him, and he turned his head to see a portly gentleman bearing down on them.

He clicked his tongue in annoyance. 'And here comes Burchill to carry you off again. He takes his duties very seriously. Shall I tell him you are indisposed or merely wave him away?'

'Neither,' she muttered. 'Hush, now, or he will hear you.'

'Ah, Your Grace.' Mr Burchill's corset creaked as he made a very low bow to Jason. 'What a splendid evening this is turning out to be! You have been most obliging, Your Grace, most obliging. And I know you will not object if I steal your good lady away from you once more. There is someone here very desirous to meet her. And if Her Grace will be so kind as to honour the gentleman with her hand for the next dance…'

Jason cast a teasing glance at Angel. 'Alas, sir, I fear my wife is feeling the heat somewhat—'

'Nonsense, I am quite recovered now.' She flew out of her chair and bestowed a brilliant smile upon the master of ceremonies. 'I shall be delighted to dance again, Mr Burchill. Lead on, sir!'

'Ah, you are too kind, ma'am, but with so many gentlemen begging for the honour of dancing with Your Grace, I fear we will not be able to accommodate them all.'

Jason had also risen and he touched Burchill's arm.

'One more thing before you go. The Duchess is at liberty to dance with anyone she wishes this evening. Except for the final dance.' He looked at Angel. 'That, madam, I claim for myself.'

His tone was deliberately autocratic and he wondered how she would respond. Her head came up and the flash of fire in those dark eyes was a mixture of surprise, anger and amusement. Then she snatched her fan from his hand and, with a look that promised retribution for his teasing, sailed off to meet her next partner.

Having sent his duchess away to dance, Jason discovered he did not want to stand up with anyone else. He feared he would not be able to give his partner sufficient attention. His eyes would be following Angel, anxious to see just how much she was enjoying another man's attentions. He remembered only too well the agony of watching his first wife flirting with her dance partners and did not wish to experience that hurt again.

Not that he had ever allowed anyone but Lavinia to see how much he cared.

At first she had laughed it off and soothed his ruffled feathers. Later he had discovered it was not only on the dance floor that she enjoyed other men's company.

Looking back, he could not recall precisely when his jealousy had faded, leaving only anger and outrage at her behaviour. He only knew that at some time, long before she had broken her neck in that carriage accident, he had ceased to love his wife.

Jason saw Rose going down the dance with Kenelm Babberton, the son of one of his neighbours. The boy was clearly enraptured. He could not keep his eyes off his partner and Jason did not blame him. At seventeen, Rose was already bidding fair to rival her mother, with her golden hair and that bewitching smile. She would break hearts, he knew it, but she would also attract any number of rogues.

Not that Babberton was a rogue, thought Jason, regarding the young man's honest, open countenance. He was more likely to need protecting from voracious females!

Nevertheless, Jason decided he should make it plain that he was keeping a watchful eye on his stepdaughter. He wandered across the room to join Mrs Watson until the dance ended, then he would stand up with Rose himself.

Angel did not sit down again for the rest of the evening. The master of ceremonies had not lied about the number of gentlemen wishing to stand up with her. Thankfully, she loved to dance and enjoyed herself immensely, but deep inside a little fizz of anticipation was building as the evening drew to a close.

Had Jason been serious when he had claimed the last dance from her? A slight shiver ran through her when she remembered his haughty tone and the hot, possessive look in his eyes as he had spoken.

He was making it plain to the world that she was his.

The sizzle of excitement increased. Did he also intend to make it clear to her, later, by taking her to bed?

Angel laughed and talked with her partners, but all the time she was aware of the Duke. His tall figure was easy to spot as he made his way around the room, with a word here, a smile there. Then she saw him dancing with Rose, and for one dreadful moment her heart stopped.

This was how it must have looked when he and Lavinia had danced together. The Duke broad-shouldered and straight-backed, a commanding presence on the dance floor, and his duchess a dazzling golden beauty at his side. Angel forced her eyes away. The black, raging jealousy she felt for a dead woman was foolish and illogical. She must not give in to it.

The evening was almost over and Angel slipped away to a shadowy corner of the room to avoid Mr Burchill, whom she knew would want her to dance again. There was an open window nearby and she moved across to it, looking down into the dark street below. She felt tired, even a little deflated, and wanted to save her remaining energy for her dance with Jason.

She had been looking forward to it so much that she was afraid that it might not live up to her expectations. It was only one dance, after all. Did she hope to impress him? At eight-and-twenty, the Duke was no stranger to society. He had danced in the finest ballrooms and with the most beautiful and accomplished dancers. Her own performance must surely compare most unfavourably.

'Well, madam, are you ready for our dance?'

Angel turned quickly. The Duke was standing beside her, as immaculate as when they had arrived. Other men were looking a little dishevelled, and some of them distinctly red-faced, after the evening's exertions, but not Jason. His raven hair was still neat, the blue-black coat lay smoothly across his broad chest and the snowy linen of his shirt and neckcloth were immaculate. Looking at his face, she noted that save for the shadow of stubble on his lean cheeks he looked cool and composed.

Which was more than she could say for herself. Just the sound of his voice had set her heart racing. She felt hot, anxious, and she was obliged to breathe deeply before she could take his hand and accompany him onto the dance floor.

They took their places in the set. The music started and her nerves steadied a little. They skipped, circled, crossed and twirled as if they had been dancing together for years rather than just this one evening. The Duke was smiling at her, which made Angel's heart soar, and when they were separated by the movement of the dance their coming together again was joyous. By the time she made her final curtsy and walked off on Jason's arm, Angel was bursting with happiness.

As soon as the dancing concluded there was a rush for the doors, with everyone making their way to collect cloaks and change shoes.

'I think we would do well to wait a little,' said the Duke, holding back.

'Very well.' Angel was content to wait with him until the crush had died down.

The servants were already clearing the ballroom and smoke from the freshly snuffed candles clouded the air. Jason guided Angel across to the open window. The shadows were deeper here, and they could hear the noise from the dispersing crowd.

'Tell me,' he said. 'Tell me about this man who broke your heart.'

Angel closed her fan. She had told no one of the pain and humiliation she had felt, but perhaps it was time. She could do this if she kept her tone light.

'It is a familiar story. We met at Almack's. He was very handsome, very charming, and I was flattered by his attentions. I was smitten, and truly thought he loved me. He gave me to understand he would be making me an offer, but then…' She was obliged to take a breath, to swallow the hurt and humiliation that had never quite gone away. 'Then a new debutante arrived in London. A fair-haired beauty who had all the gentlemen vying for her attentions. My beau was the one who won her hand. I first learned of it one night. At Almack's.'

She was so lost in the past that she jumped when Jason put his hands over hers and removed the fan from her fingers.

'You have broken the sticks,' he said gently.

A shudder ran through her, ending in a long sigh. 'It is the first time I have spoken of that night.'

'I am sorry if I have upset you.'

She glanced up and saw his face was full of concern.

'Please don't be sorry. I am glad I have told you. It was a long time ago and deserves to be forgotten.'

'And I am honoured by your confidence. Do you know where this fellow is now?'

'Why do you ask?'

'Because I want to run the villain through!'

He vehemence surprised her. She gave a shaky laugh.

'Then I am glad I did not divulge his name! He married the beauty, but sadly they were both far too extravagant, and soon their debts were such that they were obliged to go abroad to escape their creditors.'

'Leaving you with a broken heart,' he muttered, throwing the mangled fan aside.

'I thought so, at the time. But I have recovered now and I am much the wiser for it.'

He hesitated. 'You told me once that the villain had stolen a kiss from you.'

'Did I?' she looked at him, surprised. 'It is of no consequence now.'

'It has not given you a distaste for kisses?'

'Not in the least.' She blushed and looked away, saying shyly, 'I like it when you kiss me.'

He put his fingers under her chin and she felt their gentle pressure, lifting her face up, then he gently lowered his head. Angel did not wait for his lips to reach hers. She stretched up and captured his mouth, slipping her arm about his neck. What followed was a long, lingering kiss.

They were oblivious to the servants clearing the room, the squeaking chandelier chains and the scrape of chairs being moved, until one of the footmen noticed the couple in the shadows.

'Oh! Beggin' your pardon, sir, madam. I didn't see you there!' he muttered, hurrying away.

Jason lifted his head, but kept his eyes on Angel. There was no mistaking the glow of pleasure in her face.

'I just wanted to be sure,' he murmured, happiness spreading through him like a flame. 'Allow me to escort you home, ma'am.'

'Well, I think that went very well!' declared Mrs Watson when they were all in the carriage and travelling back to Rotherton.

'Oh, yes!' Rose gave a loud sigh. 'I had the most wonderful time. I danced almost every dance!'

'I am glad you enjoyed it,' replied Angel. She turned to Jason, who was sitting beside her. 'I hope you did not find it too tedious, Your Grace?'

His glowing look almost melted her on the spot. He caught her gloved fingers and raised them to his lips.

'On the contrary, it was far better than I expected.'

He continued to hold her hand and she felt quite dizzy with delight as the carriage rattled along the lanes in the early-morning light.

The rest of the journey passed in near silence. Mrs Watson was dozing in her corner and Rose gazed out of the window, most likely reliving her evening, and Angel was happy to sit quietly, her fingers snug in the Duke's warm clasp.

Could anything be more perfect?

Jason held on to the small hand, trying not to crush it. The evening had been a revelation. He had no doubts now that Angel would make him a perfect wife. He had heard nothing but compliments all evening. She won everyone over with her kindness and her gracious manners. He had seen her dancing with his neighbours, dull dogs like the crusty old General Appleton and young Lord Kennet, as well as a floridly handsome buck that Jason did not know, but whom he disliked as soon as he saw him stand up with Angel. He had watched the pair keenly as the music started, ready to step in if the fellow should become too forward, but Angel treated him with the same smiling good humour she had shown to all her partners. She was friendly, cool, and composed.

Until that final dance. Jason's pulse quickened when he remembered standing opposite her and seeing that becoming flush on her cheeks. There was an added sparkle in her eyes, too, and she gave him a beaming smile that he had not seen her bestow on anyone else that evening. His body had responded to that look. It set his pulse racing and he wanted to drag her away into the night and kiss her senseless.

Now, in the darkened coach, with Angel beside him, he had to breathe deep and slow in order to stay calm, reminding himself that they were not alone. *Not yet*, he thought, desire rapidly increasing. But they would soon be back at Rotherton, and tonight he fully intended to make Angel his wife—in every sense.

When they reached the house Jason jumped down from the coach and turned to hand out the ladies. Angel was first, but instead of hurrying away indoors she stood aside, shaking out her skirts while he helped the others to alight. Mrs Watson and Rose moved towards the door, but his heart leapt when he saw Angel was waiting for him.

He closed the door and the carriage moved off.

'Well, madam?'

She came closer and slipped her hand onto his sleeve.

'Well, Your Grace?'

In the dawn light he could see the smile lilting on her lips and he bent to brush them with his own. 'Shall it be my room or yours?'

'Either.' A very wicked gurgle of laughter escaped her. 'Perhaps both?'

Elation surged through Jason. He smothered a laugh and whispered, with mock outrage, 'I thought I had married an innocent maid!'

'I am certainly a maid, sir, but I have two married sisters. One…hears things.' She squeezed his arm. 'We should go indoors, Jason.'

Curbing a desire to pick her up and carry her to his bed, Jason walked her towards the house. As they approached the open door he could hear raised voices coming from the hall, and they stepped inside just as Rose gave a small shriek. She and Mrs Watson were standing with the young nursemaid, who was wringing her hands and looking agitated. All three were talking at once.

'What the devil is going on here?' His voice cut through the chatter.

'It is Nell, Your Grace,' said Mrs Watson. 'Edith says she has a temperature and has thrown out a rash.'

'She has been a little quiet for a couple of days,' said Angel, going forward and casting her cloak onto a bench as she passed. 'Has the doctor been summoned, Edith?'

'N-no, ma'am.' The maid wrung her hands even harder. 'I was going to ask Mrs Wenlock to send someone for the doctor when we heard the carriage. Miss Nell's burning up now something terrible.'

Rose gave a sob and started for the stairs. 'I must go to her!'

'No!' Angel caught her arm. 'She might be infectious. It would be better for you to stay away from your sister until the doctor has examined her.'

'But I must see her! What…what if she does not get better?'

'She will get better,' Angel told her. 'We shall make sure of it.'

It was clear to Jason that this news, following the excitement of the evening, was too much for Rose, and she began to weep. When Mrs Watson tried to comfort her she clung to her, crying even harder.

'Take Rose to her room and look after her, if you please, Mrs Watson,' said Angel, moving towards the stairs.

The older woman hesitated. 'But what about Nell, Your Grace?'

'I will go to her. But we need to send for a doctor.' She glanced towards the footman hovering at the side of the hall. 'You will arrange it, if you please.'

The servant shifted from foot to foot and looked indecisive. Jason recognised him as one of the footmen Lavinia had hired for their stature and handsome faces rather than their intelligence. Angel was already heading up the stairs, but when the man did not move she addressed him again, more sharply.

'Send someone for the doctor, *now*!'

'I will go,' said Jason. He turned back towards the outer door, barking an order to the hapless lackey as he passed. 'Find Adams and tell him to bring my riding boots out to the stables for me!'

With that he left the hall at a run. Whatever amorous intentions he had planned for this evening must wait. It was clear that Nell needed Angel far more than he did tonight.

Chapter Eight

Angel sat beside Nell's bed, occasionally bathing her forehead with lavender oil. The little girl was sleeping now and Angel had sent the nursemaid away to get some rest. Silence had descended on the house and the morning light was growing stronger. There was no clock in the room, but Angel thought an hour at least must have passed since Jason had set off to fetch the doctor. The window was open and she was on the alert for sounds of an arrival. All she could do until then was wait.

It was impossible to stop her thoughts from wandering. If Nell had not been taken ill she might now be lying in Jason's bed. Would there be another chance? He had warned her the children would consume all her time. He might not forgive her for putting Nell's needs before his own.

She shook her head, refusing to believe that Jason could be so selfish, but in her tired mind the sly voice of doubt would not be silenced. After all, he had resisted having the children here. He had warned her how it would be. Perhaps he would put her aside now. Annul the marriage and find himself a duchess more suited to the life he wanted.

Perhaps she should have waited until their marriage was secure before bringing the children to live with them. Now she would not just be losing Jason, she would be losing the girls, too, and she had grown fond of them.

These dismal thoughts were interrupted by the unmistakable sound of a carriage. Moments later she heard voices. The door opened and Jason came in, followed by a stocky man who introduced himself cheerfully as Dr Granger.

'Now then, what have we here?' he said, divesting himself of his hat and gloves and coming over to the bed.

Angel was aware of Jason leaving the room, but she had no time to dwell on it. She quickly explained the symptoms as she knew them to the doctor, then stood back while he made a thorough examination of the sleeping child.

'Your Grace is concerned it might be scarlet fever?'

'That is my biggest fear, Doctor, yes. I had a mild case of it as a child.'

He pulled the sheet back up over Nell.

'I have my doubts, but we must wait a few days to be sure. You will be aware that it is highly infectious. No one should leave the house until we know for certain. I think it would be best if the rest of the household kept away from this room, too.'

'It shall be arranged. The maid Edith and I can look after Nell, if you tell me what to do.'

'Sadly there is very little we can do. Time will tell. I am not in favour of blood-letting in cases like this. Keep her temperature down and get as much liquid in her as you can. Lemonade and barley water are particular good for soothing the throat. And a little soft food or broth, if she can manage it.'

'Thank you. I am sure we can do that.'

'Very well.' He picked up his hat and gloves. 'I will call again tomorrow and see how she goes on.' He looked back at the bed. 'The child looks healthy enough, and if it is not what you fear then she should recover quickly.'

* * *

Jason spoke briefly with Dr Granger before he left and, after giving his instructions to the butler, he went to bed. The doctor had assured him there was nothing more to do now but wait.

It did not surprise him to learn that his duchess had taken charge of the sickroom. That was typical of Angel. The momentary thought that she might be doing it to avoid him occurred only to be dismissed as unworthy of him. He resolved that, in the morning, he would do whatever he could to help her.

'Well, here's a to-do.' Having brought the Duke his morning coffee, Adams was now pouring hot water into the bowl on the washstand. 'Everyone is buzzing with the news that Lady Elinor is at death's door. I left Mrs Wenlock dealing with one of the housemaids, who is in hysterics because she cannot visit her family today, you having given orders that no one is to leave the house.'

'The devil she is! I thought I had explained everything clearly enough to Langshaw before I went to bed.'

'I am sure you did, Your Grace, but with the Duchess choosing to nurse Lady Elinor herself… Well, you know what servants are like.'

'Thankfully I do not!' Jason threw back the covers. 'Dr Granger is not yet certain if it is scarlet fever, but until he *is* sure we must be cautious.'

'Of course, Your Grace. I will visit the servants' hall and do my best to make sure everyone understands that.'

Jason found only Mrs Watson at the breakfast table, and saw immediately that she was looking unusually anxious.

'This is a sad business, Your Grace. I wish that the Duchess had not taken the nursing of Lady Elinor upon herself, and with only young Edith to help her.'

'Her Grace has nieces and nephews, Mrs Watson, and she has some experience of the sickroom,' he reassured her. 'And someone must look after Rose. I hope she is not still distressed?'

'No, sir, but she is so exhausted by the events of yesterday that I left her to sleep.' She paused. 'Her Grace has instructed that we move out of the nursery wing, and I wondered if you would prefer me to take Rose back to Kent? With scarlet fever in the house…'

'The doctor is not yet certain that it is,' he replied coolly. 'Your leaving might unsettle everyone even more.'

She looked relieved. 'I am pleased to hear you say so, Your Grace. Rose would be very unhappy to leave her sister, and I would not wish to go until I know Lady Elinor is out of danger. Families are such a worry, Your Grace, are they not?'

Jason was about to reply that he knew nothing about the matter, but that was not true any longer. After having the girls at Rotherton these past weeks he realised that he had grown accustomed to them being in the house. He liked the lively atmosphere, the cushions out of place, doors left open. The sudden giggles and laughter that echoed through the stately rooms and corridors. The house felt warmer. More alive.

'Yes, they are, Mrs Watson.'

He smiled at her, acknowledging that he was anxious about the girls. And Angel, too.

His family.

After breakfast Jason busied himself in his office, but he could not settle. He was waiting for the doctor to give his judgement upon Nell's illness, as was everyone in the house.

Jason missed Angel damnably. He wanted to know how she was coping, to talk to her. To be of some use. Most of all he wanted to hold her. All he could do for the moment was to go about his business and help to calm the nerves of his household.

It was late on Sunday afternoon when Dr Granger called again. He was taken directly to the sickroom, where Angel was waiting for him.

'Well, Your Grace, Lady Elinor…' He bowed to the little girl, who was propped up against the pillows, looking pale and hollow-eyed. 'At least you are awake for me today!'

Angel liked his cheerful, no-nonsense manner and she managed a smile.

'Nell is a little better, I think, Doctor. She says her throat is very sore, but she has managed to eat a slice of bread dipped in tea this morning. And last night she ate some of the excellent lemon syllabub that Cook prepared especially for her.'

'Well, well, that is good news. We can't have you fading away to a wraith, my lady, can we?'

Angel stood back, watching, as the doctor examined Nell. He continued to talk to her, and although Nell made no reply she did give the doctor a faint, wavering smile when he took his leave. Angel followed him out of the room and they stopped on the landing for him to deliver his verdict.

'I cannot rule out scarlet fever, Your Grace, so we must not relax our guard just yet. You are keeping her isolated?'

'Yes, Doctor. Only Edith and I come into the sickroom, and we keep our distance from the rest of the household.' She saw his brows rise a little and added, 'We take all our meals in the schoolroom, and I am making use of one of the bedchambers in this wing. No one else comes any further than the top of the stairs.'

'Good, good.' He nodded. 'I hope such precautions will not be necessary for very much longer, but the child's temperature is still high, and the rash has not subsided. I will send over a draught to calm her when she grows restless. However, that sore throat worries me. You might try a sage gargle twice a day, and continue to bathe her whenever she grows too hot.' He donned his hat and began to pull on his gloves. 'I shall call again in two days, but do not hesitate to send for me if you are concerned.'

'Thank you, Dr Granger.'

He nodded, and said with a twinkle, 'A message from you at any time, day or night, will fetch me. I've no fear you will disturb me unnecessarily, ma'am!'

With that he ran lightly down the stairs, leaving Angel to return to her charge.

For the next two days Angel and Edith nursed Nell, who was by turns fractious and listless. Angel was heartened though, that the angry red rash was fading, and when Dr Granger called again he declared himself almost sure that Nell was not suffering from scarlet fever.

'However, while there is the slightest doubt we must continue with the precautions,' he warned Angel. 'No visitors, and you and the nursemaid should continue to avoid the other members of the household.'

'For how long, sir? I know Nell's sister is anxious to see her.'

'Well, now…' He stroked his chin. 'These lesser infections sometimes last no more than a week. I will call again on Saturday to see how you go on.'

With that Angel had to be satisfied. She went over to the window and saw Jason on the drive, talking with the doctor. By Saturday it would be a full week since she had spoken with the Duke and she missed him terribly. But what played most on her mind was that he might *not* be missing her.

It was gone nine o'clock when Edith came in to relieve Angel, and she went into the schoolroom to eat the meal that Cook had sent up for her. The tray was already on the table, and as she sat down she saw a folded paper pushed beneath one of the dishes.

It was a note from the Duke, asking her to meet him.

Angel's throat dried as her eyes scanned the paper.

Dr Granger confirms it is safe to meet out of doors, as long as we keep our distance. When you have dined, you will find me waiting on the south lawn.

How was she to understand this? The wording was formal, even a little cold. Was he going to rebuke her? Or was it possible that he wanted her company?

'Well, you will only know once you have spoken to him,' she said aloud.

As soon as she had finished her meal Angel went down the back stairs to the garden door. This brought her out on the far side of the house, but the walk in the fresh air helped to clear her head. It was nearly midsummer, and the sun had not quite set, although it cast long shadows across the formal gardens. The air was warm and she breathed in the fragrance of the summer flowers blooming in the borders.

When she cut through the rose garden the scent was particularly heady. It was an ideal spot for a romantic assignation, she thought, before reluctantly pushing aside such a notion and walking on.

She saw Jason as soon as she reached the south lawn and her stomach flipped over.

'Dr Watson told me the fever had broken,' he said, stopping while they were still some distance apart.

'Yes.' She longed to run to him, to feel his arms about her. 'Nell is a little better. I left her sleeping.'

They began to walk, keeping a wide space between them. Too far even to reach out and touch hands.

'I was afraid you would not come,' he said. 'I know how tired you must be.'

'It is not so very bad. Edith is proving to be very capable. She is sitting with Nell now.'

He nodded. 'Dr Granger said he is hopeful that these restrictions need not last much longer.'

'He does not think it is scarlet fever, but wants to be sure.' She burst out, 'I am so sorry! I should have spoken with you before going off to look after Nell.'

'There was no time. Everything was in uproar and someone had to assume responsibility.'

'And you rode for the doctor yourself,' she said. 'That was very good of you.'

'It is nothing compared to what you have taken upon yourself.'

Angel stopped. 'I did not mean this to happen. I did not mean to abandon you for the children.'

'Hush, now. It could not be helped.'

'But this is not what you wanted!'

'I certainly did not want Nell to be ill, but I am glad that it happened at Rotherton. Granger is an excellent doctor. And he has told me he has the utmost faith in you.'

'That is very gratifying, Your Grace.' She twisted her hands together and said in a rush, 'Once Dr Granger says there is no fear of infection there is no need for you to stay at Rotherton. I am sure you have much to do elsewhere.'

* * *

Jason felt aggrieved that she could think he would walk away from his responsibilities, even though it was what he had done in the past.

'Do you think me so heartless that I would leave my daughter at such a time? I am not so uncaring.'

'I know that, but what I mean is, you must be dreadfully bored here. You might go to London. Visit your clubs. And your friends.'

He dismissed this with a wave of his hand. 'I am not bored, Angel. There is plenty here to occupy my time. And I will not leave Rotherton while Nell is sick. That is why I wanted to see you. To tell you I am here to help, in any way I can.'

'How kind of you…'

He was concerned for his daughter. That was as it should be and she was glad of it. But her spirits, dragged down by lack of sleep, slumped lower before she gave herself a mental shake. It would be foolish and very selfish to want anything more.

'Thank you, Your Grace.'

Jason heard the tired note in her voice and his heart went out to her. He wanted to cross the space between them and wrap her in his arms.

I miss you, Angel. I wish I could take you to bed and kiss away that sad look.

If only he could voice those words! It was something he had never learned—how to talk about his innermost feelings. Jason had never known his mother, and his father had discouraged displays of emotion. He had implanted in his son a belief that a nobleman should never display any sign of weakness or self-doubt.

Only once had Jason managed to overcome his natural reticence, and that had been with Lavinia. He had been infatuated, unable to see or think of anything but her happiness, her desires. He had not realised she was totally incapable of loving anyone but herself. He had laid his heart at her feet and she had trampled it into the ground. The restraint instilled in him as a boy had returned, reinforced by her cruel contempt. Now it was solid as steel. Unbreakable.

Not that Angel would want to hear such maudlin rubbish. She needed practical help from him now, and that he could give her.

'We must tempt Nell's appetite. I shall order the choicest fruits to be sent up from the glasshouses,' he told her. 'And send word to me if there is anything else you think she would like. We must get her well again.'

'Thank you, Your Grace. You are very good.'

She sounded a little surprised at this, and it pricked his conscience. He went on, 'And do not fret about Rose. Mrs Watson is looking after her, and I take her for the occasional airing in my carriage. There can be no harm in driving out, as long as we do not stop.'

'An excellent plan.'

There was still a listlessness in her voice that concerned him. He said, 'But I am keeping you from your rest. Off you go to bed now, Angel.'

She nodded. 'Goodnight, Your Grace.'

He watched her walk away, wishing he could do more, vowing that when this was over he would make it up to her. Somehow.

Over the next few days Jason was encouraged by news that Nell's condition was improving, and when Dr Granger called he declared himself satisfied that she was no longer infectious. However, he cautioned that Nell's recovery might be slow, and she would still need careful nursing.

After that, the Duchess was able to join the rest of the family for dinner each evening, but Jason was quick to note her subdued manner and the dark circles beneath her eyes. It was understandable, of course. Angel had been relieved of much of the burden, but Nell became fractious if she was away for too long and she still spent hours each day in the sickroom. She was exhausted, and Jason ruthlessly suppressed his own desires while he gave her time to recover.

As for Angel, emerging from the nursery wing after a week of constant nursing duties, she felt thoroughly dispirited by the Duke's behaviour. The easy camaraderie between them had quite disappeared. She found she could not confide in him and explain that Nell's recovery was proving quite as draining as her illness. Angel now only attended the nursery during the day, but her time was spent soothing Nell when she was tearful or trying to find ways to entertain her.

The Duke's warning that the children would consume all her time had been proved correct. Not that he reminded her of it. Whenever they met, Jason was invariably polite but he had withdrawn from her. At dinner he entertained her with light conversation, helped her to the choicest cuts and delicacies on offer and was solicitous of her care, but at the end of every evening he was keen to say goodnight, giving her the barest peck on the cheek before leaving her to go to her bed alone.

Angel wanted desperately to talk to him, but her tired brain could not find the words, and beneath it all was the fear that he might finally say what she already suspected. That he no longer wanted her for his wife.

* * *

Towards the end of the second week Nell had improved sufficiently for Mrs Watson to resume her duties in the nursery. Rose was also allowed to visit, amusing Nell with games and books as well as passing on to her all the messages and little gifts that had arrived at Rotherton from their kindly neighbours.

Angel knew she should be happy that she was no longer needed in the sickroom but, strangely, it only added to the depression that was clouding her spirits. She could not shake it off and when, a few days later, she went up to her room to change her gown she sat down at her dressing table, looking at herself in the mirror and wondering what the future might hold.

She and Jason had been getting on well until the night of the assembly. Since then they had been more like polite strangers. Not that she could share these dismal thoughts with anyone… So she put on a brave smile as she went downstairs to join the family in the garden.

The gentle breeze carried their laughter across the lawn to Angel. Mrs Watson was sitting on a chair in the shade of a large chestnut tree. Rose and Nell were on rugs at her feet and Jason was sitting beside them. He was very much at his ease with the girls now, and that at least was a good sign, thought Angel, determined to be cheerful.

As she approached the little group, Mrs Watson waved to her.

'Ah, there you are, Duchess! Would you like this chair? I can easily have another fetched.'

Angel declined, smiling. 'Thank you, but no, ma'am, I am very happy to sit on a cushion,' she said, suiting the action to the words.

This was such a lovely spot, with the lawns stretching

down to the lake that sparkled in the sunshine and everyone gathered together so comfortably. Angel felt some of the tension easing out of her. Perhaps things were not so bleak after all.

Jason had watched Angel as she walked across the lawn, his insides twisting with desire. He wanted to jump up and go to meet her, but he knew if he touched her he would not be able to let her go, and he was uncertain of her feelings for him. Travelling back from the assembly, everything had seemed so right. She had been happy, laughing, but he had barely seen her smile since that night. She looked cheerful enough now, but there was no light in her eyes. Her face was pale and drawn, and guilt smote him.

She had exhausted herself, looking after Nell. By marrying her so precipitately he had placed the burden of his family on her shoulders and, being Angel, she had accepted it without question.

Ironic, he thought bitterly. He had no doubts now that he wanted Angel as his wife, but he was no longer sure of what *she* wanted, and her happiness was paramount.

'What do you think, Duchess?' exclaimed Rose, breaking into his thoughts. 'Papa Duke is sending us all to Brighton.'

'We are discussing it,' Jason corrected her quickly. He glanced at Angel, but could read nothing from her face. 'You will recall I have a villa there. It has been standing empty since your brother's visit. I suggested Mrs Watson should take Nell and Rose to Brighton for the rest of the summer, rather than returning directly to Kent. A little sea bathing will benefit Nell's recovery.' He picked a few dried leaves off the rug. 'I think you would enjoy it too, Duchess. You have worn yourself out with all the constant nursing. You deserve a rest and a change of air.'

* * *

Not by the flicker of an eye did Angel react, but she felt as if a splinter of ice had lodged itself in her heart. There could be no misunderstanding his words. He was sending her away!

'It would be much better if you came too, Papa,' said Nell. 'Do come with us!'

'Alas, I have important business here that requires my attention.'

'But it cannot be more than fifty miles,' argued Rose. 'That is not too far to ride in a day. You might at least come and visit us.'

'Sadly that will not be possible. But I am sure you will all enjoy yourselves equally well without me.'

Angel listened in silence as the conversation swirled around her: the delights of Brighton in the summer, the drives they might take, the shops and libraries.

Inside, she was protesting vehemently.

Do I have no say in this? Are my wishes of no account?

Then, as if her thoughts had reached Jason, he turned to her.

'You are very quiet, Angel, what think you of the plan?'

'I think it is an excellent idea,' declared Nell happily. 'I shall take care of the Duchess and look after her, just as she looked after me!'

'Hush, Nell.' Rose was watching Angel, her blue eyes shadowed with concern. 'Her Grace might prefer a little time away from us.'

Angel could not allow the girls to think that. She said quickly, 'Nonsense! I love being with you all. How soon…? That is, when are you proposing we go to Brighton?'

'A week today,' said Jason. 'If Dr Granger approves.'

'You have everything arranged, then.' She felt brittle as glass, but summoned up a beaming smile. 'Well, well. Sea bathing, girls. How exciting.' She scrambled to her feet. 'Excuse me. I have just remembered something I need to say to Mrs Wenlock.'

She hurried away, blinking back the tears that threatened to blind her.

'Angel.' She heard Jason's voice close behind her. 'Angel, what is wrong? Is aught amiss?'

She walked faster. 'Go away, Duke. I am too angry to talk to you!'

He put his hand on her arm but she pushed him off.

'Leave me alone!'

She almost ran towards the house, not stopping until she had reached the seclusion of her own bedchamber. It was blessedly empty and she walked quickly up and down, taking deep, shuddering breaths. She did not know if she most wanted to lash out in anger or to weep.

She had no time to decide before Jason came into the room.

He closed the door. 'Are you angry with me, Angel?'

She rounded on him. 'How dare you! How *dare* you arrange everything without a word to me?'

'If you mean the visit to the coast, I told you we were merely discussing it. Nothing is settled.'

She gave a furious huff of disbelief.

'It did not sound like that to me! You are packing us all off to Brighton in a week's time. Out of your way.'

'That is nonsense.'

'Is it?' She began to stride back and forth again. 'Family life has been everything you warned it would be. Noisy, disruptive, all-consuming. Inconvenient!'

'Yes, but—'

'I am not surprised if you have had enough of us.' She threw the words over her shoulder as she continued her angry pacing. 'But why did you not talk to me first?'

'I barely see you, save at dinner,' he retorted. 'And even then our conversation consists of the merest commonplace remarks!'

'Yes.' She dashed a hand across her eyes. 'Because you c-cannot bear to be in my company!'

'That is not true.'

'You have come up with the most elegant solution, have you not?' she went on bitterly. 'Sending everyone off to Brighton is the perfect excuse to rid yourself of a wife you no longer want in your house!'

'You have that all wrong!' He stepped in front of her and caught her wrists, forcing her to stop. 'I am sending you away because...because...confound it... *I want you too much!*'

Chapter Nine

Angel was staring up at him, eyes glittering with rage. Jason was still holding her wrists and he gave them a little shake.

'Do you understand what I am saying, Angel? I want you. Too. Damned. Much.'

He struggled to get out those last words. He was painfully aware of her breasts pressing against him every time she took a ragged breath. The heat of her body, the flowery perfume she used. She was irresistible. He bent his head and captured her lips, subjecting them to a bruising kiss. For a moment Angel did not move, then she whimpered, deep in her throat. He should stop, pull away, but she confounded him by leaning into him, her mouth working against his.

She was giving him back kiss for kiss and there was no anger now, only white-hot passion. Jason swept her up into his arms and carried her across the room. They tumbled onto the bed, lost in a frenzy of kissing and caressing, tearing off the clothing that prevented them from exploring each other fully. Angel's eager, innocent responses inflamed him. The gasps of pleasure as he kissed her breasts heated his blood. She responded eagerly to his touch and stroked her hands over his skin until he was a heated mass of pure need.

It was over all too quickly. A rapid, urgent coupling when her cries mingled with his. And then they were lying together, spent and exhausted. Angel gave a long, shuddering sigh and he gathered her into his arms.

'I hurt you. I am sorry.' He rested his cheek against her hair. 'It was your first time. I should have been more gentle with you.'

'No, it was not painful. At least, not very much.' She pressed a kiss on his naked chest. 'I did not know what to expect. Certainly not such…such incredible *pleasure*.'

'Truly?'

She pushed herself away a little, so she could look at him, and he saw that her eyes were shining with happiness.

'Truly.' She blushed and hid her face in his shoulder.

Smiling, Jason pulled her close again.

'You understand that there is no going back now,' he murmured. 'Our marriage is binding. For life.'

'Are you sorry about that, Jason?'

His arms tightened around her.

'No, Angel, I am not sorry.' He dropped a kiss on her hair. 'I am not sorry at all.'

When Angel woke she found Jason propped up on one elbow and looking down at her.

'Time to get up,' he said. 'We must find the family and tell them you will not be going to the Brighton with them.'

'We could all go. I should like to see the villa.' She added daringly, 'Barnaby and Meg said it is perfect for lovers.'

She had expected Jason to laugh at her remark, but instead she had the impression he had turned to stone. His expression was inscrutable and her brow furrowed with concern.

'Jason?'

The hard look disappeared and he dropped a light kiss on her nose.

'Another time,' he said lightly. 'For the present I want to

keep you at Rotherton, all to myself.' He rolled away from her. 'Come along now, Madam Duchess, we must get dressed.'

Angel followed him off the bed and said nothing more, but she could not help thinking she had touched a raw nerve.

When the children learned that Angel would not be joining them they were disappointed, but this was overridden by their excitement for the forthcoming treat, once Dr Granger gave his full approval of the plan.

A week later, Angel and Jason waved off the rather ancient berline, which was large enough to carry Mrs Watson, Rose and Nell, as well as the maid Edith and a large quantity of baggage.

Once the carriage was out of sight Jason turned to Angel. 'Would you like to walk down to the lake with me?'

'I thought you were meeting with Mr Merrick?'

'Not for an hour yet.'

She smiled. 'Then, yes, I should like a walk.'

He pulled her hand onto his arm and they strolled off towards the lake.

'At last, we have Rotherton to ourselves!'

'Have the children been too much of an inconvenience?' she asked him.

'I have to confess there have been times when their presence has stopped me from carrying you off to bed!'

Angel blushed. Just thinking of the nights she and Jason had spent together during the past week turned her bones to water.

'However, despite that,' he went on, 'I was thinking that perhaps the children should make Rotherton their home. What do you say?'

Her heart skipped a beat. 'I say it is a wonderful idea, Jason. You know I have long thought so.'

'I would not arrange anything without consulting you.' He gave her a quick, glinting smile. 'I do not want you flying into a temper again, as you did over my suggestion you should go to Brighton.'

'Pray, do not remind me of that!'

'The quarrel did not end so very badly, though, did it?' He stopped and pulled her round into his arms. 'In fact, I think it is resolved most satisfactorily.'

Angel felt the now familiar tug of desire curling inside her, and when he bent his head to kiss her she responded eagerly.

It was several minutes before they could resume their walk, and as they did he remarked, 'Do you know, you blush most delightfully?'

'Hush!' she begged, a laugh trembling in her voice. 'You are only increasing my confusion.'

'Well, you may take comfort from the fact that there is no one near enough to see you. Which is why I have…er… "packed the children off" to Brighton, as you phrased it. Although it was not the only reason.'

Angel waited for him to continue, wondering where this was leading.

'You may recall that Rose was quite a hit at the assembly. You were in the sickroom, and may not have heard, but several posies of flowers arrived for her the following day. I thought little of it at the time, and with all the concern for Nell I forgot all about the flowers. However, Mrs Watson tells me that whenever she takes the girls into town there are always numerous young fellows wanting to speak with Rose. I even found one young rascal loitering in the lane, and was obliged to tell him he would not be welcome at the house.'

Angel chuckled. 'I am surprised it was only one young man lying in wait for her! Rose is a very pretty young lady. I doubt it will be any different in Brighton.'

'True, but there are other diversions in Brighton—the sea bathing, for one thing. And Mrs Watson has been charged to keep a close eye on her.' He swung his cane at a weed that had dared to spring up in the grass. 'She is too young to be thinking of marriage.'

'She will be eighteen in December, Jason. It is quite natural that she should be thinking of it. And she must meet young gentlemen at some time, you know.'

His jaw tightened. 'And what if she takes it into her head to elope?'

'Goodness! Why on earth should she do that?'

'Because she is her mother's daughter!' He beheaded another weed with a flick of his cane. 'It concerns me.'

'Yes, Rose is bidding fair to be a beauty, is she not?' Angel hesitated. 'That is why I think it would be better if the girls made their home at Rotherton. Between us, I am sure Mrs Watson and I could ensure that Rose is never without a chaperon.'

She said no more. It was better that Jason should take his time to consider the idea.

They strolled alongside the lake for another half-hour before turning back to the house.

'What do you propose to do with yourself today?' Jason asked her when they reached the hall.

'I have arranged to take the carriage into Middlewych at twelve, to do a little shopping, including collecting a few things for Mrs Wenlock.'

He glanced across at the clock. 'It is gone eleven now. I am sorry if I kept you.'

'Not at all.' She added shyly, 'I enjoyed it.'

'So too did I.' That glinting smile appeared again. 'Of course, we could send word that you no longer need the carriage.'

A little shock of excitement rippled through Angel at the thought, but she shook her head.

'Mr Merrick is waiting for you, Your Grace.'

'I am sure I can fob him off.'

Angel laughed at that. 'No, indeed. I would not have you neglect your duties. And your housekeeper is relying on *me* to fetch her shopping.'

'What a cruel woman you are, Duchess. Very well, then, but one final kiss before we part.'

He drew her to him, kissing her so thoroughly that she was very tempted to change her mind about going to Middlewych. At last he put her away from him, but he kept his hands on her shoulders for a moment and looked at her with narrowed eyes.

'How the devil do you expect me to concentrate on estate matters after that?' he demanded.

She blushed and stepped away from him. 'Go you about your business, sir, and let me go to mine!'

With that she hurried away up the stairs to change, but her heart was singing.

Arriving at Middlewych, Angel left the carriage at the Rotherton Arms and was soon walking along the high street with her maid. First she would fulfil Mrs Wenlock's request for cotton and thread at Chapmans, an establishment that combined the offices of a haberdasher and a draper. Having been there before, she knew that the shop would be bursting with every sort of sewing aid, from needles and thread to bolts of material. It left little space for customers, and when she reached the shop, she suggested Joan should wait for her outside.

It being a warm day, the door had been propped open, so no bell announced her entry, but Angel did not mind this.

She was not yet accustomed to the deference the townsfolk considered was due to a duchess. There was no one behind the counter, and a display of muslins, worsteds and calicos obscured Angel's view of the back of the shop, but she could hear voices, suggesting that there were ladies gathered there, waiting to be served.

Angel moved further in to inspect a pretty patterned chintz. She still could not see the other customers, but their conversation floated clearly across to her. She recognised one of the voices as that of Lady Hutton. They had met a few times, but Angel had been warned that the woman was a notorious gossip and she had not pursued the acquaintance. She was glad of it, too. She could hear the lady holding forth, blackening the character of some unfortunate creature.

'Did you see them dancing together at the assembly? So diverting! He scarcely took his eyes off her the whole time they stood up together.'

'But then, why not?' replied a second voice. 'She is quite as beautiful as her mother.'

Lady Hutton snorted. 'I must say I thought it most unbecoming.'

'Aye, quite scandalous.' Someone tittered. 'His own stepdaughter, too!'

Angel froze. She stared at the brightly coloured material in her hand as the voices continued relentlessly.

'My maid saw the carriage driving by this morning.' Lady Hutton's voice again. 'The girls and their chaperon are off to Brighton, I understand.'

'Yes, that is what I heard, too. No doubt the Duchess insisted upon it. Trying to nip the affair in the bud before it gets out of hand.'

'Oh, I do not accuse His Grace of anything of *that* nature.' Lady Hutton disclaimed hastily. 'I do not say he is *enam-*

oured of the chit…merely that the girl's likeness to her late mama must bring it all back to the poor man. Such a lovely creature. He was devoted to her, you know. How it must grieve him to be constantly reminded of what he has lost.'

There could be no doubt now of the subject of their conversation. Angel forced her numb fingers to release the chintz. She must put a stop to this. But she needed to breathe deep and compose herself before her limbs would move, and the gossip continued on the other side of the display.

'He must be regretting his hasty wedding now.' This was a third female, her voice full of spurious sympathy. 'Not that his new duchess isn't a most agreeable lady, and I am sure she is very good at keeping house, but she is no beauty, compared to his first wife…'

Angel stepped into view and the words trailed off into silence. She kept her chin up, regarding the three women with as much hauteur as she could manage. She recognised them all: Lady Hutton, her widowed sister Mrs Pole, and Mrs Nisbet—pillars of the community and stalwarts of the church. Hypocrites, every one of them, she thought angrily.

The three ladies goggled at her, then they each dropped a deep curtsy, muttering embarrassed greetings.

'Your Grace!' Mrs Chapman came bustling out of the backroom, her arms full of boxes. 'Oh, dear…oh, dear. I beg your pardon, ma'am. My serving maid has gone off somewhere or I would have come out immediately!'

'It is no matter.' Angel turned her back on the three now-silent crones. 'I shall return later. Pray deal with your other customers.'

Then, without a backward glance, Angel sailed out with her head held high.

She collected Joan and they walked briskly back to the Rotherton Arms. She had been looking forward to spending a happy hour browsing the shops, but now her pleasure was at an end. She wasted no time on the contemptible hints that Jason might be attracted to Rose. Not for one moment did she believe that. But she did believe that he was still in love with Lavinia. She remembered now his reluctance to take her to Brighton. The villa there had been a present to his first wife, and it was clearly too full of treasured memories to share with his second.

Angel fought down a painful stab of jealousy and reminded herself that Jason had never pretended to love her. Theirs was a marriage of convenience, and it was naïve of her to expect anything more. She had spent most of her four-and-twenty years living quietly in the country. She knew so little of the real world, or of men. And as for love, her one experience of that had ended in bitter disappointment and heartbreak.

'And you would do well to remember that,' she told herself. 'Don't fall in love with a man who cannot love you back. One, moreover, who prefers beauty to every other womanly quality.'

But in her heart Angel knew it was already too late.

When they reached the Rotherton Arms, Angel bespoke a private parlour. She treated her maid to a glass of lemonade and for herself she ordered coffee. It was hot and strong and she sipped it slowly while she composed herself. Gossip of any sort was abhorrent, and she was determined to forget all about it. On Sunday she would be obliged to attend church, and she had no doubt the three crones would be there. She would say nothing and ignore them, which was all the attention they deserved. For now she could only hope that they were as mortified as she was by today's encounter.

After a suitable time Angel sent Joan back to Chapmans to buy the items required by Mrs Wenlock while she remained in the private parlour. She had quite lost her appetite for shopping.

It had turned sultry by the time she returned to Rotherton. A storm was brewing. The air was very still, and heavy clouds were bubbling up on the horizon as she hurried into the house. Angel's head ached, and she sent her maid to the housekeeper with her purchases while she went to lie down in her room.

She had hoped to sleep, but her mind would not rest. She stared up at the carved tester, going over and over what she had heard in Chapmans. How ever much Angel told herself that it was mere gossip and should be ignored, she could not forget Lady Hutton's words. True, she was no beauty, like his first wife, but that did not mean Jason was unhappy with her. Or that he regretted marrying her. Angel clung to that thought.

She needed to tell someone about the encounter, and who else was there but Jason? He would most likely laugh when she told him about the gossip. He would take her in his arms and kiss away her fears. Wouldn't he?

Eventually she dozed, and woke later to find the room growing quite dark as the storm clouds gathered. She went over to her dressing table and sat down to tidy her hair. She was not at all refreshed from her sleep. She felt dull, listless. The encounter in Chapmans was still preying on her mind and she knew she would not be easy until she had spoken with Jason about it.

Downstairs, she found the butler in the Marble Hall. He was standing at the open door, looking out at the empty drive.

'Langshaw, is His Grace still with Mr Merrick in his office?'

'No, madam, they rode out to visit Holts Farm.' He glanced up at the black rain clouds and a shadow of concern flickered over his usually impassive countenance. 'We must hope they return before this storm breaks.'

Even as he finished speaking the first fat drops of rain fell, splashing on the gravel and quickly turning into a steady downpour.

'It's very likely they have taken shelter somewhere until this passes,' he went on, closing the door. 'Is there anything I can do for you, Your Grace?'

'No. No, thank you.'

Angel was disappointed that she would have to wait to see Jason, but decided against returning to her room. Better to find something to do until it was time to change for dinner.

Her first thought was the library, but when she went in the grey skies had made the room so dark and uninviting that she quickly changed her mind and wandered back to the hall. It was empty now and she walked around it, too restless to settle to anything. Then, finding herself at the door of the Yellow Salon, she went in.

The bright colours were somewhat muted by the heavy clouds and the rain, but that only seemed to enhance the colours in the portrait of the late Duchess. Angel stood before it, looking up at the beautiful creature with her golden hair and blue eyes. Lavinia gazed out over Angel's head, a faint smile curving her red lips. She was an alluring figure, confident and enchanting. Triumphant.

Angel's spirits were already low, but now they fell into an abyss. Compared to such a goddess she felt plain and insignificant. Jason could never love a woman whose talents, such as they were, amounted to an ability to run his houses. Perhaps that was why he had married her. Because she posed no threat. She would arouse in him no aching desires.

With a sob, Angel turned away and covered her face in her hands. What a timely reminder not to give her heart to a man who did not want it.

* * *

'Home at last!'

Jason cantered through the gates with his steward beside him. He had never been more glad to see Rotherton. They had already turned back when the heavens had opened, but they were still both soaked to the skin.

There was a sudden flash, and a loud clap of thunder exploded above them.

'We need to get under cover,' declared Merrick.

As they slowed to trot past the house a movement in one of the windows caught Jason's eye. Someone was in the Yellow Salon. He looked again and saw a figure, head bowed and shoulders drooping.

He stopped. 'Simon will you take Major back to the stables for me?'

'Of course.'

Jason jumped down and handed over the reins, then he ran into the house.

'Ah, you are back at last, Your Grace.' Langshaw came hurrying across the hall to greet him. 'I saw you on the drive and I have already sent word to Adams…'

'Yes, yes, I will go up in a moment.'

He thrust his hat, gloves and riding crop into the butler's hands and strode off to the Yellow Salon. Even as he opened the door he heard a sob.

'Angel! What is it? What is the matter?'

She jumped at the sound of his voice but did not turn towards him.

'N-nothing. I am being foolishly melancholy,' she said, hunting for her handkerchief. 'Forgive me. Please go away and forget you have seen me thus. I shall recover in a very short while, I promise.'

But he had already crossed the room. He took her shoulders and gently turned her around to face him.

'I cannot leave you while you are so upset.' She was still searching for her handkerchief so he pulled out his own. Thankfully it was dry, unlike most of his clothing. He handed it to her. 'Come. Sit here with me and tell me who or what has upset you.'

He guided her to the sofa and pressed her gently down, searching to say something that would cheer her.

'Are you missing the children? Is that it?' he asked, kneeling before her. 'We agreed this morning that they should live here, and if Mrs Watson will agree to come, too, then she will be able to look after them. I am sure that between us we can prevent Rose from making any undesirable acquaintances. At least until we go to London. There—does that make you happy?'

'It does, of course. I am sure it is the right decision.'

She finished wiping her eyes and then sat silently, gazing down at the crumpled handkerchief between her fingers.

'But that is not why you were crying.'

'No.'

'Then tell me. I have never seen you like this before, Angel. I want to help you.'

'You cannot help!' She jumped up and moved away from him. 'Forgive me, I am being very foolish. I overheard someone gossiping in the town.'

He watched as she walked across to the window and stared out at the rain-soaked landscape.

'And what did you hear?'

'That you are still in love with L-Lavinia.'

Jason flinched, waiting for the punch in the gut that always occurred when he heard that name. It did not come. Rage, regret and mortification were all there, but they were muted, superseded by an overwhelming need to comfort Angel.

'Not that I care for myself,' she went on, raising her chin a little. 'But the gossip made me think that perhaps we were wed too quickly. Six months was not time enough for you to grieve properly. I would quite understand if you were regretting our hasty marriage.'

He desperately wanted to deny it. The words were screaming around in his head, but he could not bring himself to say them. He had always envied the way Angel and her family could speak so freely with one another, laugh or cry, confide or argue with equal frankness. He had been reared to believe it was his duty to lead the way—not to show fear or doubt. Not to show any emotion.

He wanted to explain that it was his first marriage that he regretted, not this one, but he could not. His eyes strayed to the portrait of his first duchess. Words had come easily with Lavinia. Protestations of love and devotion had often tripped from her lips. But in her case it had never been true. And for himself…? Looking now at that beautiful face, he realised it had been a youthful passion that had soon burned itself out, only he had been too proud, too foolish, to see it. Even now he could barely admit it to himself.

And yet he must speak! Angel was distressed. She needed reassurance. She needed *him*.

He walked over and wrapped his arms about her, resting his cheek against her hair.

'I regret many things, Angel, but not marrying you,' he murmured. 'Never marrying you. You are my wife, my duchess. I would not want any other.'

Jason turned her about and put his fingers beneath her chin, gently urging her to look up at him. She was so dainty, so fragile, that he was almost overwhelmed by the need to protect her, to keep her safe. To make her happy. He kissed her eyes, tasting the salty tears on his lips before trailing kisses down her cheek. He captured her mouth and she trembled for a moment, then she was responding, giving him back kiss for kiss.

Reassured, he lifted her into his arms.

She gave a shaky laugh. 'What are you doing?'

He dropped another kiss on her mouth. 'Taking you to bed, madam.'

He saw the flash of fire her eyes before she buried her face in his shoulder.

'You are very wet.' Her voice was muffled.

'Then the sooner I am out of these clothes the better,' he declared, carrying her out of the room.

'But the servants…'

'Damn the servants!'

Jason went up the stairs two at a time, Angel held firmly in his arms. When they reached her room he somehow managed to open the door without dropping her and stepped inside. Joan, her dresser, was at the linen press and turned quickly, surprise and alarm in her face when she saw Jason.

'Leave us,' he said, kicking the door closed behind him. 'No, not this way. Go out through my room. And take Adams away with you.'

Joan stared at him. 'But he has p-prepared your bath, Your Grace!'

'Excellent. Tell him I will deal with it from here. Now, off you go.'

He waited until the woman had hurried away through the adjoining door, then lowered Angel to her feet. She was shaking and he held on to her, afraid she was too distressed to stand, but when she looked at him he saw she was laughing through her blushes.

'Poor Joan. I have never seen her so nonplussed!'

His lips twitched. 'She had best get used to it.'

He took her hand and led her through into his room, where a steaming bath stood before the fireplace.

Angel cleared her throat. 'J-just the thing if you have had a soaking in the rain,' she remarked, clearly trying to act as if this was an everyday occurrence.

'Yes, isn't it?' he replied. 'Will you help me out of my wet clothes?'

'I…um…'

He pulled her around into his arms again. 'Perhaps we should both undress,' he suggested. 'After all, I made your gown quite damp when I carried you up the stairs.' He saw her glance towards the bathtub and went on softly, 'It is large enough for the two of us. Trust me.'

She looked up at him, her eyes shadowed, and for a moment he thought she was going to make her excuses and leave. Then her fingers were unfastening the buttons of his coat and elation soared through him.

Silently they undressed one another, leaving their discarded clothes tangled together in a heap on the floor. Jason left Angel's shift until last, drawing it slowly over her head and tossing it aside. Then he gazed at her, standing naked before him.

'By heaven, but you are lovely!'

Angel's spirits soared. The blood sang in her veins and she felt like a princess, a goddess, when Jason helped her into the bath. She breathed in the heady spice-scented steam as Jason followed, folding his long limbs around hers in the confined space of the tub. He ran his finger down her breast and caressed one hard, rosy nub. She drew in a ragged breath and her body tingled. This was intimate. Exciting and daring.

'Comfortable, Duchess?'

'This is very…decadent.'

'Not at all,' he murmured, sliding his hand down her body. 'It would only be decadent if we had wine, and if the floor was strewn with rose petals for my lady to walk on.'

She closed her eyes, trembling deliciously at the idea. 'I think I should like that.'

'Next time.' He leaned forward to kiss her.

Angel gasped as his fingers slipped gently between her thighs. She moved against his hand, feeling the waves of pleasure building inside. She could feel the hard, knotted muscle beneath the skin as she gripped his shoulders. Every nerve was tingling, her breasts felt hot and full, and she pushed against him, almost swooning with the dizzying excitement of his touch.

Jason groaned. 'Damme but this tub is not big enough for all I want to do with you!'

Angel laughed, a low, seductive sound that surprised and pleased her. She might not be as beautiful as his first wife but she felt alluring, desirable. He rose and held out his hand to help her up. The sight of his glistening muscled body, his unmistakable arousal, made her throat go dry. He pulled her to her feet and her breasts tightened as they grazed his chest. Her whole body was now a mass of desire.

'Enough. I cannot wait for you a moment longer.'

Jason dragged her into his arms and Angel's body responded instantly to his kiss. Her heart was thudding so loud she was sure he must hear it as he swept her up and carried her over to the bed. Impatiently she reached out for him, pulling him down beside her and covering his freshly scented body with kisses. She explored him with her mouth, excited by the crisp smattering of hair on his chest and the smooth plane of his stomach. She had no idea if what she was doing was right, and when she heard him gasp she hesitated.

'No, no, don't stop, Angel.' He drew her back against him, his voice low and unsteady. 'You are driving me wild.'

He whispered encouragement and she followed his lead, kissing, touching and stroking, moving against him and exulting in her growing sense of power. Until he flipped her onto her back and began to kiss her. His caresses sent her body quite out of control. She writhed and twisted beneath him, weeping with the sheer pleasure of his touch.

She was almost beyond thought when he entered her and they moved together as one, slowly at first, then faster, more urgently. Something was building inside her…a wave of pleasure lifting her higher, higher. Jason shuddered and she clung to him as he gave one final thrust. The wave crested, flooding her body, and she tumbled into unconsciousness, her mind shattering into a thousand jagged pieces.

It was several moments before Angel recovered sufficiently to think coherently.

Jason was holding her. He brushed his lips against hers. 'How was that?'

'I… I hardly know… Wonderful.'

She felt him relax a little and he said quietly, 'I cannot stop the gossip, Angel, but it is not true, believe me. It is not easy for me to tell you what I feel, but I hope you will know. I hope I have shown you just how much I…value you.'

'Thank you.'

He *valued* her. The word sounded mundane, sensible. She snuggled closer, stifling a sigh. She should be content with that, but she was aware of doubt gnawing away at her.

Angel thought Jason had gone to sleep until he said suddenly, 'The portrait will be removed from the Yellow Salon. We will find something else to go in its place.'

For a moment Angel was too surprised to answer him. Then she said, 'But the whole room is designed around it.'

'Then we will redesign it. You shall decorate it as you wish.'

'Oh, that…that is so kind, so generous of you, Jason. But… where would we put the painting?'

'The long gallery, perhaps. We have family portraits there going back generations.'

'I do not think we should move it. At least not yet.'

He raised himself on one elbow and frowned at her. 'I do not understand. I found you crying in that room.'

'But not about the painting!' Angel was not prepared to admit she was jealous of Lavinia. She said gently, 'It is a portrait of the girls' mother, Jason. They have told me she was this…this glorious, beautiful creature who would descend upon them, bringing gifts or taking them out for special treats. She was their mama, and that room, the portrait, is all they have left of her.'

'They saw little enough of her in life!'

'But they have memories.'

'No. It upsets you, and I will not have that.'

His concern warmed her heart. That wayward lock of black hair had fallen across his brow and she reached up to push it back.

'It is only a painting, after all.'

He lowered his head and brushed his mouth over hers.

'You are an Angel indeed,' he murmured.

When he kissed her again her body responded instantly, pushing against him as their naked limbs tangled together.

'We should stop,' he murmured, his lips against her cheek. 'It must be almost time for dinner.'

'Oh…' Angel's eyelids fluttered as he laid a trail of kisses down her neck, then began to kiss her breasts, and she moaned softly. 'I have quite lost my appetite.'

'Well, that is most fortunate, because I have, too.'

He shifted his position and began to work his way down her body. He trailed a line of butterfly kisses over her belly before easing himself between her legs. He set to work with his tongue on the hot space between her thighs and her body arched. She clutched at his shoulders.

'Oh, Oh! What…what are you doing?'

He broke off and glanced up at her. 'I am pleasuring my duchess. Do you want me to stop?'

She saw the black fire in his eyes and her breath hitched.

'No.' She forced the word out. 'Oh, no, Jason, don't stop now!'

When Angel woke up the rain had stopped and the house was very quiet. She stretched, catlike. In fact she almost purred.

Jason was asleep beside her. She could hear his steady breathing, feel the warmth of his naked body next to her. She turned towards him and he stirred, gathering her against him before sinking back into a deep slumber.

Chapter Ten

For Angel, the summer months alone with Jason were almost idyllic. They enjoyed a delayed honeymoon at Rotherton, riding or driving out together and spending the evenings companionably indoors, talking and laughing. The nights were equally blissful. Jason was a skilful lover, and Angel tried not to be anxious. If Jason was still in love with his late wife there was nothing she could do about it. She told herself she was content to know that Jason cared about her.

She wrote to Mrs Watson, informing her that the Duke had decided to move the girls to Rotherton permanently and asking her to join them and continue as governess and companion to her charges. The widow replied by return, expressing her pleasure at the idea, and Angel set to work refurbishing the nursery wing. It needed little more than fresh paint on the walls, and she'd have everything ready by the time Mrs Watson and the girls returned to Rotherton at the beginning of September.

Angel and Jason were strolling through the gardens at Rotherton the night before the Brighton party were due to arrive when he surprised her by saying, 'It is Nell's tenth birthday this month. I think we should give her a pony. Mrs

Watson arranged for the girls to learn to ride in Kent, but only on hired hacks. They had no horses of their own.'

'An excellent idea,' she exclaimed, heartened to see Jason taking such an interest in his daughter.

'Good. I will set Thomas to work finding a suitable mount for her.'

'And we might do the same for Rose on her birthday in December,' said Angel. 'Although if we are all going to London this winter, she might wish to wait until we return.'

He turned his head to look at her. '*Are* we all going to London?'

She gave him a sunny smile. 'I very much hope so, Jason.'

His reply was nothing more than a scowl and Angel held her peace. For now. She was confident now that Rose would have her London come-out and she hoped that at some point Jason would tell her why he was so against it.

The arrival of the Brighton party brought a change to Rotherton. Jason might grumble at the noise and disorder in the house, but secretly he was delighted to have his family back with him.

His family!

Rose and Nell's joy that Rotherton would henceforth be their home pleased him greatly. He thought a little disruption a small price to pay for having them here. He was also pleased that Mrs Watson was happy to remain as their governess and chaperon. It meant that Angel need not devote all her energies to the nursery.

He was honest enough to admit that he wanted her to himself, at least some of the time.

Nell was ecstatic to be presented with a pony for her birthday, and spent a great deal each day at the stables with her new acquisition. Jason appointed one of the senior grooms to look after her and take her riding whenever he or Angel were not available.

Rose appeared to accept her sister's good fortune with equanimity and declared herself content to wait for a horse of her own. In the meantime she was happy to borrow Apollo, and to walk or drive out in the carriage with Edith beside her, if there was no other chaperon.

By October the weather was turning and Angel began to make her preparations for London. The Duke had still not agreed to Rose being presented in town, and he avoided her every attempt to discuss the subject. She could only hope that he would change his mind.

Jason had spent the morning at Home Farm, discussing plans for improvements to the drainage and new farming methods. The meeting had gone surprisingly well. As he was riding back to Rotherton he noticed the changes to the distant hills. Soon, for a few short weeks, the wooded slopes would blaze with gold. He sat up straighter in the saddle and looked about him with a satisfied eye. He had forgotten how much he loved autumn.

It was not only progress on his estates that accounted for his good mood. He was enjoying life at Rotherton far more than he had for a very long time. He had known things would change when he married Angel, but he had never expected it to be like this. He had guessed she would be a good housekeeper, but it was in bed that she surprised him. Angel was a revelation, eager to learn, and matching him for passion. Their nights together were exciting, fulfilling.

But it was even more than that, he thought now. She filled the house with laughter. He enjoyed her company, their conversations and even their occasional disagreements. She had reunited him with his family and whenever he was away from her, for any time, he could not wait to get back. Just like today.

Jason spurred his horse on and hurried into the house just as Angel was coming down the stairs.

'Are you going out?'

Even before he had finished speaking he was laughing at himself. The answer was obvious. She was wearing a walking dress that admirably suited her slender figure and there was a straw bonnet tied with a jaunty bow covering her dark curls. When had shy little Angel in her practical gowns changed into this enchanting creature whose very presence could turn him into such an idiot?

She continued down the stairs, her eyes twinkling. 'As you see. I am going to visit Mrs Elnet in the village. Her little boy is sick and I hope a few treats will restore his appetite. I have asked Cook to include some thick broth and a jar of Gloucester Jelly. I have also added a late peach or two from the glasshouses, I am sure we can spare them.' She gestured towards the window. 'It is such a fine day I thought I might take the open carriage. I hope you do not object? I was about to send word to the stables before I go and collect the basket—'

'Yes, yes, but let me take you in my curricle.'

She looked surprised. 'But you have just this minute come in.'

And I should very much like to go out again. I shall drive you.'

Twenty minutes later they were bowling along in the Duke's curricle, pulled by a pair of handsome matched bays.

Sitting up beside Jason, Angel sighed happily. She loved driving out with Jason, especially alone like this, without even a groom.

She turned her face up to the sun. 'It is such a fine day, it might almost be summer,' she remarked.

'Make the most of it. I was at the Home Farm this morning and old Ted was telling me there is bad weather on the way.'

She chuckled. 'Country lore, Your Grace?'

'Ted is a shepherd. He has lived out of doors all his life and is rarely wrong about these things.'

'Well, the harvest is in now, is it not?'

'Yes. And it is a good one. I looked in the barns before I left the farm this morning.'

She asked him more questions and they whiled away the rest of the journey discussing his plans for the estate.

When they reached Mrs Elnet's neat little cottage Angel climbed nimbly down from the curricle.

'How long do you expect to be?' asked Jason, handing her the basket.

'No more than fifteen minutes. Twenty at most. Mrs Elnet will not wish me to be under her feet for longer than that.'

'Then I shall walk the horses on to the crossroads and return for you.'

She thanked him and watched him drive off before making her way to the cottage door.

Her visit was soon accomplished and Angel left the cottage just as the Duke's curricle bowled into sight. The bays were coming to a halt as she walked up the path, and it was then she noticed Jason was not alone.

'Rose! What on earth—?'

'It will be a crush, but it cannot be helped,' said Jason, reaching across his stepdaughter to help Angel up into the carriage.

'No, no, there is plenty of room.' Distracted, Angel squeezed herself into the remaining space on the seat. She glanced anxiously at Rose's flushed countenance. 'But what has occurred? I thought you had taken a walk with your maid.'

'She sent Edith off to visit her family in the village.' Jason ground out the words. 'I found her flirting with a damn-dashed scoundrel!'

'Kenelm Babberton is not a scoundrel!' exclaimed Rose angrily.

'He is for keeping a tryst with you.'

'What else can we do when you have banned him from calling at the house?'

Angel was surprised at the uncharacteristic vehemence of Rose's response. She saw the Duke's jaw tighten and said quickly, 'I do not understand. Who is this Mr Babberton?'

'The damned scoundrel lying in wait for Rose when her sister was still in the sickroom!'

'You met him at the assembly, Angel,' said Rose. 'Mr Burchill presented him to you before we danced together.'

Angel searched her memory. 'Ah, yes. A fresh-faced young man with a shock of curly hair. I had forgotten. Coming home that night to find Nell so ill drove almost everything from my mind. I am very sorry.'

'No need to be sorry,' Jason snapped, whipping up his team. 'I have forbidden Rose to see the fellow again!'

Rose was about to retort, but Angel gripped her hand and squeezed it hard.

'We can discuss all this when we get back,' she said firmly. 'For now, Your Grace, pray look to your driving. You frightened that poor oxcart driver by cutting in too close.'

There was more than a hint of gritted teeth when he answered her.

'I am perfectly capable of handling this team, madam!'

'Pho,' said Angel, not a whit intimidated by his sharp

retort. 'You have already jerked on the reins twice. Look to your horses, sir, before you ruin their mouths!'

Jason bit back the words that sprang to his lips. She was right, damn her. He was angry. Furious, in fact, but it would not do to take it out on the bays.

He drove on in silence, determined to give his duchess no further cause to criticise his driving. Steadying his breathing, he concentrated on getting the equipage swiftly but safely back to the stables, and by the time they approached Rotherton he had his temper under control. He drove through the gates at speed and saw from the corner of his eye that Angel was gripping the side rail. He allowed himself a moment of ignoble satisfaction and pulled up at the house with a spray of gravel.

A servant ran out to help the ladies alight, and Jason drove the curricle to the stables. He returned to find Angel had left word for him to join her in the family drawing room.

'Rose has gone up to her room,' she said, when he came in. 'The poor girl is very distressed.'

'She deserves to be. Conducting herself like a hoyden.'

Angel nodded. 'Yes, she told me you called her that. She tells me she and Mr Babberton were just talking.'

'They were arm and arm in the lane. With their heads together!'

'Is that all?'

'*All*, madam? Anyone might have seen them flirting. They were making themselves the subject of gossip!'

His anger flared again and he paced the room, unable to keep still.

'It was very wrong of her to send the maid away,' said Angel, after a moment. 'But Rose is no longer a child, Jason.

She tells me it is the first time she has met Mr Babberton alone and admits that it was imprudent.'

'Imprudent! It was damned irresponsible!'

'It was,' Angel agreed, trying to calm the situation. 'You are right, and I hope I have made it clear to Rose that concern for her welfare made you act the way you did.'

Jason nodded.

Angel went on, 'Rose is anxious about Edith, too. She thinks you will dismiss the poor girl.'

'Damme, she is right!'

'I told her I will not allow that.' Angel carried on calmly, as if he had not spoken. 'That is the way to ensure that gossip spreads. I am certain your anger frightened Edith out of her wits and she will not neglect her duties again. Besides, she was very useful when Nell was sick. I shall give her another chance.'

He said stiffly, 'You are in charge of the house servants, madam, you must do as you see fit.'

He waved a hand, dismissing the maid from his mind. But Rose was his stepdaughter, it was his duty to keep her safe. The devil of it was that he knew nothing of dealing with young people. His upbringing had not prepared him for this. He was out of his depth, like an inexperienced swimmer struggling to find a way out of stormy waters.

'Damme, I should have left the children in Kent!'

'The same thing would have happened there,' Angel told him. 'Rose is a very pretty young lady, Jason. She is bound to attract the attention of local gentlemen.' She paused. 'She says she and Mr Babberton are in love.'

'Hah! That is absurd. They are both children. They do not know their own minds.'

'She is nearly eighteen, Jason.'

Jason walked over to the window. He looked for solace

in the landscape and found none. He had made the most disastrous decisions at that age.

He said, 'Babberton is not much older.'

'Mr Babberton is one-and-twenty.'

'The fact that he was willing to meet her so clandestinely shows he is not a fit companion for her!'

'If he is in love he might well act foolishly.'

'Love—hah! If they met at the assembly then they cannot have known each other all that long. We were all confined to the house after that.'

'Only for a week.' Angel rose and crossed the room to join him at the window. 'Rose told me they met again by chance on her first outing to Rotherton. And since then they have met at the circulating library, or when Rose has been visiting her friends. Your neighbours, Jason. Surely Mr Babberton would not be allowed into their houses if he was not respectable?'

'Oh, he is very respectable.'

'Then why has he not called here?'

'Because I caught him loitering outside the house and made it clear that he was not welcome.'

'Oh.' She digested this. 'Is he so ineligible, then?'

'Not at all. His father is Lord Winchcombe, and he will inherit a very pretty little property in due course. But that is not the point.' He turned to face her. 'They are both far too young.'

'You were no older when you defied your family and married Lavinia.'

'I forbid you to mention her name!'

Angel went white and recoiled.

Jason rubbed a hand over his eyes. The reminder had caught him on the raw.

'I b-beg your pardon,' she said, while he was still struggling to speak. 'I did not realise just how much you still…'

'No!' He took a step towards her. 'Confound it, you have it all wrong!'

She retreated, shaking her head. 'We will continue this another time. Excuse me, I n-need to change.'

She almost ran to the door.

Call her back, man. Explain yourself.

But the words would not come. He was left with nothing but remorse for his own weakness.

They met again at dinner. Angel appeared to be quite herself, save that she would not meet his eyes. Rose came in, pale and subdued, and returned only monosyllabic answers to his attempts at conversation. Eventually he gave up, leaving it to Angel, Nell and Mrs Watson to keep a flow of small-talk going throughout the meal.

When dinner was finished, Jason took his obligatory glass of brandy alone in the dining room before joining the others in the family drawing room. The atmosphere was still strained, and after half an hour Mrs Watson bade Nell say goodnight before she carried her off to bed.

Rose jumped up. 'I shall go with you.'

'Would you not like to stay for a little longer?' Jason made a last attempt to make peace. 'We have not yet seen the tea tray.'

Flushing a little, Rose shook her head and hurried out of the room. Jason was left alone with his duchess, who ignored him and bent her head over her embroidery. He went across and sat down beside her on the sofa.

'I have made a mull of everything today, Angel, have I not?'

'She will come around in a few days.'

'I did not mean Rose. I meant with you.' Her head bent

lower over her work as she set another stitch and he went on, 'I beg your pardon. I did not mean to fly at you.'

'I am sure I, too, will come around.'

'I…' He sat forward, hands clasped, elbows resting on his knees. 'I apologise, Angel. You said…you *did* nothing wrong. I reacted badly when…' He drew in a deep breath. 'When you mentioned… Lavinia.'

She did not reply, but he saw her fingers hesitate before she pushed the needle into the fabric again. He forced himself to continue.

'I have never said…never spoken about her with anyone.' She had stopped sewing, he noted. 'Hearing her name brought everything back again.'

She touched his arm. 'Oh, Jason, I am very sorry. I know how hard this must be…losing someone dear to you. If it is still so painful perhaps it is best that we don't talk of it.'

He knew he should correct her. Describe the pain, the anguish of falling out of love. The humiliation of discovering that the goddess he'd worshipped was nothing but a spoiled, heartless beauty.

Then he heard his father's voice, echoing down through the years.

'Never show weakness, boy.'

He could not do it. He was the Duke. He cared too much for Angel's good opinion to confess how weak he had been to be deceived by a traitorous woman.

'Let us talk instead about Rose,' said Angel.

'Rose?'

'Yes.' Angel began to pack up her embroidery. 'She is in the throes of her first love affair. Most likely it will come to naught, if it is allowed to run its course, but you will not persuade her to believe that. Any attempt to prevent her meeting Mr Babberton could make her rebellious, but I have explained to her that no guardian would countenance an engagement before a young lady has had her come-out. I believe I can persuade her to come to London with us, if you will agree to it. After all, what girl would not want to be brought out in town, to acquire a little town bronze before she settled down?'

'I have already given you my views on taking Rose and Nell to London.'

'Yes, but that was before they made their home with us.'

The shy twinkle had returned to her eyes and the last remnants of his anger faded.

He laughed. 'You have me there, madam!'

'I am glad you think so,' she responded cheerfully. 'But, Jason, you are much better acquainted with your family now. You know they are not the onerous responsibility you expected. And think how much they would both enjoy the sights and entertainments of the capital! Think what pleasure *we* would derive from that.'

'Nonsense. I can think of nothing more tiresome!'

But his resistance was weakening, and Jason knew she had seen through his bluster.

'Then Mrs Watson or I will take them out,' she said. 'You may go about your business and we will tell you of our outings when we see you. Oh, do say they may come, Jason! Rose will go on much better in town—there will so much more to occupy her mind there.'

'And until then? What of Babberton?'

'I think you should allow her to meet him, as long as there are no more clandestine assignations. There will be ample opportunity for them to see one another in company, and Mrs Watson and I will be much more on our guard now. We must hope that if we do not oppose the friendship they will discover it is just that. And once Rose is in London there will be any number of town beaux to divert her attention.'

'There will also be any number of rakes and rogues, ready to take advantage of an heiress,' he warned.

'But when it is known she is under your care, very few will attempt to go too far.' Angel folded her embroidery and put it on the table at her elbow. 'Well, sir, do you wish to consider further? Or will you let me give Rose the good news that she and Nell are coming to London with us?'

With a sigh he threw himself back on the sofa. 'Do I have any choice?' he said.

'Of course you do, Your Grace. It is for you to decide.'

He turned to look at her, his eyes narrowed. Angel was regarding him, her hands folded in her lap and with a look of such innocence that another laugh escaped him.

'Very well, madam, it shall be as you wish. We will take the girls with us to town. It will at least remove Rose from Babberton's company for a few months.'

'And may I tell her that if, by the time we return to Rotherton, she is still of the same mind, you will not object to Mr Babberton as a suitor?'

'No, you may not.' She raised her brows at him and he released his breath in a long hiss. 'You may say that we will discuss it at that time.'

Immediately she beamed at him. 'Thank you, Jason. I shall go upstairs, and if Rose is still awake I shall tell her of the treat in store!'

With that she hurried away and Jason was left alone, wondering what had just happened. He had quite decided that Mrs Watson would bring Rose out quietly, in Kent. Certainly he had been determined she would not be presented in London, where she would hear gossip about her mother that would upset her. Old rumours would be unearthed, old scandals recalled. He had lived through it all once and had no wish to do so again. Yet it seemed that now he would have to, and to protect Rose, too.

He turned his eyes to the ceiling. Angel made so few demands upon him, no tears or tantrums. She did not wait until she was lying in his arms, beguiling him with her kisses and caresses, to ask for favours, but for all that he had given in to her on almost every point.

How the devil did she do it?

Chapter Eleven

London. Angel had only visited the capital once, for her come-out, when her parents had hired one of the smaller properties in Hanover Square for the season. Now she was on her way the Duke's neo-classical townhouse overlooking Green Park.

They reached Darvell House shortly after noon. The travelling carriage drew up at the door and Angel looked out at the building that was to be their home for the next few months.

'It is not as impressive as Spencer House,' said Jason, helping her to alight. 'Nor as large as Cleveland House, but it has a pleasant garden adjoining the park.'

'I like it very much.' Angel glanced back as the commodious berline turned the corner. 'Here come Mrs Watson with the girls now. We shall see what they think!'

An army of servants were gathered in the hall, and Angel was glad of Jason's hand on her back, supportive, comforting.

'This is Marcuss,' he said, leading her up to a stately figure standing a little apart from the liveried servants. 'He has been in charge here since before my time. Anything you need to know, just ask him.'

'Welcome to Darvell House, Your Grace.' The butler bowed low. 'Perhaps you will allow me to present your household to you?'

Reassured by the man's kindly smile, Angel nodded. The formalities were cut short by the entrance of Mrs Watson and her charges and the arrival at the door of the baggage coach.

The Duke and Duchess's personal servants came in quickly, followed by the trunks which needed to be distributed to the various bedchambers. Jason carried Angel away from the chaos to the morning room, ordering refreshments to be brought into them.

'That's better,' he said, closing the door upon the noise and bustle. 'We will stay here until everything has settled down.'

He took her pelisse and threw it over a chair while Angel looked around her at the silk-lined walls and Carrara marble chimneypiece.

'This is a very elegant apartment.'

'Aye, one of the more restrained rooms of the house. The most splendid apartments are on the first floor. Due to a number of distant relatives dying without heirs, the Darvells inherited several large fortunes, which enabled them to build this house and decorate it to impress.'

'It will certainly do that.' She bit her lip. 'I confess I find it all a little daunting.'

'No need—you will be a splendid mistress. You are the most capable woman I know.'

Angel looked away from the glow in his eyes. Capable, yes. Sensible Angeline. How she wished he would call her beautiful!

Thankfully, the servants entered at that moment with their refreshments and she did not need to reply.

After they had finished a glass of wine, and Angel had been persuaded to nibble on one of the fancy cakes brought in for their delectation, the Duke suggested it would be safe now to go upstairs.

'I should very much like to see the rooms prepared for

Rose, Nell and Mrs Watson,' she told him, as he escorted her from the room. 'I want to assure myself that they are comfortable.'

'Of course, if you wish. We shall do that first. I should have known you would put their comfort before your own.'

'But not before yours, Jason!'

She cast an anxious look at him and was reassured by his smile.

'No,' he murmured, bending to kiss her cheek. 'Not before mine.'

They set off up the grand staircase and had reached the landing when Adams appeared.

'Your Grace, if I might have a word with you...'

'Not now, Adams.' Jason waved him aside and guided Angel towards the plain staircase leading up to the second floor. 'I must admit I am curious to see the children's apartments for myself. I have not been in those rooms for years.'

'I hope you will not be disappointed. Sometimes places feel smaller once we are grown.'

'That would be an advantage. These nursery apartments always seemed too large for an only child.'

Angel's heart tightened at his bleak tone, and she tucked her hand into his arm in silent sympathy.

Mrs Watson and the girls were happily settled in their rooms, which appeared far more comfortable than Jason remembered. Angel, too, was content with the arrangements, and after agreeing with everyone that they would convene in the drawing room before dinner she was ready to see her own bedchamber.

'I shall draw up a list of things to entertain the girls,' remarked Angel, as he guided her back through the corridors and down the stairs. 'It is a pity we are nearing winter, so there will be no military reviews in the Park, but Rose is old enough to visit the theatre, and I think they would both enjoy a visit to the British Museum. Oh, and Astley's Amphitheatre, of course. You might like to join us there?'

'I might, indeed! But you must not run yourself ragged over the children. You will be presented to the ton as my duchess and you must be prepared. There may be…talk.'

'Because you did not wait a full year's mourning before marrying me?'

'Yes.'

She nodded. 'I am aware there will be gossip, but I shall not mind it if you are with me.'

He kissed her cheek. 'I shall do my best to support you.'

'I know it,' she replied, smiling at him in a way that lifted his heart. 'The Queen is not holding her drawing rooms, which is understandable while the poor King is so unwell, so at least we do not need to prepare for that ordeal! But there is Almack's.'

She stopped, and Jason sensed a reluctance to think of it. He asked gently, 'Does that evoke unpleasant memories for you?'

'Yes, a few,' she admitted. 'But Rose will want to go. I am sure the hostesses will not refuse vouchers to a young lady brought out under your aegis.' She hurried on, 'Of course it will not be necessary for you to go with us if you dislike it so.'

He did dislike it. He hated the place with its intrigues and gossip. but he would be there to look after his duchess.

'Of course I shall come with you.'

She squeezed his arm. 'Just once, then, Jason.'

Her understanding struck him like a heavy blow. He would not leave her to face the ordeal alone. And he would do all he could to protect her. Not only from the gossip but from her own unhappy memories.

'I shall accompany you whenever I can, but there are other matters that require my attention, too. The sale of the Kent house, for instance, since it is no longer required.'

'I understand that, and I shall not expect you live in my pocket, as they say. Besides, Mama is coming to town in a few weeks, and she is going to see to the purchase of gowns for myself and Rose. But, Jason, I know these events are horrendously expensive. I hope you will advise me how much I may spend?'

Jason relaxed a little. He was far happier to discuss money than the necessary social events they must attend.

He said, 'You must spend as much as you wish.' They had reached the Duchess's bedchamber and he threw open the door. 'I trust you not to ruin me!'

The happy smile she gave him before preceding him into the room warmed his heart.

'Oh!'

She had taken only a few steps inside the room and Jason, stopping beside her, felt his blood run cold.

Rich red silk still adorned the walls, but the tester bed with its satin hangings was gone, along with all the original furniture. Lavinia had turned the room into a sumptuous private boudoir. He even imagined a trace of her scent lingering in the air.

How the devil had he forgotten about this? And how the deuce was he to explain it to Angel?

Then, unexpectedly, he heard her laugh.

It is either laugh or cry, thought Angel.

The first sight of what was supposed to be her bedchamber had shocked her, but she was also amused by the dazzling brashness of the room.

All the furniture had been painted gold. The window was

framed by rich golden curtains and a large dressing table and mirror stood before it. To one side of the marble fireplace was a daybed with scrolled and fluted ends, its sides and seat deeply padded, and everything was covered in the same gold silk damask as the curtains. The red walls were hung about with mirrors, all of them in wildly ornate and gilded frames. Even the ormolu clock on the mantelshelf was flanked by a pair of Chinese vases with bronze-gilt banding.

Taking up most of the room was a bed unlike anything Angel had ever seen before. It had no canopy, and she saw the four corner supports were carved into the shape of quivers, presumably for the benefit of the Cupid perched atop the footboard and looking across at a naked goddess draped artistically across the carved and padded headboard. The space between these figures boasted fat, gold-embroidered pillows and a scarlet coverlet exquisitely embroidered in gold thread.

Angel thought it all far more suited to a courtesan—or at least what she imagined a courtesan's room might look like—than a duchess.

She heard the Duke swear quietly.

'I beg your pardon, madam. I had not… I would have thought—' A sound from the corridor made him turn. 'Adams—wait!'

He strode away to the valet, who had stopped at the door of the Duke's room.

'Is this why you wanted to speak to me?' Jason waved one hand in the direction of the bedchamber behind him.

'Yes, Your Grace.' Adams replied woodenly. 'I only discovered it when I overheard Her Grace's maid complaining to the housekeeper.'

Angel saw the valet shift his gaze to somewhere beyond Jason's shoulder.

'I am informed that it was decided, since Your Grace

made no mention of the room, that you wished it to remain as it was.'

'Remain?' Jason had lowered his voice, but every word was audible to Angel, still standing in the doorway. 'Why the devil would I want it to remain like that?'

No, thought Angel with a sigh, *you would not.*

She had known from the moment she saw the room that it had not been prepared for her. She went across to a concealed door in the wall and peeped in. Her dresser was unpacking her trunks there, a look of the utmost disapproval on her face. Joan opened her mouth to speak, but Angel shook her head and retreated as she heard Jason come back into the bedroom.

'Angel, this is not what I intended.'

Having shut the door to the dressing room, Angel ran her hand along the back of one of the gilded chairs.

'No, I am sure it is not,' she said, with admirable calm.

He raked a hand through his hair. 'I had quite forgotten. I—'

'Yes.' She put up a hand to stop him, all desire to laugh gone. 'You have no need to explain. I quite understand.'

She saw a dull flush darken his cheeks.

He went on, 'Everything should have been restored. I did not expect it to still be like this. I am very sorry, Angel.'

'It is no matter. I am sure there are plenty of other rooms I may use.'

She looked around the room again, taking in the garish luxury. This was a room for lovers, she thought. Her eyes moved from the extravagant bed to the couch and back again. She did not know whether to rage at him or to weep.

'It should have been attended to!' he exclaimed angrily. 'My people should have known what needed to be done.'

'Oh, Jason,' she said, her voice mocking. 'You married me

within six months of becoming a widower, which argues a man violently in love! If you sent no instruction to the contrary, what did you expect them to think?'

'Angel, let me explain!'

He came towards her and she flinched away. She would dissolve into tears if he touched her.

'Oh, there is no need for that,' she said with brittle cheerfulness. 'Perhaps you would have a guest room prepared for me until this is put right? In the meantime, the dressing room is very well appointed, and there is plenty of room in there for me to change into my evening gown.' She walked back to the concealed door. 'We will meet again at dinner, but we will not refer to the matter, if you please. I am sure we will both find it highly amusing. In time.'

'Angel, wait—' Jason put out his hand, but the door had already closed behind her with a snap.

'Hell and damnation!'

He walked over to the fireplace and stood staring down into the empty grate, one booted foot resting on the fender.

How could he have forgotten?

In the white-hot passion of his early years with Lavinia he had agreed she might do as she wished with his properties, not caring as long as she was happy. But this transformation had happened much later, and he had only seen it once before, when he had come to London in the weeks after she'd died. He had known immediately she had done it to punish him. She'd no longer had the power to hurt him with her lovers and her outrageous behaviour, so she had sought to do so by turning the room into something resembling a bagnio.

It had been a calculated insult to his family, and as such she would have known he would feel the desecration deeply. His mistake had been to walk away. Not by a look or a word had he revealed to his staff his displeasure. He could hardly blame them now for thinking he had wanted it left that way.

He rubbed a hand over his face. 'You have had your revenge, then, Lavinia!'

He heard a soft cough and looked up to see his valet in the doorway. There was no one Jason trusted more—and, by heaven, he needed to speak to someone!

'I am in the suds now, I fear, Adams.'

'Yes, Your Grace. Is there anything I can do?'

'Have the Blue Room prepared for the Duchess, if you would. Send out today for a new feather mattress for the bed in there, no matter what the cost. Make sure it is in place before she retires tonight.'

'Very well, Your Grace. And this room?'

Jason looked about him, grimacing at the gaudy ostentation.

'Have it all put back as it was. Everything. No, wait, you will buy a new mattress for here, too. My duchess deserves only the best!'

It was some hours until dinner. Angel knew she could not hide away in the dressing room until then, but neither did she want company. She changed from her travelling clothes into a warm day dress and matching pelisse of holly-green and went out to explore the garden. High railings separated the garden from Green Park, but shrubs and trees provided an effective screen and she was able to wander the paths without fear of being spied upon by strangers.

The Duke's obvious chagrin at finding the bedchamber just as he and his first wife had left it went some way to assuaging her anger with him. She could even find it in her heart to sympathise. It must remind him of his lost love. She recalled how he had looked when his father had died, and he'd visited Goole Park for the last time as a boy. Angel's young heart had ached for Jason as he'd tried to act normally, to do his duty. He was so brave, yet always so alone.

The crunch of footsteps on the gravel path broke into her reverie. The Duke was coming towards her.

'What can I say, Angel?' He hurried up to her and took her hands. 'I am more sorry than I can tell you for this.'

'Pray do not make yourself unhappy over it, Jason. I unders—'

'No, you don't!' he interrupted her, his grey eyes stormy, troubled.

She waited while he appeared to wrestle with himself.

Then, 'I need to tell you, if you will listen?'

'Of course.'

He nodded and fell into step beside her.

'I had not seen that room for years.'

'There was no reason for you to do so if she was sharing your bed.'

'That's just it.' His jaw tightened. 'She was not. At least, not so much after Nell was born. Lavinia kept putting it off. At first it was on the doctor's advice, then there were other excuses… Until she wanted something from me, that is. Then she would be so sweet, so loving, that I would succumb to her blandishments. Then, some years ago, I came to London unexpectedly to join her and she was here. With her lover. Or rather, one of them.'

'Oh, Jason!'

'After that, if I was obliged to come to town when Lavinia was at Darvell House, I stayed at my club and left my duchess to hold court here. My only demand for keeping up the pretence of our marriage was that neither she—nor any of her lovers—should ever enter the Duke's bedchamber.' His mouth twisted. 'I no longer had any interest in entering hers.'

Listening to the tragic tale, Angel felt a hollow ache growing inside her. 'Did,' she swallowed. 'Did my brother know of this?'

'Call it pride, if you will, but I could not bring myself to tell anyone, even Barnaby.' He shrugged. 'The ton does not expect husbands and wives to appear often together, but there were rumours.'

'I am so sorry.'

She could only guess how difficult it was for him to go into public with such gossip swirling about him. She squeezed his arm and he nodded, briefly putting his hand over hers.

They strolled on in silence for a few moments before he spoke again.

'This is a wretched start, Angel, I would not have had it so. I have ordered the room to be put back as it was in my parents' time, for now, but believe me, you may make any changes you wish to the furnishings.' He glanced down at her. 'I am sure you will exercise a little more taste.'

She was heartened by the glimmer of a smile she saw in his eyes but she made no reply. It was one thing for Jason to criticise his dead wife, quite another for her to do so.

'So now you know it all,' he said. 'I should have told you at the outset. I apologise.'

And do you still love her, Jason?

Angel could not bring herself to ask him that question.

He went on, 'The Blue Bedroom is being prepared for you now. I hope it will only be a night or two before your own bedchamber is restored.' He paused. 'Or, of course, you might share my bed.'

She stepped in front of him.

'Is that what you wish?' she asked, searching his face.

'Yes.' He pulled her into his arms. 'Oh, yes, I want that. More than anything.'

He lowered his head and kissed her then, and Angel responded.

She was his solace, his comfort. His practical duchess and that would have to suffice.

But it did not stop her yearning for more.

Once it was known the Duke and Duchess of Rotherton were in residence morning callers arrived, and the inevitable invitations. Jason was not always available to accompany Angel, but friends of her family and of the Duke were quick to make themselves known, and before long her circle of acquaintances had grown sufficiently to ensure that she rarely found herself completely amongst strangers. But she still found going into society a challenge.

She was aware that she was being compared to Jason's first wife and made no effort to try and outshine her. With her dark hair and slender figure Angel would never be a voluptuous, dazzling beauty, like Lavinia, but she refused to be daunted. She restyled her hair and bought several more gowns. The finest modistes in town were eager for custom from the new Duchess and put aside their other commissions in order to rush through her orders.

Her latest purchase had arrived in time for her to wear it to Lady Tiverton's ball. It would be the most glittering occasion, and she was very glad Jason was coming with her. Once she had changed into the gown—a daring creation in deep coral silk embroidered with gold thread—she went downstairs to join him in the drawing room while they waited for their carriage to be brought around. His look of admiration when she walked in warmed her immensely.

'You do not think it is a little too…grand?' she asked him, looking down at the brightly coloured skirts.

He grinned. 'You are a duchess—how could it be? And you have a new way of dressing your hair, too. It suits you.'

She blushed, pleased beyond measure that he had noticed.

'You do not object?' she asked shyly, putting a hand up to the topknot. 'The coiffeuse told me it is becoming all the fashion.'

'Not at all. I like it. Very fetching.' He kissed her cheek, sending a flutter of pleasure running through her from head to toe. 'Now, shall we go?'

Tiverton House was bustling when they arrived. Torches flared at the entrance and liveried servants were waiting to help guests from the carriages as they pulled up. Jason escorted Angel into the ballroom, where the dancing had already commenced.

'By heaven, this is a sad crush,' he muttered.

'That means it is a success,' replied Angel, smiling and nodding to an acquaintance. 'We need not stay too long.'

Their hostess came up and carried Angel off to meet some especial friends. This resulted in several invitations to dance, and it was not until supper time that she was free to look for the Duke. She had last seen him dancing with a dashing redhead in an emerald gown spangled with gold. Now, as she looked in vain for his tall, imposing figure, she felt a small stirring of unease. The redhead had been gazing up at him in a way that could not be described as anything other than inviting…

Then he was there, moving through the crowd towards her.

'I was looking for you,' she said, almost dizzy with relief.

'I have been doing my duty on the dance floor.'

'Yes, I too was doing my duty.' She hesitated. 'I hoped you might dance with me.'

He said, a hint of a smile in his eyes, 'Do you really wish to dance with your husband?'

'But of course!' She opened her eyes at him. 'You dance better than anyone I know.'

Flatterer!' He laughed. 'Come along then, madam. Two dances and then I shall take myself off to the card room.'

They were just leaving the dance floor when Angel spotted a familiar face in the crowd.

'Barnaby!' She hurried towards him. 'But this is a surprise! I did not know you were in town.'

'I arrived earlier today. I have an appointment tomorrow with my man of business.' He leaned forward to kiss her cheek before turning to the Duke. 'Jason.'

'Good evening, Barnaby. Is your wife with you?'

'No, alas. It is a very short visit, just a couple of days, and not worth subjecting her to the journey.' He grinned and said, colouring a little, 'She is in an…*interesting* condition. We thought it best she should rest.'

'Oh, Barnaby, how marvellous!' exclaimed Angel, beaming at him. 'I shall write tomorrow, to congratulate her.'

'Yes, do. She will be delighted to hear from you.' He looked past her. 'A new set is forming for the Scotch reel. My favourite! Will you stand up with me, Sister?'

'Why, yes, gladly.' She threw a mischievous glance at the Duke. 'Unless you wish to claim this dance, sir?'

'No, no, I am off to play cards. Go and enjoy yourself.'

'I shall join you after this dance,' Barnaby called after him as he led Angel away to take their places in the set. 'By Jove, Sis, you are looking very well. That orange gown is very stylish. You are dressing your hair differently, too.'

Angel beamed at him. Jason was not merely being polite, her looks must be improved if her brother had noticed them! They leapt and skipped their way through the reel and then

Barnaby carried her away for a glass of punch before heading off to the card room.

When he had gone Angel went back to the ballroom. The dancing had not yet recommenced, and it was more crowded than ever. As she moved between the guests she heard her name. The speaker, a woman, had her back to Angel, but she immediately recognised the red hair and the green and gold gown. It was the lady she had seen Jason dancing with earlier. The redhead was part of a little group of ladies and gentlemen, and Angel heard her say, in a voice dripping with scorn, 'I could not believe it when I heard that Rotherton had married again. How could he, after the ravishingly lovely Lavinia?'

The backs of two large gentlemen in the group provided a convenient screen for Angel. She knew she should walk on, but she could not help herself. More ladies were joining in, their disdainful voices carrying with disastrous clarity.

'I saw them dancing earlier. She is well enough, I suppose, but when one remembers his last duchess there can be no comparison.'

'Indeed! Poor Rotherton. Whatever can have possessed him to settle for such an ordinary little thing when he might have had his pick of the London beauties?'

'Perhaps that was the point.' It was the redhead again. 'Lavinia led the Duke a merry dance with her tantrums and her lovers! From what I have seen of the new duchess, *she* is unlikely to cause him any heartache…'

Angel made herself move away. She could no longer hear them, but she could not forget their words. She moved aimlessly through the crowd, her thoughts bleak. How drab and dull she must look, compared to the late duchess. It would be no wonder if Jason began to regret that he had married her.

'There you are.'

The Duke's voice at her shoulder made her jump.

'Oh… Jason. I could not see you!'

Well, I am here now, and I have come to take you down to supper,' he said, pulling her hand onto his sleeve.

'If you do not object, I would much rather leave.'

He gave her a searching look. 'You are pale. Has anyone upset you?'

'Of course not. I am a little tired, that is all.'

He stopped. 'Would you really like me to take you home?'

She hesitated and he went on, with a smile.

'Pray do not say you want to stay for my sake. I have had quite enough society for one night.'

'Then, yes, please, Jason. I should like to go now.'

In a very short while they were in their carriage, bowling through the darkened streets towards Darvell House, and Angel could no longer ignore the question that was lodged in her head.

'Who was the lady you were dancing with, Jason? A pretty matron with red hair.'

'Mrs Sharrow. An acquaintance, merely. Lavinia knew her better than I. Why do you ask?'

'Oh.' She waved an airy hand. 'I merely wondered who she was.'

He pulled her closer. 'Jealous?'

With his arm around her, and that teasing note in his voice, she felt much better. Well enough to chuckle.

'Not at all.'

'Good. You have no need to be, you know.'

'No, I know that.'

But the hollowness inside her persisted.

She was not jealous of any *living* rival.

Angel was her usual smiling self at breakfast, but as Jason drove to the city to see his man of business he was haunted by the sadness he had seen in her face at Tiverton House last night. She had told him she was tired, but she had seemed more out of spirits—which was certainly not warranted by the occasion. He had seen the admiring glances she had received, accepted any number of compliments on her behalf, and knew that she deserved them all. She had been a hit, but she was so modest, so unassuming, that perhaps she did not realise it.

'Damnation, man, you know women like to be told these things!'

His outburst surprised his groom, sitting beside him in the curricle, and he felt obliged to explain.

'I was talking to myself, Ben. You know I've never been one for making pretty speeches, but I think perhaps I need to make the attempt with the Duchess.'

'Women's like horses, Your Grace,' opined the groom, sagely. 'Unpredictable, but most of 'em respond to a kind word. Although, if you'll forgive my saying so, sir, I have always found Her Grace very easy to talk to.'

'You have?' Jason threw a frowning look at his groom. 'I didn't know that.'

'Aye.' The groom sat back, folding his arms across his chest. 'She came to the stables regularly while we was at Rotherton, to see that horse of hers and to talk with the stable hands. Very keen that the younger ones should learn their letters, she is, and to make sure everyone has comfortable quarters.'

Jason gave a bark of laughter. 'I am sure Crick has something to say about that! He's not one to endure anyone interfering in his domain.'

'Well, that's the thing, Your Grace,' said Ben, rubbing his chin. 'Old Thomas don't mind it at all. He won't hear a word against the new mistress—especially since she had the roof mended and new windows put in the loft.'

Jason digested this. Angel had asked who maintained the outbuildings at Rotherton. He had told her to speak with Simon and then forgotten all about it.

'In fact,' Ben continued, 'the stable lads think the world of her. She has a pleasant word for everyone, and time to listen to their worries.'

Jason felt a stab of conscience that he had not known of this. He had told Angel to run his houses as she wished, and she did, not bothering him with details. But confound it, he *wanted* to be bothered. Clearly he should spend more time discussing these things with his duchess.

His business with Telford was soon completed and Jason drove directly back to Darvell House. He was impatient to see Angel, to talk to her. To make sure she realised how proud he was of her, and how well she had been received last night.

He drove to the front door and jumped down, leaving Ben to take the curricle away to the stables. He ran up the steps and hurried inside just as an elegant figure in a dove-grey suit and a curly brimmed beaver hat was strolling across the hall.

Jason stopped, his mouth twisting with dislike. 'Knowsley! What the devil are you doing here?'

'Dear me, Cousin, you are devilish impolite today.'

'Is there any reason why I should be polite to you?' Jason retorted. A glance showed him that the footman had closed the door and disappeared, but he still lowered his voice. 'I say again: what is your business here?'

Knowsley waved one hand towards the morning room. 'I have been paying my respects to your new duchess.'

Jason stiffened. 'The devil you have!'

'Yes. As behoves a close relative and…er…your heir.'

Jason's temper flared at the smug look on that handsome face but he curbed it, schooling his own features into a look of indifference.

He said coldly, 'Then, if you are done here, I will not detain you.'

Jason went to pass him, but his cousin raised his elegant silver-topped cane and barred his way.

'Do you not want to hear my verdict on your new bride? Can't hold a candle to Lavinia, of course, but pretty enough. I don't doubt she'll fulfil her purpose and give you a son to cut me out.'

Jason snatched the cane and Knowsley stepped back quickly, holding up his hands and laughing.

'No, no, Rotherton, don't call me out. That would cause the sort of scandal you'd most abhor! I meant no harm, I assure you.'

'Then you had best leave now.' He thrust the cane back at Knowsley and turned away.

At that moment there was a burst of girlish laughter from the landing, and Jason swung back to see Rose and Nell at the top of the stairs. What damned ill timing!

Knowsley had dropped his cane but he quickly scooped it up and was already walking towards the stairs.

'Lady Elinor and Miss Haringey, if I am not mistaken,' he drawled, touching his hat. 'Good afternoon to you. I am Tobias Knowsley, your cousin.' He threw a mocking glance at Jason. 'Well, to be accurate, I am the Duke's cousin—but that makes us all somehow related, what?'

The girls had reached the hall by this time, and he bowed first of all to Nell, who was regarding him silently.

'Lady Elinor.'

He turned to Rose.

'Miss Haringey.'

Jason noted the searching look, the faint hesitation before he inclined his head to her. 'You are very like your mother.'

'Why, thank you, Mr Knowsley.'

'No, no, I will not have such formality! You must call me Toby. I hope we are all going to be great friends.'

This jovial declaration received nothing more than uncertain smiles from the young ladies, and Jason stepped up, determined to put an end to this charade.

'Rose, Nell, you will find the Duchess in the morning room. Off you go now. I will show Mr Knowsley out.'

'Charming girls,' observed Knowsley, when they had run off. 'I look forward to our being better acquainted.'

'I will not hear of it.'

'No? You may scoff, Duke, but I am quite sincere. I am of an age now to understand the importance of family.'

'You will stay away from this house, Knowsley, and from my family. Do you hear me?'

'Oh, yes,' he said softly. 'I hear you, Cousin.'

He touched his hat and Jason watched him saunter out, not at all convinced by his cousin's sober tone and demeanour.

Jason went into the morning room, where he found Angel, Rose and Nell about to begin a game of spillikins. He was invited to join in, but declined.

'I shall sit and watch, if I may.'

'I do not think it will take long,' said Rose. 'Angel is very good at this!'

He sat down on one of the sofas to observe the play. How long had it been since this house had echoed to the sound of so much laughter? How long had he lived such a lonely life?

It was not just since Lavinia's death. It had started years

before that. When Nell was born, in fact. Lavinia had hated carrying a child, bemoaning the damage to her figure, but it had taken him a long time to realise why no more children were forthcoming. And even then she had assured him that the poisons and potions she used had been necessary to protect her own health.

He had believed her at first, so besotted had he been. But not any more.

A cheer roused him from his dismal reflections. The game was over, and Rose and Nell were congratulating Angel.

'Do let us play again,' cried Nell. 'Then Papa Duke can join in!'

Angel laughed and shook her head. 'I think not, I want a little time to savour my victory. Besides, it is very nearly time for your walk.'

Both girls protested but after a glance at Jason Angel was adamant. 'We can play again before dinner, if you wish, but off you go now and find Mrs Watson.'

She shepherded them out of the door and closed it with an exaggerated sigh.

Jason smiled. 'You are very good with them.'

'They are delightful,' she said, coming to sit beside him. 'Mrs Watson has brought them up very well. She is truly fond of them.'

'What did Toby Knowsley want?'

She blinked at the sudden change of subject. 'To introduce himself. He was most apologetic for calling when you were not at home, but thought, as your cousin, there would be no objection.'

'You saw him alone?'

'Why, yes. Was I wrong to do so?'

She was looking up at him, her dark eyes so innocent that Jason felt himself relaxing.

'No, but I would not want him running free in this house.'

'You do not like him? He appeared to be very pleasant.'

'As a weasel may appear harmless!' She frowned and he added, bitterly, 'Knowsley was Lavinia's lover.'

Chapter Twelve

Angel gasped. 'I—I cannot believe it!'

'Why not? My cousin is handsome, charming and sociable. He has a great deal of address.' Jason scowled at the carpet. 'He is everything that I am not!'

Angel did not agree with him, but she was still taking in what he had told her about Mr Knowsley.

'Lovers!' she said. 'B-but how? I mean why did you…'

'Why did I not put a stop to it?' He shrugged. 'He was not the first. I had given up caring by the time I discovered the truth.'

Angel felt sick at heart for Jason. She wanted to take him in her arms and kiss away the darkness she saw in his face. Instead she put her hand on his sleeve.

'I think perhaps you cared too much.'

'No. Not about them. I cared only for my family's name.'

She said quietly, 'I do not believe that, Jason.'

'No?' His lip curled. 'While she was discreet, I was prepared to put up with her infidelities.'

'That must have been very painful for you.'

'It was not so bad. After I discovered the truth about her and my cousin we lived separate lives.'

Angel bit her lip, thinking of the gilded boudoir upstairs.

He said, as if reading her mind, 'She redecorated that

bedroom to spite me, but I do not believe she used it often. There are servants here who have been with the family since before I was born. I have no doubt they made it clear what they thought of her behaviour.' A pause. 'The villa in Brighton, however, was another matter.'

'Is that why you will not go there?'

She read the answer in his face and her hands clenched into tight fists as she fought down her anger at his own cousin and the spoiled woman who had caused him so much pain.

'I will instruct the servants to tell Mr Knowsley we are not at home if he calls again. But if we meet in public…?'

'A nod will suffice. You need not acknowledge him.' He sighed. 'The devil of it is that now he has met Rose. He was very taken with her.'

'Do you think that will be a problem?'

He shrugged. 'He might think she is like her mother.'

Angel shook her head. 'Rose is not like that at all. She is a very kind, sweet-natured girl. But, Jason, I do not wish to spoil her memories of her mother. Would you object if we do not tell her anything of your cousin, save that you do not get on?'

'If you think that will suffice.'

'I hope so. We can tell Mrs Watson the same. We will none of us pursue Mr Knowsley's acquaintance.'

He nodded, the darkness lifting from his countenance.

'Are you sure you would not like Mrs Watson to take the girls back to Kent?' he said, coming back towards her. 'I have not yet sold the house.'

'No! They are your family, Jason. They are our responsibility. Also, I feel Rose will be much safer under our eye.'

'Bless you.' He pulled her to her feet and into his arms. 'Dearest Angel, would you have married me if you had known we would have such problems?'

'Of course. You are…' *You are my whole world.* 'You are a duke, sir. That outweighs everything!'

It was not what she wanted to tell him, but she had her pride, too. He had never sought her love and she could not bear to have him reject it.

It took a full week for the servants to return the Duchess's bedchamber to its former order, and even in that short time London life became even busier than ever. More families arrived in town for the winter and the number of invitations increased, not only for Her Grace the Duchess but also for Rose, who was quickly making friends amongst other young debutantes.

There might be whispers about her mother, but if the Duke of Rotherton and his new duchess supported the lovely Miss Haringey, then fond mamas with daughters to launch into society saw every advantage in befriending her. Angel and Mrs Watson accompanied Rose whenever they could, but they also allowed her to attend parties of pleasure with only her maid to escort her, if they were sure a responsible chaperon was present.

When Jason was dealing with business matters Angel had her household duties, plus morning visits and charitable causes to occupy the days, and she was always careful to hide her disappointment if he could not accompany her to the routs, soirées and parties that filled her evenings.

It was not fashionable for a husband and wife to be constantly in each other's company. Theirs was a marriage of convenience and Angel could never forget it. She did not want Jason to think she could not manage quite well without him, although in truth she found little amusement in going out alone.

* * *

Jason, however, was wishing that his wife would show just a little less independence. If he was engaged to dine out with friends he could not help but wonder what Angel was doing. He began to drop in at the parties and balls she attended, arriving late but always in time to claim a dance with his wife and accompany her back to Darvell House.

Coming in earlier than usual one evening, he was disappointed to discover that Angel had already gone out.

'Her Grace has escorted Miss Haringey to an engagement,' Marcuss informed him. 'Mrs Watson being a trifle under the weather.'

'Oh, yes. The Westberes' evening party. I recall they were talking about it at breakfast.'

Nodding, he went on to his room. He knew the hosts slightly. They had come to town with three daughters to marry off and were forever inviting other debutantes and eligible bachelors to their evening parties. Jason was sure it would be a dull affair, but he missed Angel and decided he would change and go there rather than wait at home for her to return.

He arrived at the Westberes' just before supper and went in search of Angel, whom he found sitting with a group of matrons at one side of the ballroom. His arrival caused a stir amongst the ladies—as he remarked when he eventually managed to draw Angel away.

'I thought they would never stop talking,' he muttered. 'I was hoping to dance with you, but it is too late for that now.'

'You cannot blame them,' she said, a laugh in her voice. 'Dukes are something of a rarity. I am not sure any of them has met one before. It will give them something to talk of for weeks to come, I should imagine.'

'You speak as if I was a freak!' He grinned down at her.

He added, looking around the room, 'I suppose Rose is on the dance floor?'

'Yes, but there is no need for us to wait for her. She is having supper with Mrs Westbere.'

'Better and better. I shall have you to myself!'

Angel went down to supper in the best of spirits. They found a quiet corner, and although any number of eyes were turned upon them, no one was brave enough to interrupt their *tête-à-tête*. Angel enjoyed herself immensely, and she was surprised when she heard the musicians striking up again.

'Goodness, the dancing is recommencing. I did not realise we had been here so long.' She laughed and looked around her, saying guiltily, 'Nearly everyone else has gone upstairs.'

Jason rose and offered her his arm. 'And I suppose we must join them.'

Together they went back to the ballroom, where a lively reel was in progress. The throng was too great for Angel to see over the heads of those watching the dancing, but the Duke had no such problem and she was glad to have his tall, imposing presence at her side to carve a path through the crowd.

When he stopped, Angel glanced up and saw that he was staring at the dancers.

'What is it?' she asked. 'Jason?'

'Is this why you were happy to keep me at supper, madam?'

He looked down at her, all trace of humour gone from his eyes. They were now as hard as slate.

'What is it?' she asked him again. 'What can you see?'

He said grimly, 'My cousin is here, and he is dancing with Rose.'

A chill ran through Angel. 'Mr Knowsley? I had not seen him…'

'You were too busy enjoying yourself!'

She flushed. 'That is unfair, Jason. I did not know he was here.'

'Rose is your responsibility tonight,' he retorted. 'It is your duty to make sure she is safe.'

'She is hardly likely to come to harm dancing a reel!'

She tried to pull her hand free but he clamped it to his arm.

'Oh, no, madam. You will not disappear now. We need to sort this out as soon as the music ends!'

'That is what I intend to do!' she retorted. 'Pray remember that we decided Rose need be told nothing about Mr Knowsley. You cannot blame her for standing up with him.'

'I do not blame her. I blame *you*, madam!'

Angel bit her lip. She accompanied Jason through the crowd, ready to meet Rose and Mr Knowsley when they finally walked off the floor. Rose was looking flushed and happy after the exertion of the dance, and when she saw the Duke she beamed at him.

'Your Grace! I did not think you would come tonight.'

Her greeting was quite unaffected. Angel thought that should tell Jason that Rose was innocent of any intrigue, but she answered quickly, before he could speak.

'Nor I. Is it not the most delightful surprise?'

She smiled up at him, holding her breath and praying that he would not lose his temper.

'No, I had not planned it.' He nodded to his cousin. 'Perhaps you will give me a few moments of your time.'

Toby Knowsley was looking wary, but he could hardly refuse the Duke.

Angel stepped across to Rose and linked arms with her. 'Yes, let us leave the gentlemen to their talk and we will go and sit down. I vow you have been so busy this evening I have scarce seen you!'

She led Rose away from the dance floor, heading for the side of the room, away from the crowd.

'Is the Duke angry with me?' Rose asked her, when they had found two empty chairs in a window embrasure.

'Now, what makes you think that?

'He was frowning so heavily when he looked at me. He looked most displeased.'

'Not with you, my dear. He had not expected to see you dancing with his cousin, that is all.' Angel took a moment to rearrange her skirts while she chose her next words. 'The Duke would not wish it known, but he, he does not quite approve of Mr Knowsley. His manners are not those of a gentleman.'

'Oh.' Rose digested this. 'He is always very friendly, but I have never felt quite at ease with him.'

'You have met him before tonight, then?'

'Oh, yes. We have met several times, in various shops, and in the library, for instance. But now I think of it, it has always been when you or Mrs Watson were absent. He was at Almack's last week, when Mrs Westbere took me there with her daughters. I only stood up with him to be polite, because he said we were as good as cousins.'

'You do not like him?'

Rose shook her head. 'No. Jane Westbere thinks he is very handsome and charming, but he stares at one so.'

Angel hid her relief.

'You are free to refuse him the next time he asks you to dance,' she said, patting Rose's hand. Although she thought it was unlikely Toby Knowsley would ask again, after this evening.

They remained at the side of the room until Rose's next partner came looking for her. Since it was young Mr Westbere, the son of the house, Angel sent her off with a smile, but she herself moved closer to the dance floor, from where she could do her duty as chaperon.

She was still there when Jason came back into the ballroom. She saw him making his way towards her. In repose, his expression was naturally reserved, even a little forbidding, and it was impossible to read his mood until he was much closer. Then she saw the cold, angry light in his eyes.

'Where is Mr Knowsley?' she asked him.

'Gone.' He noticed her anxious look and added, 'We did not come to blows. I merely warned him what would happen if he came near any of my family again.'

'I am glad.' She took his arm. 'Let us walk a little. Rose will come to no harm while she is dancing with Mr Westbere.'

She cast a glance up at him as they began to stroll about the room.

'I beg your pardon. I shall not forget my responsibilities again this evening.'

'So that rankled, did it? It was as much my fault, for carrying you off to supper with me.'

She acknowledged this with a slight nod, much encouraged. Her husband was not one to readily admit he was at fault.

'Rose has told me she does not much like Mr Knowsley.'

'Then she is a better judge of character than I thought.'

'You hardly know her, Jason.' She hesitated. 'I told her you did not approve of Mr Knowsley's manners.'

'An understatement!'

'I know, but I believe it was enough. Rose knows now you will not be offended if she refuses to dance with him again.'

'Thank you.' He looked down at her, his face relaxing into a rueful smile. 'I am not yet experienced in the role of guardian.'

She squeezed his arm. 'It is only right that you are cautious where your ward is concerned.'

He looked over her head. 'I shall be more than cautious where Tobias Knowsley is concerned!'

A few days later, at the beginning of November, Lady Goole arrived at Darvell House.

'I can stay only a few weeks,' she told Angel, when she joined her to take tea in the morning room. 'Meg is increasing—but you know that. She told me you saw Barnaby when he was in town recently. They are coming to Goole Park for Christmas, because Barnaby wants the baby to be born there.' As Angel handed her a cup of tea she said, 'I was wondering, perhaps, if *you* had anything to tell me, my dear…?'

'No, Mama. Not yet.' Angel felt a blush stealing to her cheeks and she busied herself filling her own cup.

'Ah, well, it is early days.'

Angel quickly changed the subject. 'I have put you in the Blue Room, Mama. It overlooks the park, so it is blissfully quiet at night, and the bed is very comfortable.' She added airily, 'It has a new feather mattress.'

'Goodness, I hope you did not go to such an expense just for me!' exclaimed Lady Goole.

Angel shook her head, but did not explain. She had no wish to tell her mother just how that particular purchase had come about.

She said, 'Mrs Watson has taken Rose and Nell on an outing to Green Park, but they will be back in time to see you before dinner.'

'Ah. I hope the children are not taking up too much of your time?'

'Not at all. They are very well behaved. And Rose is nearly eighteen. She is very good company.'

'And the Duke?' Lady Goole sipped at her tea. 'Is he good company?'

'Why, yes. He is very attentive. Although I do not think he is comfortable going into society. There are too many reminders of his first wife.'

'Ah.'

'People make...comparisons. Between me and the late Duchess.'

'That is understandable, my dear. You must not let it upset you.'

'I do not. Well, not much.' Angel bit her lip. 'But... I cannot bring myself to like the late Duchess. Her behaviour...' She tailed off, unwilling to confide everything to Mama. 'It is not merely jealousy. I cannot like the way she convinced Jason it would best to set her daughters up in their own establishment.'

'You must remember, my dear, that Jason was brought up in very much the same way,' reasoned Lady Goole. 'His parents were rarely at home with him. He would see nothing wrong in it. But all that has changed now, I believe?'

'Why, yes. We are all pleased with the arrangement.'

'And you still have Mrs Watson to look after the children.' Her mother nodded. 'That means you have more time for your husband when he needs you.'

'Yes.'

Angel hoped she did not sound unsure about that. She knew Jason wanted her, that he found comfort in her arms. And she was useful, but did he really *need* her?

Lady Goole was watching her closely. 'Are you regretting marrying the Duke, Angeline?'

'No. Oh, no. It is just... I wonder if *he* regrets marrying *me*.'

'Oh, my poor girl! Did he tell you he was in love with you?'

'No, of course not. I never thought, never expected...'

Lady Goole put down her teacup. She said delicately, 'I hope he is not unkind?'

'No, no! Jason is the very kindest of men. And attentive. Generous, too.'

'Does he have a mistress? Oh, do not colour up so, my dear. That would not be unusual for a man such as Rotherton.'

'I know that, but I am almost sure he does not have a mistress.' Angel plucked at her skirts and said, in a burst of confidence, 'I think he is still in love with his first wife.'

'I see.' Lady Goole sighed and shook her head at her daughter. 'Life is not a fairy tale, Angeline. You have an exemplary husband. Many women would envy you your good fortune. Give Jason time, my dear. It has been just over a year since his wife's untimely death. Let him grieve and mourn. As his wife, you are well placed to win his affections when he is ready. In the meantime you must show the Duke that you are the perfect partner for him!'

She gave Angel a smile of reassurance and drained her cup.

'Now, tomorrow we shall go shopping. I need to buy some new gowns to take home with me, and I am sure you could do with more.'

'Oh, no, Mama, I have already purchased any number of gowns!'

'Nonsense. A duchess can never have too many. We shall visit the finest modistes in London. Oh, my dear, I am so looking forward to going out and about with you! We must make a plan. But first let us have more tea!'

With Lady Goole in London, Angeline found her days became very full indeed. There were trips to silk warehouses, plus visits to linen drapers, modistes, mantuamakers and hosiers. Angel might protest that she could not possibly wear so many new clothes, but her mama was adamant.

'A duchess attracts attention every time she ventures out. You will be scrutinised from head to toe. Every detail will be noted and discussed.'

Angel gave a wry smile. 'I think that happens already.'

'So you must always look your best. Now, there is a very good shawl and linen warehouse in Fleet Street that we must visit, but because of its proximity to the prison I think we should take along a second footman when we go, don't you?'

It was not only shopping that kept the ladies busy. Lady Goole was anxious to be out and about as much as possible, and Angeline accepted far more invitations than she had done prior to her mama's visit.

Thankfully, she was growing accustomed to hearing talk of Lavinia. Without exception it was agreed that for beauty she had no equal, but Angel soon discovered that not everyone had been enamoured of the late duchess. There were rumours of excessive gambling, even hints of her numerous lovers, although Angel already knew about that. What she had not heard before was that Lavinia had been high-handed and demanding with those she considered inferior—until Joan informed her of it.

'Not that one should always believe everything one hears below stairs,' added Joan, after she had passed on yet another instance of the late Duchess's petty tyranny. 'But I have been told enough, and from several sources, to believe at least *some* of it must be true. Don't you think so, Your Grace?'

'Very possibly,' Angel agreed. 'But we will not repeat any of this outside this room.'

'Oh, no, indeed, ma'am. I wouldn't dream of it,' replied Joan, much affronted. 'I just thought you should know, seeing as how you might be thinking your predecessor was such a paragon.'

Touched by Joan's loyalty, Angel thanked her and said they should now put it from their minds. However, she could not forget. It saddened her to think Jason still worshipped such a flawed goddess.

When an invitation arrived from the Countess of Cherston, Angel took it immediately to her mother.

'She has invited us to her masquerade tomorrow night, Mama. She apologises for the late notice, but says the card slipped down behind her desk and she has just this minute found it! I do not think it would be suitable for Rose, but I should very much like to go. I have never been to a masked ball. What say you?'

Lady Goole tapped her lip. 'These affairs often turn a little rowdy after midnight…'

'We need not stay late, Mama. And there could be no harm in it if you were to come with me.'

Lady Goole sighed. 'It is a long time since I attended a masquerade. But where would we get costumes at this late date?'

'Do we need them? I believe many people simply wear a domino over their evening clothes.'

'Yes, it would be easy enough to purchase dominos, I suppose. And masks.' She laughed. 'What fun it would be!'

Before making a final decision, Angel asked Jason for his opinion.

'I have never been to a proper masquerade,' she told him. 'Mama held one at Goole Park once, but it was only for our neighbours and I recognised everyone immediately, despite their masks.'

'How disappointing! Then go, if you wish. I have not

seen Cherston for years, but I recall he was ever a dull dog and very respectable. I have no objection if Lady Goole is going with you.'

'Would you not like to come?'

He grimaced. 'Not unless you especially wish it. And besides, Westbere has invited me to join him for a dinner at Boodle's tomorrow. I thought it would be politic to attend.'

She chuckled. 'Yes, you owe him that after we left their party so precipitately. Very well, Mama and I will go, and I shall tell you all about it when we get back!'

Jason watched her trip away, thinking that if he hadn't accepted Westbere's invitation then he might well have gone with her, just to share her pleasure in the novelty.

He frowned. This growing desire to be in his wife's company was concerning. Angel might be nothing like his first wife, but he still did not want to lose his head over her!

No, he thought, setting off to join Westbere the following evening. Far better that he did not follow her everywhere.

Besides, there was no need. Angel would have Lady Goole on hand to look after her.

Angel adjusted the hood of her domino and checked that her half-mask was in place before stepping down from the coach. She accompanied her mother into the house, where all was bustle and noise. There were a number of black dominos on display in the ballroom, but these only enhanced the colourful and garish costumes of most of the guests.

'Heavens, I had forgotten how abandoned these affairs can become!' exclaimed Lady Goole. 'But then, I only ever attended masquerades with your father. Perhaps you should have pressed Rotherton to come with us.'

'Yes, perhaps.' Angel quickly moved back as a shepherd

and shepherdess barged past her, laughing immoderately. 'I do not think we will remain here long.'

'No, I agree. We shall certainly leave before midnight,' said her mother. 'Until then, we must stay together.'

But this was not possible. They were pressed to dance and, as Lady Goole remarked, it would have been extremely ill-humoured of them not to join in.

'We will meet here, by the door, at a quarter to twelve,' she assured Angel, before being whisked away by a jovial Falstaff.

The room was still cool enough to make skipping around in an enveloping domino possible, and once on the dance floor Angel began to enjoy herself. Everyone was very jolly, if a little loud, but so happy and good-natured that she had no qualms about standing up with strangers.

As she glanced at the large ormolu clock on the mantelshelf she felt this was like a fairy tale, where she must be gone by midnight.

At Boodle's the dinner was good, but Jason found himself one of the younger members of the party. Talk meandered between politics and sport, but when the gentlemen began to discuss the merits of various blends of snuff his mind began to wander. Only to be brought back when he suddenly heard a name he recognised.

'I've no doubt there will be some of the more exotic mixtures available at the Cherstons' ball tonight,' remarked his host. 'I understand the Earl thinks himself something of a connoisseur, but it's all an affectation. He himself favours taking snuff from the wrist of his latest paramour.'

'Cherston?' Jason's brows went up. 'I thought he disapproved of mistresses—or has he changed now he is in his dotage?'

'Good God, Your Grace, where have you been?' laughed someone further down the table. 'The old Earl has been dead these two years or more. No, I mean his son. A very rakish fellow. And his wife is no better.'

Jason picked up his glass. He was out of touch. His visits to town had been purely for business in recent years, and while Lavinia had been alive he had made a point of avoiding their friends and the gossip pages of the newspapers.

He said casually, 'What exactly is happening tonight?'

'They are hosting a masquerade,' Westbere told him.

The man beside him laughed. 'That's what they call it! But knowing Cherston and that trollop he married there'll be plenty of high-flyers present, and any number of young bucks. It will be a dashed romp by midnight, mark my words!'

Jason pushed back his chair.

'Anything wrong, your Grace?' enquired his host.

'No, no,' Jason replied, trying to remain calm. 'Just remembered something I need to do tonight. Excuse me!'

It was not far to Portland Square and Jason set off on foot, striding through the dark streets and ignoring the icy wind that cut at his cheeks. If what he had heard about the Cherstons was correct, it was possible that Angel and her mother would already have left, but he could not risk wasting time going back to Darvell House to find out.

The square frontage of the Cherstons' hired mansion was illuminated by torches, and the windows glowed with candlelight, but no carriages waited outside.

And nor would they, he thought grimly. It was not yet midnight, and no one would leave before the unmasking.

The ballroom was growing warmer and Angel decided she would sit out the next dance. She walked around the edge of the room, enjoying the spectacle. Her mother was dancing with an ageing Harlequin and laughing so much that Angel smiled. Mama rarely came to London and it was good to see her enjoying herself.

When the musicians struck up for a Scotch reel, Angel knew it was likely to be the last dance before the midnight unmasking. She had already refused two gentlemen, both of whom were clearly inebriated, but stood up with a third, whose plain coat suggested a certain sobriety.

The music started, the tempo very quick, and soon everyone was reeling and skipping. Such was the energy that before long Angel's hood came free of its pins and slipped back, but she hardly noticed, too busy keeping pace with the dance. It was extremely fast, everyone was whooping and laughing, and Angel was enjoying it immensely.

They had reached the final movement of the dance when her partner took her hands to spin her about, only instead of releasing her at the required time he clung tighter and spun her away from the dance floor. Angel was off balance and could do nothing but try to keep her feet. Those watching fell back, screeching with laughter, as he pulled her through an open doorway and into an inner hall.

Angel tried to free her hands but her partner held on and pushed her backwards into the shadows.

'This is no longer amusing, sir,' she told him, too angry to be afraid. 'I insist you let me go.'

He fell against her, pinning her to the wall. 'Not before I have claimed my prize, fair maid.'

His hot breath was on her cheek. Angel was no longer a shy debutante, and she gathered herself to fight, but then, quite suddenly, she was free. A tall figure in a black cloak had pulled her would-be attacker away.

The man squawked ineffectually as he was lifted off his

feet and thrown aside like a rag doll. The cloaked figure followed and stood over him like a dark knight, tall and menacing.

'Get up,' he ordered savagely. 'Stand up, you dog. We will finish this now!'

'No!' Angel knew that voice. 'No. I am not hurt!'

She ran across and caught the Duke's arm. She could almost feel the rage radiating from him, and beneath his sleeve the knotted muscle was hard as steel.

She said again, 'I am not hurt, sir. Pray, take me away from here.'

Jason felt the red-hot anger cooling. Angel's hand had slipped down and wrapped around his clenched fist. She was unhurt, and still masked.

'Cover your head,' he ordered. 'We might yet get out of this without being recognised.'

When she had pulled the hood up he took her arm and escorted her quickly back through the ballroom. Thankfully everyone was too drunk to take any notice of them.

'Are you very angry with me?' she asked him.

'Furious!'

Although mainly with himself for not taking better care of her.

'I did not need your help,' she said, her little chin raised defiantly.

'Hah!'

'It is true! I was about to send him about his business when you came blundering in.'

He stopped. 'My *blundering*, as you call it, madam, saved you from being mauled by that rogue!' Her eyes glittered through the slits of her mask and he added savagely, 'I have told you, I know how to protect my own!'

He looked so menacing that Angel shivered. Beneath his reserve she detected a wild spirit in her husband that made him very dangerous.

But not to me. Never to me.

Aloud, she said, 'We must find Mama.'

'I met her when I came in and told her to wait by the door.'

'You must not blame her, Jason.'

'I don't.'

She sighed. 'You blame me.'

He stopped. 'After what you told me about your previous visit to London, I should have thought you would have more sense!'

'I do!' she retorted, bridling. 'Since then I have always made sure my hairpins are long and sharp. As you will discover if you keep glaring at me like that!'

Jason's eyes narrowed, and Angel braced herself for a stinging retort, but instead he set off again, keeping a tight grip on her arm.

She said suddenly, 'Your domino smells of camphor. Where did you get it?'

'There was a drunkard in the square. He did not require it any longer.'

'If he is still there when we go outside you can return it.'

He laughed.

It sounded harsh, but even that was better than his remaining stubbornly angry with her.

They found Lady Goole pacing by the ballroom entrance.

'Oh, my dear! I would never have brought you here if I had known how it would be!' she cried, taking Angel's hands. 'And then I could not see you! There were so many people milling around, blocking the way.'

'Pray do not upset yourself, Mama. I have enjoyed myself prodigiously.'

She threw a challenging look at Jason, which he met with a scowl.

'It is growing rowdier by the minute,' he muttered. 'Time to be going.'

'I have summoned the carriage,' said Lady Goole as they made their way downstairs. 'It should be here by now.'

They found their town coach waiting at the door and Jason handed the ladies in.

'Wait!' Angel put up a hand as Jason jumped in and began to close the door. 'You must return that cloak to its owner.' He hesitated and she added, 'If for no other reason than it smells so atrociously.'

She thought he might explode, but a sudden grin replaced the irritation in his face. He disappeared, coming back a few minutes later to announce that he had given the domino to one of Cherston's servants.

'The fellow is gone, but he can collect his property tomorrow. If he can remember where he left it.'

It was a subdued party that returned to Darvell House. Lady Goole went up to her room immediately, but Angel hesitated, looking at the Duke. He was abstracted, a slight crease in his brow, but then he looked up and saw her waiting.

'I beg your pardon. My thoughts were elsewhere.'

'I wondered if we might take a glass of wine together,' she suggested.

He shook his head. 'Alas, no. I have business that requires my attention.'

'Immediately?'

'Yes. And you must be tired after your...exertions.' He took her hand and lifted it to his lips. 'Goodnight, Angel. Sleep well.'

'Goodnight, Your Grace.'

She made her way up to her bedchamber, her spirits drooping. He had dismissed her. Not in so many words, but she knew he would not come to her room tonight. He was still angry at having to rescue her from a scrape—not that she had needed rescuing!

The sudden spurt of rebellion died away. How she wished that she had never gone to that silly masquerade. But it was too late for regrets. Jason was disappointed in her and that was not at all what she wanted.

Almost before Angel had said goodnight Jason turned and went into his study. He had shut the door on the sight of her walking up the stairs, but he could not shut her out of his mind. He had told her he was furious, but it was not anger he had felt when he'd learned the sort of masquerade she was attending. It was fear. Ice-cold dread at what might happen to her in such company. And when he'd found that scoundrel trying to molest her it had roused all his protective instincts.

He walked over to the side table and poured himself a glass of brandy. Damnation. His worst fears had been realised. He had vowed he would never lose his head over a woman again and here he was, just as besotted and even more in love than he had ever been.

Chapter Thirteen

Returning to Darvell House from a morning visit to a new acquaintance, Angel was glad Mama had insisted she buy a fur-lined pelisse to wear beneath her cloak. It helped to keep out the icy November wind that whipped through the London streets and even permeated the town coach.

She hurried into the hall and heard a merry laugh coming from the morning room, followed by the murmur of voices.

'Oh, do we have visitors?' she asked as she removed her bonnet and gloves.

She realised the waiting servant was another of the handsome but slow-witted creatures Lavinia had taken on, and when he gave her nothing more than a startled look she smothered a sigh.

'No matter. I will go in directly.' She shrugged off her pelisse and handed everything to the hapless footman, saying, 'And, no, I do not need you to announce me!'

Really, she thought as she hurried towards the morning room, *I shall have to talk to Jason about turning the man off.*

But all thoughts about the unfortunate lackey fled as soon as she opened the door.

'Mr Babberton!'

The young man was sitting on the sofa with Rose beside

him. They both jumped to their feet as she came in, Kenelm Babberton flushing to the roots of his curly brown hair.

Angel shut the door quickly behind her. 'What is the meaning of this? You know you should not be here. Alone, too.'

'We are not alone,' said Rose. 'I mean, Lady Goole was here.'

'Well, she is clearly not here now!'

'She w-went off to speak to someone…' Rose twisted her hands together and threw a despairing look at Mr Babberton.

He turned to Angel. 'I beg your pardon, Your Grace. I know we agreed not to see one another, but I could not stay away any longer.'

'Evidently.'

He flushed and spread his hands, searching around for the words to express himself.

'When Rose went off to London I felt… It was as if part of me was missing! I—'

He stopped as Lady Goole rattled the doorhandle and came in, saying, 'There, that is settled— Oh! You are back, Duchess.' She smiled brightly, but not before Angel caught her look of guilty dismay.

'Did you admit Mr Babberton, ma'am?' Angel demanded.

'Why, yes,' replied Lady Goole, adopting an innocent demeanour. 'Rose said he was an acquaintance from Rotherton.'

'And it is true!' declared Rose. She reached out and took the young man's hand. 'We are *very* good friends!'

Angel's heart was touched, but she said, trying to keep her voice calm, 'I think, sir, it would be best if you left before the Duke comes in.'

Mr Babberton pulled himself up straighter. 'I am not afraid to meet His Grace, ma'am. In fact, I should very much like to talk to him.'

'That may be so, but not today,' she said firmly, imagining Jason's reaction if he found the young man in his house. 'Pray go now. I shall talk to the Duke on your behalf.'

'You, you will?' said Rose.

'You have my word.' Angel nodded. 'If Mr Babberton is staying in town then the Duke must be informed.'

'Of course,' he said quickly. 'That is why I called today—to see him. But I was informed His Grace was not at home.' He stopped, looking a little uncomfortable. 'And then I asked for Miss Haringey.'

An awkward silence fell over the room. Lady Goole was regarding the young couple with every appearance of sympathy, but Angel knew it would not do. She walked across to the chimneypiece and tugged at the bellpull.

'I suggest you go now, Mr Babberton, and you must not contact Miss Haringey again until you hear from me.'

'But, Angel—'

'No, Rose. That is how it must be. At least until I have spoken with the Duke.'

'But you will plead my case for me?' asked Mr Babberton, his blue eyes fixed upon Angel.

'I shall do my best. Now, go, sir, and wait until you hear from me.'

The footman was at the door. Kenelm Babberton threw one last, longing look at Rose before he recovered himself, bowed formally to the ladies and went out.

No one moved. They listened to his booted footsteps crossing the hall and the clunk of the street door. Rose gave a sob and Angel went over to take her hands.

'There really is no need for you to weep, Rose. The Duke has already agreed to discuss the situation when we return to Rotherton.'

'But that will not be until the spring! It is too cruel when we are in love!'

Angel's heart went out to the girl, but Rose was the Duke's ward, not hers, and she dare not raise false hopes.

As if reading her mind, Rose gave a little cry and ran out of the room.

'Ah, the poor dears!' Lady Goole sank down onto the sofa. 'Was I very wrong to leave them alone?'

'I am afraid you were, Mama,' said Angel. 'They formed an attachment while we were at Rotherton and the Duke was furious when he discovered it. Mr Babberton was forbidden to come to the house. That is in part why Jason allowed the girls to come to London. We neither of us expected Rose's swain to follow her. I thought, with time and all the distractions of the capital, she would forget him.'

'And now I have spoiled all that.' Lady Goole sighed and shook her head. 'I am very sorry, my love, but it was a genuine mistake. When the footman asked if we were at home to Mr Babberton, Rose looked so pleased that I assumed he had called before. If I had known…'

'How could you know, Mama? Pray do not torment yourself. Rose should have told you, although I cannot find it in my heart to be angry with her when she thinks herself so much in love.'

Lady Goole said nothing. She spent a few moments smoothing out her skirts then she said, without looking up, 'Far be it from me to criticise the Duke, but I have always thought it unwise to keep young people apart. It is far too easy for them to convince themselves that they are star-crossed lovers. Much better to let them get to know one another. They very often discover that they are not in love at all. In some cases they do not even *like* one another very much! But that is only my opinion, of course.'

'It is mine too, Mama, but Jason thinks differently and he is Rose's guardian.'

'Well, you must talk to him,' said her mother. 'Rotherton is not an unreasonable man. I am sure you can persuade him to let them meet. As long as they are supervised, of course.'

'Of course.' Angel nodded. 'I shall speak to him at the earliest opportunity.'

Not that she could be sure when that would be. She had seen very little of Jason for the past week. Since the Churstons' masquerade, in fact. He had taken to spending most of the day at his club, or locked in his study not to be disturbed. If he joined the family for dinner he was quiet, preoccupied.

Angel suspected he was still angry with her. Disappointed, perhaps, that she had shown such a lack of judgement in attending the masquerade. However, she must speak to him about Rose and Kenelm Babberton before he discovered for himself that the young man was in town and jumped to his own conclusions.

The following morning, therefore, she went to his study as soon as she had finished her breakfast, entering upon the knock.

'May I speak to you, Your Grace?'

'Can it not wait?' He scowled at her and waved at the documents spread out over the desk. 'I have an appointment with Telford and I need to finish these papers first.'

'It will not take long.'

She sat down across the desk from him and quickly explained about Rose and Mr Babberton.

'Are you telling me the young devil had the audacity to come to Darvell House?' he demanded, when she had finished.

'Yes. I believe he really did want to speak to you, which I think, in the circumstances, was very brave of him.'

'It was damned foolish! I expressly told him he must not see Rose.'

'I think they might truly be in love, Jason. Will you not reconsider—?'

'No!' He slammed his hands on the desk. 'I will not countenance it, madam! It was you who suggested she should have a London season.'

'Yes, and I still believe it is the right thing to do. Is there any harm in allowing her to see Mr Babberton while he is in town? After all, you cannot prevent him from being here.'

'I can and I will!'

She shook her head, smiling a little. 'What, will you become a tyrant, Jason? I think not.'

Jason almost ground his teeth at that. How did she always manage to find his weakness. Of course he was no tyrant!

She went on. 'I believe Mr Babberton was sincere when he told me he called here with every intention of speaking with you. Surely it is better to let them meet? Under strict supervision, of course.' She hesitated. 'If you do not trust me to do it, then there is Mrs Watson, and also Mama. Now that she understands the situation I am sure she would agree to play chaperon sometimes.'

'Good God, woman, will you not let it be?' he exclaimed, jumping to his feet. 'I have said no and I mean it. Be warned, madam: I won't let you coax and cajole me this time.' He glared down at her. 'Have you not done enough damage already? Not content with bringing the children to live at Rotherton, you have now thrust them into the London house! Confound it, you have done nothing but turn my ordered world upside down! I should never—'

He broke off, turning away from her with an angry growl.

Angel pressed her hands to her chest, trying to stop the fearful thud of her heart.

She finished the sentence for him. 'You should never have married me.'

She blinked rapidly and fixed her eyes on the Duke's broad back, stiff and yielding under the black coat. It was true, then. She had long suspected it, but now she knew the truth.

She drew in a deep breath. 'Perhaps you are right, sir. I have certainly not done well by Rose, have I? First I allowed your cousin to dance with her when I should have prevented it. Although Mrs Watson and I have seen Mr Knowsley at several balls and parties since, and even if he does stare a great deal at Rose, he has made no attempt to approach her. But I beg you, Jason, do not let your anger with me cloud your judgement. Allow Rose and Mr Babberton to meet. Watch them together and judge their affection for yourself.'

Jason stared out at the street. Marrying Angel was the very best thing he had ever done, so why did he not say so? Why could he not bring himself to tell her?

He was on the edge of a precipice.

To admit how much he cared was to risk everything he had struggled for years to repair. Everything Lavinia had destroyed. His life, his happiness. His heart.

Angel went on, the unhappiness in her voice slicing into him.

'I will say no more. I am clearly not the best person to act as advocate for the young couple. However, I thought it important you were informed that Mr Babberton is in London. I would not have you think that anyone in this house is trying to deceive you.'

There was a pause, then he heard her sigh.

'Excuse me. You have business in the City today and I have taken up too much of your time.'

He heard the click of the door and swung round, but she had gone. All that was left was her perfume…a faint trace of summer flowers.

It was gone noon when Jason left Telford's offices and he made his way to a nearby tavern. After a gruelling interview with his man of business he felt in need of sustenance, and a little quiet reflection.

The lowering sky matched his mood, which had not improved since he had quit Darvell House that morning. The encounter with Angel concerned him. He was frustrated that he could not explain his true feelings. He had always struggled with a natural reserve, but these past few years it had become an almost physical barrier. He had worn his heart on his sleeve for Lavinia and her betrayal had left deep scars. Pride had stopped him denouncing her, and they had continued with their sham marriage until her death, when he had withdrawn from Society to lick his wounds.

Jason knew he would be hiding away still if Angel had not rescued him. She had coaxed him back into the world, brought his family to Rotherton and filled the old house with warmth and laughter. He owed her so much, and she deserved a great deal more than his morose reticence. He should have told her everything about his first marriage…how his first wife had broken his heart. Perhaps then he might have been able to tell her that she had mended it.

Confound it, he was a fool of the highest order!

And now Telford had shown him just how much of a fool he had been. And not just over Lavinia.

When they had married, Jason had been content for Lavinia to retain control of her properties, including the house in Kent, which she told him she would settle upon Rose. He had trusted her word, and it had come as a shock today to find that it was mortgaged to the hilt. Its sale would bring in only a pittance.

Galling as he'd found this news, it was not financial matters but Angeline who was uppermost in his mind as he sat in the tavern. He had arrived at Goole Park for Barnaby's wedding troubled and angry, but she had soothed his soul. He'd found peace in her company and had married her for purely selfish reasons.

The first glimmer of a smile lightened his spirits as he finished his meal and poured more ale into his tankard. Yes, she had turned his world upside down, there was no doubt about that, but it was for the better. She endured his moods with patience and good humour, and she had even taken on responsibility for Rose and Nell. Compared to Lavinia, Angel gave so much and asked for very little in return.

Jason drained his tankard. By heaven, he might not be able to *say* the words, but he could show her how much he valued her. A grand gesture was required, and he knew just what to do.

Jason made his way to his bankers on the Strand and was shown into an inner office, where one of the elderly partners was waiting to do his bidding.

'I want you to fetch the family jewels from the Darvell vault.'

'Of course, Your Grace. Which ones?'

'All of them,' said Jason.

'All?'

'Yes, of course.'

'As Your Grace wishes.'

The man bowed and left the room and Jason sat down to await his return. The only jewellery he had given Angel was his wedding gift—a few paltry diamonds and pearls. Now she should have her choice from all the family jewels. He was only sorry that he had not thought of it earlier.

Just what was in the collection he could not recall. There were pieces going back several generations, plus the jewellery that he had lavished upon his late duchess. Jason had instructed that all the jewellery should be sent to the bank for safekeeping when she died, and then he had forgotten all about it.

He wondered which of the family pieces would best become Angel. Rubies, perhaps. Or sapphires. Some of it would be unfashionable now, but the stones could be reset if Angel liked them. He had a vague memory of seeing a parure of emeralds set in gold that would look magnificent against Angel's creamy skin…

The door opened and the senior partner came back with several velvet boxes in his hands. He was accompanied by a minion carrying a large jewel case.

'Here we are, Your Grace.'

The clerk withdrew and the elderly partner spread the boxes over the desk and began to open them. In the large box Jason recognised the garnets that his grandmother had worn: a necklace, earrings and a pair of bracelets all set in gold. There was also his mother's necklace of blue jasper cameos, linked with gold chain.

Soon the whole desk was glittering with gold and silver jewellery set with seed pearls and diamonds, emeralds and rubies. The last box revealed Jason's wedding present to Lavinia—a diamond and sapphire necklace with matching eardrops and bracelets.

'I must say I was a little surprised that Your Grace wished to leave all these pieces in our vaults,' remarked the banker. 'No doubt some of the more recent additions have sentimental value for you.'

'No, none at all.' Jason was surprised to find how little he cared about the money he had lavished upon Lavinia. His only regret was that he had allowed her to manipulate him for so long.

The banker continued. 'Some of the gems are extremely well-made—one would hardly know they were paste.'

Jason looked up. *'Paste?'*

A shadow of concern flickered over the man's face.

Jason picked up one of the necklaces and studied it, then another. Fine, tell-tale scratches on the stones revealed that they were imitation.

He fixed the banker with a hard, steady gaze. 'What the devil has been going on here? What has happened to my family's jewels?'

The banker sat down. 'There are *some* genuine pieces here, Your Grace. The blue jasper, for example. And the garnets. Also some of the early sets, pieces that have remained in the bank since your father's time.'

'And all the rest are paste?' Jason dropped the necklace he was holding back onto the table.

'Why, yes, Your Grace. It was assumed you knew of it.'

'The devil I did! Tell me.'

The old man gazed down at his clasped hands and said in a colourless voice, 'The late Duchess came in to collect them, Your Grace. Not all at once, you understand. She made several visits to the bank over the years. I remember the first occasion most particularly, because I checked the records myself, to make sure that you had signed the necessary permissions.'

Jason felt a chill hand clutching at his insides. Yes, he remembered now, all too clearly, putting his seal and signature to a letter. In those early days he would have given his new wife anything she asked for.

The sombre voice continued. 'I was also present when your secretary brought all the jewellery into the bank last winter and I made a full and detailed inventory of all the pieces.' The old man paused and added gently, 'Your secretary signed for them all, Your Grace. Perhaps you would like to see the ledger entries?'

'No, that will not be necessary.'

Jason rubbed a hand over his eyes, thinking of the receipts Simon had brought him. He had sent his man away and stuffed the papers in the drawer without a second glance. How could he have been so stupidly naive? Even the stones in his wedding gift to Lavinia had been sold and replaced with cheap replicas.

He had given her a very generous allowance, refused her nothing, but it had clearly not been enough.

Chapter Fourteen

Jason left the bank, anger and depression weighing heavily on his spirits. It was growing dark, and he hunched himself into his greatcoat as he set off to walk back to Darvell House.

How had he allowed himself to be so deceived? And how would he tell Angel?

He could buy her new jewellery, of course. He would take her to Rundell and Bridge and beg her choose whatever she liked. But at some point he would have to explain to her what had happened to the family jewels.

As he turned off St James's Street he thought it would not be such a bad thing. He wanted no more secrets between them. She needed to know the truth. About everything.

He quickened his step, eager now to see Angel. Perhaps, at last, they could put the past behind them and start again.

He turned the corner and Darvell House was there before him. His mood lightened, just knowing Angel was in there, waiting for him. Looking up, Jason saw the golden glow of candlelight shining through the thin under-curtains in the morning room window. A shadow fell upon the muslin: a woman's figure.

Angel, he thought, smiling. His wife. His duchess.

He saw a second shadow, a man this time, and as he watched, the two joined together in an embrace.

The world tilted. Jason shook his head and looked again at the window, but the image had not changed. There could be no mistake. Angel was kissing a man, a lover. Under his own roof!

Cursing under his breath, Jason crossed the road and strode into the house, tossing his hat, gloves and cane at the footman before taking the stairs two at a time. He burst into the morning room, his hands bunching into fists.

'Take your hands off her, damn you!'

The couple jumped apart, staring at him in alarm. Only it was not Angel he saw in front of the window, but Rose.

'Jason, pray do not be angry. It is not what it seems!' Angel had been standing by the fire but now she came hurrying across to him, hands held out.

He said icily, 'I am quite capable of seeing what is going on, madam.'

'No, no! Mr Babberton is going back to Surrey. His father has broken his leg and he is needed at home.'

She was standing before him, shielding the errant lovers from his wrath.

Kenelm Babberton stepped forward. 'I set out for Winchcombe Lodge in the morning. Her Grace was kind enough to allow me to come in and take my leave of Miss Haringey.'

Jason snarled. 'You were doing a dam—dashed sight more than that when I came in!'

Babberton flushed a little and inclined his head. 'I beg your pardon. I was overcome by the violence of my feelings.'

'We are in love!' cried Rose, taking his hand. 'You cannot blame Kenelm for his actions, Papa Duke. No one with a heart would blame him!'

Jason was almost grinding his teeth. Now there were two females standing between him and Babberton! Confound it, did they think he was going to run the man through in the morning room?

He breathed deep and, with an effort, unclenched his fists.

'I should leave.' Babberton picked up his hat. 'I have booked a place on the morning mail and have yet to pack.'

He turned to Rose, taking her hand and bowing over it. He gave her a brief sustaining smile before releasing her and turning to Angel.

'Goodbye, Your Grace. And thank you for all your efforts on my behalf.'

'I am only sorry that it could not have turned out better,' replied Angel, as he bowed low to her. 'Pray, give our regards to your mother, and wish Lord Winchcombe a speedy recovery.'

'Thank you, ma'am, I shall.' Then he bowed to the Duke. 'Your Grace. We shall speak again when you return to Rotherton.'

With that, he went out, leaving a heavy silence behind him.

'Well,' muttered Jason. 'You have to admire his nerve.'

Rose glared at him, her eyes sparkling with unshed tears. '*He*, at least, behaved like a gentleman!'

Angel saw Jason frown and quickly stepped forward.

'It is time to change or we shall all be late for dinner. Have you forgotten, Rose? We are going to the Westberes' soirée tonight.'

She ushered the girl out of the room and watched her run up the stairs before closing the door and turning back to the Duke.

'Poor child. I doubt we shall see her at dinner.'

'Do you think I was too harsh on her?'

'You lost your temper.'

She waited, wondering if he would deny it, or fly into a rage.

'I thought it was you,' he said. 'When I looked up at the window and saw the figures embracing I thought it was you.'

Angel pressed one hand to her breast. That was quite a revelation, but she was not ready to forgive him just yet.

She said coldly, 'Am I supposed to be flattered that you think I would break my marriage vows?'

He raked his fingers through his hair. 'I did not *think* anything. I was afraid I had lost you.'

The quiet words and the bleak look that accompanied them tore at her heart. It was the closest the Duke had ever come to expressing his feelings and she could only guess what an effort it had been for him.

The clock on the mantelshelf chimed and Jason glanced at it.

'There is no time now, but I need to speak with you. Tonight. After dinner. Can Mrs Watson accompany Rose to the Westberes'?'

'Why, yes, if you think it necessary.'

'I do.' He nodded. 'It is essential we talk. Until dinner, then, madam.'

He gave a little bow and went out, leaving Angel a prey to such conflicting emotions she doubted she would be able to eat anything at all this evening.

In the event, no one from Darvell House attended the soirée. When Mrs Watson brought Nell to the drawing room she announced that Rose was feeling too unwell to go out, or even to join them for dinner.

'The poor child was looking so pale and drawn I sent her straight to bed,' she went on. 'I only hope it is nothing infectious.'

Angel was duly sympathetic, but as they all went in to

dinner she wished that she too might be spared the ordeal of sitting through a long meal. She had no idea what it was the Duke wished to say to her, but she wanted it over.

The atmosphere in the dining room was strained. The Duke said very little, but that was not unusual, and if Mrs Watson noticed that Angel was quieter than usual she made no mention of it, and was happy to encourage Lady Elinor to tell the Duke and Duchess about her day.

The widow had taken her to the Tower to see the wild animals, and it took very little effort on Angel's part to keep Nell chattering away on the subject for most of dinner and afterwards in the drawing room, until Mrs Watson carried her charge off to bed.

If Angel had found the meal difficult, then sitting alone in the drawing room with the Duke was even more uncomfortable. He was clearly distracted, replying mechanically to any subject she proposed. She wished she could put her arms around him and kiss away the frown that darkened his brow, but she lacked the courage. There had never been any words of love between them and she did not think she could bear it if he pushed her away.

She took up her embroidery, deciding that they would sit in silence until he was ready to talk.

Jason watched his duchess ply the needle, her dark head bowed over the tambour frame. Seeing the shadow at the window earlier and thinking it was Angel had thrown him. Only then had he realised just how much she meant to him. How much he would hate to lose her.

Then tell her, you dolt.

But the clock ticked on while he wrestled with his inner demons. It had been so easy with Lavinia. He had declared himself constantly, but her loving smiles, her kisses and caresses, had been nothing but a sham and learning that had broken him. He had started building a wall around his feelings, brick by brick, vowing he would never again leave himself so vulnerable.

And he had made an excellent job of it, he thought, bitterly. That wall was so impregnable now even *he* could not breach it.

Angel began packing away her embroidery.

'It is growing late,' she said, rising. 'I should retire.'

Jason jumped to his feet. 'No, don't go!'

'We have been sitting in silence for nigh on an hour, sir.'

'Yes. I beg your pardon. A little longer, I pray you.'

Silently she inclined her head and sat down again, folding her hands in her lap while Jason paced the room. He reminded her of a caged tiger, like the ones at the Tower that Nell had described earlier.

She prompted him. 'You said you wanted to talk to me.'

'Yes. I meant to do so when I returned from the Strand today, but when I discovered Rose and Babberton—'

'You were enraged,' she said, nodding. 'But they were only taking their leave of one another.'

'Hah! If only I could believe that!'

'You can believe it, Jason. You should. I have no doubt that Mr Babberton's intentions are quite honourable—'

He interrupted her roughly. 'It isn't Babberton's intentions that concern me!' He stopped and raked his hand through his hair. 'It's Rose. What if…?'

He paced again, clearly wrestling with himself.

He stopped and looked at her, and the pain and uncertainty in his eyes made her catch her breath.

'What if she is too much like her mother?'

Angel jerked upright in her chair. 'Why on earth should you think that?'

His chest heaved, and when he spoke his voice was grim.

'After I left Telford today I went to the bank, to look at the Rotherton jewels.' He threw her a quick, diffident glance. 'I thought you might like to wear some of the family pieces. The last time I checked there was a king's ransom in the vaults. Now there is almost nothing.' His lip curled. 'My late wife sold them—and with my blessing, apparently.'

Angel was even more mystified, but he was scowling so blackly she was loath to speak.

At length he went on. 'I was besotted, Angel! In those early years I would have given Lavinia anything her heart desired. I took her to the Strand, introduced her to my bankers and, very foolishly, signed a paper giving her free access to the jewels. Complete freedom to do whatever she wished with them.'

He turned away, walking over to the fire, where he stood, staring down into the flames.

'She chose to sell them all and replace them with paste copies.'

'And she never told you?'

'No.' A sigh shook him. 'What she did with the money I have no idea. Certainly I never saw any sign of it.'

Angel recalled the rumours she had heard. The tales of wild parties. Extravagant gowns. Lovers.

'Oh, Jason, I am so sorry.'

He raised one hand as if to ward off her sympathy.

He went on. 'I came back today to find Lavinia's daughter embracing young Babberton. Proclaiming her love for him just as Lavinia declared hers for me, years ago. If, as I fear, she is like her mother, Babberton will never be rich enough to satisfy her. Damme, he is the son of a neighbour. I have a responsibility for him, too. I cannot let him fall into the hands of a fortune-hunter.'

'Rose is no fortune-hunter, Jason. I would stake my life on it.'

'No? London has gone to her head. Even if she thinks herself in love with Babberton, he is not man enough to keep her in check.' He shook his head. 'I should never have agreed to her coming here. It is not too late to stop the sale of the Kent property. Mrs Watson can take both girls back there, out of the way.'

'Oh, no, pray do not do that! They are enjoying themselves so much, and learning a great deal, too.' Angel went over to him. 'Rose is too honest, too kind, to deceive anyone, Jason. You know that in your heart.'

'I thought the same of Lavinia, once.'

'Jason, I am sure it is not so.'

'You are *sure*?' He turned his head and fixed her with a glacial stare. 'You have spent your life hidden away in the country. What can *you* know of the world?'

Angel could see the hurt in his eyes. He had been tricked by his duplicitous wife and felt ashamed to admit it.

She said gently, 'Not much, perhaps, but—'

'Let be, madam. They are not your children, after all!'

Angel winced, but she raised her head and looked him in the eye.

'True, they are not,' she said coldly. 'But I am well enough acquainted with Rose and Nell to know that I should be *proud* to have them for my daughters. As should you, Your Grace. In fact, I know you will admit it. Once your damned temper has cooled!'

With that she turned in a swish of silken skirts and walked away, praying her legs would support her long enough to get out of the room.

* * *

As the door snapped shut behind Angel, Jason rubbed a hand over his eyes. That was badly done of him. Badly done indeed. He had lashed out at Angel and she did not deserve that. Confound it, she was trying to help him! It was his damnable temper that had prompted him to talk of sending the girls away. He did not mean it. They were his family now. As was Angel.

He stood for a while, thinking of all he should have confessed to her. Not only his first wife's perfidy but his own.

Somehow during his appointment with Telford today the talk had come around to marriage and annulments. A simple enquiry from Jason had elicited the information that these were extremely difficult to obtain and involved almost certain public humiliation for the woman.

Why had he not looked into the matter further before he had subjected Angel to the indignity of sleeping alone for so many weeks? He had demeaned her. It would serve him right if she never forgave him for that.

With sudden decision he strode out of the room and took the stairs two at a time. He stopped at the Duchess's bedchamber and tapped on the panel.

'Angel, may I come in?'

There was no answer. He walked on to his own room. A single lamp was burning but there was no sign of Adams.

He went over to the connecting door and knocked softly.

'Angel, I want to talk to you. Please, let me come in.'

She did not reply. His hand went towards the doorhandle but he drew it back. Even if it was unlocked he would not enter her bedroom uninvited.

He tried again. 'Please, Angel. I want to apologise.'

Silence.

Sick at heart, Jason turned away. He must talk to Angel

tomorrow and hope that it was not too late to put everything right. That she would give him one last chance to be the husband she deserved.

'Your Grace—*Miss Angeline*! We should go in now. You'll catch your death out here.'

Angel was tempted to tell Joan she did not care what happened to her, then berated herself for such foolishness. When she had reached her bedroom she had been too hurt and angry to sleep, and had immediately gone out again to walk in the gardens. Her maid had been scandalised and insisted on coming with her.

'Please, Your Grace, come inside.'

Angel sighed. None of the disasters that Joan had envisaged had happened. No intruders were skulking in the gardens, waiting to molest them, and Angel had not tripped and fallen in the darkness. However, she was grateful for the cashmere shawl the maid had put about her shoulders, and she could not deny that her feet in their thin satin slippers were icy cold. Which was no more than she deserved.

No matter how much she tried to tell herself she had acted for the best, Angel knew her attempts to help Rose and Mr Babberton had failed. And now Jason was going to send the girls back to Kent. She had made everything worse, not better.

Joan had asked no questions about her mistress's heavy sighs. She obviously knew the Duke was in a rage because of Mr Babberton's visit to the house and Miss Rose's subsequent absence from the dinner table, and she had already informed her mistress that everyone in the household knew it too.

'It was inevitable word would get around, ma'am, when you think of it, His Grace storming in like he did, and the second footman being right outside the morning room and hearing every word. It was all that was talked of in the servants' hall this evening, even though Mr Marcuss did his best to stop it. Trouble is, some of the younger maids see Miss Haringey and Mr Babberton as doomed sweethearts, and think the Duke a villain for keeping them apart.'

'But he is not a bad man, Joan! His Grace is trying to do what he thinks is right.'

'Whisht, now, Miss Angeline. *I* know that, and so do most of the servants. They remember the Duke's first duchess, and not with much affection either. I am not one for gossiping, but they all say she led His Grace a merry dance from the start, truth be told, what with her extravagance and wicked ways. And His Grace never allowing a word to be said against her! It's impossible to keep things from servants, as you well know. Not that anyone would dare to speak of it outside these four walls, for it would be instant dismissal if they did, the Duke not being one to pardon such disloyalty.'

No, thought Angel sadly, Jason did not forgive easily.

She shivered and turned to her maid, grasping her hands.

'Was it a mistake, Joan? Was I wrong to marry the Duke?'

If Angel was hoping for a strong denial it was not forthcoming. She felt tears prickling in her eyes. What a silly, naïve fool she had been to think she could ever make him happy.

Joan put a comforting arm about her shoulders and turned her towards the house. 'Come, now, Miss Angeline, it's not like you to be so downhearted. Come inside. 'tis growing late and you know you will feel better after a good night's sleep.'

Angel woke to a grey, overcast dawn and a pressing sense of foreboding which was not lessened when her maid informed her that the Duke had requested his duchess's presence in the morning room before breakfast.

She dressed quickly, but before she left the bedchamber she asked Joan to look in on Rose.

'Mrs Watson is taking Nell to the Ragholmes', and I am very much afraid that if Rose is left to herself she will keep to her room. I hope you can persuade her to come down to breakfast, Joan. It will do her no good to mope.'

'Very well, ma'am. I will do my best, just as soon as I have finished in here.'

'Be kind to her, Joan, the poor child is heartbroken,' said Angel.

She gave a little sigh, straightened her shoulders and went out.

The Duke was already in the morning room when Angel went in. He was standing by the window, his broad shoulders blocking out much of the already poor morning light.

He said, as she shut the door, 'I thought you might not come, after the way I ripped up at you last night. Are you very angry with me?'

'I am, Your Grace.'

'Ah, don't call me that, Angel! I wish you had flown at me last night, told me that I was being quite unreasonable.'

'Would it have done any good?'

'Possibly not. But I need my duchess to remind me that I can be damnably ill-mannered at times.'

'Yes, you can be,' she told him. 'You are often odiously overbearing. High-handed, too.'

'Then I give you leave to tell me whenever you find me being so *odious*, as you put it.'

When she made no reply, he sighed. 'The problem with being a duke is that one is rarely contradicted. One is fêted, fawned upon and allowed to ride roughshod over everyone without ever being corrected.' He bit his lip. 'A duke is also expected to be some sort of superior being. To have no feelings. To show no sorrow or remorse.'

Her anger melted away. She said, remembering the fifteen-year-old Jason, 'And you became a duke far too young.'

'Help me, Angel.' He reached out to her. 'Help me to be a better man. A better husband and father. Tell me when I am being a fool or a tyrant.'

She went to him, saying, as she took his hands, 'And will you promise not to rage at me?'

'I will do my best to curb my temper. And who else is to correct me, if not my duchess?' He shook his head at her. 'I know you did not marry me for love, Angel, but I hope, in time, you could come to care for me.'

'Oh, I do,' she said quickly.

'Truly?' His eyes searched her face. 'As much as you cared for that scoundrel who broke your heart?'

Something between a laugh and a sob escaped her. 'Far, far more than that, Jason. In fact, I have quite forgotten him!'

His look softened. 'You do not know how happy that makes me.' A small sigh of relief escaped him. 'I shall not be sending Rose and Nell away, Angel. That was said in the heat of the moment and I regret it now, very much. But believe me, it was not born of malice. It was inadequacy. I am at a loss to know how to go on as a parent.'

Angel felt a sudden constriction in her chest. Jason was not a man to admit any weakness. She knew it had cost him dear to say that.

'Then we shall learn together,' she said, squeezing his fingers. 'We will make mistakes, I am sure, but I believe, if we both try, we can be a happy family.'

Her spirits sang at the warm look in his eyes. He pulled her closer, holding her hands against his heart, and she held her breath, waiting for him to say the words she longed to hear. Waiting for him to say that he loved her.

'Angel—' He broke off as a knock sounded and the door opened. 'Yes, Marcuss, what is it now?'

The butler did not flinch at his master's impatient tone.

'Her Grace's dresser wishes to have a word with the Duchess, sir.'

'The devil she does!'

Angel shushed him and instructed the butler to send Joan in.

'She would not interrupt us if it was not urgent,' she said, as Marcuss disappeared.

He returned a moment later, with the dresser hurrying in behind him.

'Well?' barked Jason. 'What is it?'

Joan was clearly not to be put off, even by a duke. She said, 'I should like a word my mistress, if I may, Your Grace. Alone.'

Angel went to move away, but Jason held on to her hand. 'You can say whatever it is here, before both of us. And it had better be important!'

Angel tutted. 'Odiously high-handed!' she murmured, before turning back to her dresser. 'Go on, Joan, what is it?'

'It's Miss Haringey, madam,' said Joan, throwing a fulminating glance towards the Duke. 'She has eloped!'

Chapter Fifteen

'*Eloped!*' Angel's hands flew to her cheeks. 'I do not believe it. Excuse me, sir, I must go and talk to her maid—'

'No.' Jason stopped her. 'We will deal with this together. Bring the girl in here, if you please.'

When the dresser had gone, he turned to Angel.

'Rose is my ward, my responsibility. It is only right that I should be involved in this.' He saw the uncertainty in her eyes and added, 'I shall not lose my temper. I give you my word, but if she has eloped, time will be crucial in finding her. It is best I know everything from the start.'

'I am hoping there is some misunderstanding,' said Angel, clasping and unclasping her hands. 'I cannot believe she would be so lost to all sense of propriety.'

He said grimly, 'Believe me, young people in love are capable of anything.'

They did not have to wait long until the dresser returned, bringing with her Rose's maid.

The girl was shaking as Joan led her forward, saying, 'Now, then, Edith, tell them everything you told me.'

'But I don't *know* anything, and that's the truth!' cried the unfortunate maid, screwing her apron between her hands. 'Miss Rose went out in the early hours and she d-didn't come back.'

'But that's not the whole of it, is it?' put in Joan, folding her arms. 'You must tell them about the letter.'

'Letter?' said Angel. 'She received a letter?'

The maid looked more frightened than ever.

'Y-yes, ma'am. It c-came last evening.'

'Not with the post, then,' muttered Jason. 'Who took it in?'

The girl looked up at him, her eyes wide with fear.

'Well?'

He kept his tone calm, but just the fact of being addressed by a duke was too much for Edith. She threw her apron over her head and burst into tears.

He swallowed an oath of frustration and Angel put a hand on his arm, giving him a warning glance before stepping up to the girl.

'There is no need for this, Edith,' she said firmly. 'No one is going to punish you as long as you tell the truth now. How did Miss Haringey come by the letter? Did you give it to her?'

'Yes, ma'am.' The words were almost lost in a fresh bout of weeping.

'And who gave it to you?'

'The under-footman. He'd been sent to the mews last night, to tell them that we wouldn't be needing the coach after all, and on his way back a man came up with a letter for my mistress.'

'And where is the note now?' asked Angel.

Joan put her hand in her pocket and pulled out a folded paper. 'I have it here, safe.'

Angel took the letter and unfolded it.

Jason looked over her shoulder and scanned it, muttering some passages aloud.

'*"My dearest Rose...cannot leave without speaking to you once more...the Bull and Mouth...will send a carriage for you...waiting at the end of the street at five o'clock tomorrow morning...*" And the rogue has signed it with a K!'

He slammed a fist into his palm.

'Damned scoundrel! So Rose *has* eloped!'

'No, no, look!' exclaimed Angel. 'It says "to bring you to the inn and back again". Do you not see? She intended to come back.'

Joan nodded. 'Aye, and that's what she told her maid. With your permission, Your Grace,' she went on, looking at the weeping servant. 'I will take Edith to her room now. I doubt she can be of any more use to you.'

'Yes, yes, off you go.' Jason waved them away. 'But try if you can to stop her from chattering with the rest of the household.'

Joan nodded. 'I will, Your Grace, never fear.'

Angel said, as the door closed behind them, 'If Rose has not returned, then Mr Babberton must have persuaded her to run off with him.'

'Aye, dashed rogue!' declared Jason. 'I will send out runners to find which way they went.'

He had not gone two steps towards the door when Marcuss came in again.

'Mr Babberton to see you, Your Grace.'

The young man himself strode into the room even before the butler had finished announcing him.

'I beg your pardon for the intrusion,' he said, sketching a quick bow. 'I have just—'

Jason cut him off. 'Where is Miss Haringey?'

'That lady is the reason for my calling here,' replied Mr Babberton, in his measured way. 'I believe she has been abducted.'

'But not by you?' exclaimed Angel.

The young man looked offended. 'No, no, of course not.'

Jason dismissed the butler.

'I think you had best tell us the whole,' he said. 'Quickly, man!'

'Well, Your Grace, I was in the street here earlier, about five o'clock.'

'Wait—what were you doing here at that time in the morning?' demanded Jason.

'I had ordered a hackney to take me to Cheapside, from where I was taking the coach to Surrey. Having a little time to spare, I asked the driver to stop at the corner of Piccadilly and I, er, strolled down here.'

'In the early hours?' exclaimed Angel. 'What on earth did you think to achieve by that?'

'Nothing.' He flushed. 'I just wanted to be near Rose.'

Angel looked bewildered, but Jason understood completely. He remembered how he had felt, standing outside Darvell House yesterday.

He nodded. 'Go on.'

'A post-chaise pulled up at the door and I saw someone come out of the house. She was wrapped in a cloak, but I recognised it as Miss Haringey. She climbed into the waiting carriage, which set off immediately, and at pace.'

'Good God!' exclaimed Jason. 'She has been flirting with some other fellow all this time.'

'No, I will not believe that,' declared Angel.

'Nor I,' said Babberton. 'Rose would not do that. She had no baggage with her, not even a bandbox. The chaise rattled past me but it was too dark to see who was inside, so I ran back to Piccadilly and told my own cab driver to follow. At first it was not difficult, because we took the narrower streets, but it was more difficult after the tollgate at Tottenham Court Road. However, by making enquiries I tracked them as far as Barnet.'

'In a *hackney cab*?' asked Jason.

'Yes, although I had to pay the fellow handsomely to do it, and we were considerably slower than a post-chaise. Only at Barnet he refused to go any further, so I thought it best to come back and tell you what had occurred.'

'Then you did not send this?' Jason thrust the note at him.

Babberton studied it closely and shook his head. 'No.' He handed it back. 'That is not my writing. Also, my coach leaves from Blossoms Inn, not the Bull and Mouth.'

'Rose would not know that,' Angel pointed out.

'And I should never sign a letter in such a familiar manner, even to Miss Haringey.'

Jason looked again at the curly 'K' at the bottom of the paper and his blood chilled.

'Knowsley,' he ground out. 'She has run off with Toby Knowsley. Hell and damnation! He would know the Bull and Mouth. In all likelihood he hired the post chaise from there.'

'And he is your heir,' said Babberton in dismay. 'Could it be she never really cared for me?'

'No, no, I cannot believe that,' Angel told him. 'She would never go off with Mr Knowsley willingly. She does not even like him.'

'Whether she likes him or not is immaterial. She ain't going to marry him,' muttered Jason, ringing the bell. 'I am going after them. They are a few hours ahead, but my curricle will give me a good chance of catching them before nightfall.'

A servant entered and he barked out a series of orders.

When the man had withdrawn Babberton stepped forward. 'I shall come with you, Your Grace.'

'The devil you will!'

'Sir, I insist. You may need me when we catch up with

them, and I am sure I can handle a yard of tin as well as your groom. I will not slow you up, Your Grace.'

Jason saw the determined look in his eyes and nodded. 'Very well. Wait here while I go and change!'

Jason dashed away, and Angel was left alone with Mr Babberton.

'You will have missed your coach to Surrey,' she remarked, to break the silence.

'That is not important. All that matters is finding Miss Haringey and bringing her home safe.' He coughed, and looked slightly embarrassed. 'I took the liberty of bringing in my bags and depositing them in the hall, ma'am. The cab driver was not inclined to wait.'

'No, of course.' She nodded. 'I fear, when the Duke catches up with them, he will challenge Mr Knowsley to a duel.'

The young man's rather cheerful face took on a very black look. 'If he doesn't, then I shall!'

Angel relapsed into silence, realising it was pointless to ask him to keep the Duke out of trouble.

Ten minutes later Jason ran down the stairs to find his curricle at the door and Babberton and his wife waiting for him.

'God speed, Jason,' Angel clutched at his hands. 'Bring Rose home safely.'

'I will. Do not worry.'

He kissed her fingers and smiled down at her, but the anxious look was still in her eyes when he left her.

The hours ticked by. Angel took a solitary breakfast and then wandered disconsolately through the empty rooms. She could not settle to anything, she was far too anxious. She was fearful that Jason would not find Rose and Tobias Knowsley, and even more concerned that he would. The idea of the Duke fighting a duel terrified her. She could not bear the thought of him killing a man or being killed himself.

When the butler came to find her, carrying a folded missive on the silver tray, she snatched it up.

'Oh,' she said, her spirits dipping. 'It is from Lady Ragholme, requesting that Lady Elinor and Mrs Watson might be allowed to remain for dinner.'

At least it meant she need not tell them about Rose until later. She forced a smile to her lips.

'She assures me she will provide outriders to escort them back to town later tonight. I shall pen a reply immediately, Marcuss. Please have a servant ready to carry it to Ragholme Hall.'

The task took only a few minutes, and then she was back to pacing the floor and trying to prevent her imagination from conjuring up the very worst scenarios. The ones in which Jason was lost to her for ever.

The short November day dragged on into darkness.

Angel instructed that dinner should be put back, and settled down in the morning room with her embroidery, plying her needle by the light from a branched candlestick.

Mrs Watson returned with Nell, who was too full of her splendid day out to question Angel's explanation that Rose was at a party of pleasure with her friends.

Once Nell was tucked up in her bed Angel went to find Mrs Watson and tell her what she knew, which seemed pitifully scant, but she refused to allow the widow to sit up with her.

'There is nothing we can do until we have some news,' Angel told her. 'It would be best if you get some rest now. Then you will be fresh to deal with anything that is required in the morning.'

'Very well, Your Grace, I will go to my bed. Although I doubt I shall sleep until I know my darling girl is safe.'

She went off then, and Angel went back to her embroidery, only to be interrupted shortly after by the butler.

'Cook has asked me if you wish him to put dinner back again, Your Grace.'

Angel hesitated, and Marcuss gave a little cough.

'I would suggest another hour, ma'am. It is important that the household thinks we expect the Duke to return shortly.'

She looked up at him. 'Does everyone know what has occurred?'

The butler shook his head. 'No, Your Grace. There was some speculation this morning, of course, but that was confounded when His Grace went off with Mr Babberton.'

'Yes, that is something, I suppose.' She sighed. 'Very well. Another hour, then.'

Bowing, the old retainer withdrew, and Angel was left with her thoughts. She knew Jason would not rest until he had found Rose, but could he bring her home unharmed? And if not, what vengeance might he wreak upon his cousin?

The sound of voices intruded.

Angel threw aside her embroidery and jumped to her feet just as the door opened.

'Jason!' She stared at him, her eyes widening in dismay to see he was alone. 'What…? Where…? Oh, thank goodness!'

The frantic worry faded when she saw Mr Babberton coming into the room, one arm firmly around Rose. He was holding her close against him, but when Rose saw Angel and put out her hands he released her immediately.

'She is unharmed,' he said, as Rose fell into Angel's arms, 'But she is naturally distressed and exhausted.'

'We shall get her upstairs as soon as possible,' said Angel. 'I have already ordered hot bricks to be put in her bed.'

'Not yet!' cried Rose, clinging tighter. 'I could not sleep just yet.'

'Very well, then. You shall sit with me until you are ready.' Angel guided Rose to the sofa. 'But I should very much like to know what happened. Would you mind if we talk of it?'

'N-no.'

They were just sitting down when the door opened again.

'I have ordered refreshments to be brought in,' explained Jason as the butler and a footman put down their trays upon the side table. 'Marcuss says it will be an hour before dinner is ready. I thought some wine and bread and butter in the meantime might not go amiss.'

'And there is a cup of hot chocolate for Miss Haringey,' added the butler, his kindly eyes shadowed with concern. 'If she would care for it?'

Rose did care for it. She declared that the warm drink and a slice of bread was all she required.

Kenelm Babberton immediately fetched them over to her, placing the cup and plate on a table beside her while the Duke poured wine for everyone else.

'How far were you obliged to travel?' asked Angel, when they were all seated.

'To Huntingdon,' said Jason.

'It would have been a lot further if Miss Haringey had not had the presence of mind to pretend that she was a poor traveller,' put in Kenelm, smiling fondly at Rose. 'She insisted she would be violently ill if the postboys did not slow down.'

Rose shuddered. 'It was horrible. Mr Knowsley k-kept calling me L-Lavinia…and saying he w-worshipped me.' She sat up a little straighter, saying angrily, 'He tricked me!'

'By signing himself "K," knowing you would think it was Mr Babberton?' asked Angel.

'No, that, apparently, was mere coincidence, but it worked

in Knowsley's favour,' said the Duke, draining his glass. 'He knew Rose would not consent to an elopement, so he promised to bring her back here.'

'I would n-never have left the house if I had known it was not Kenelm!' exclaimed Rose, sending the young man a look full of apology. 'And I *should* have known. I should have realised that he is too good, too honourable, to suggest a meeting after he had given his word to Papa.'

'You are quite correct, I would not,' replied Mr Babberton, returning her look with an ardent one of his own. 'Even though it was breaking my heart to leave London without you.'

'Yes, well, we can talk more of this tomorrow.' Jason rose abruptly. 'Rose can hardly keep her eyes open. She needs to go to bed.'

'Yes, of course,' said Angel. 'Come along, my dear, I will take you to your room.'

Rose got up meekly and went with her towards the door, but as she passed Kenelm Babberton she stopped. 'I would like to properly express my gratitude to you for rescuing me today,' she murmured. 'Shall I see you in the morning?'

It was the Duke who replied.

'You can hardly avoid it. Babberton is sleeping here tonight.'

Both Rose and Angel stared at him.

'It would be nigh on impossible for him to find anywhere to stay at this time of night,' he said gruffly. 'I have had his bags taken up to one of the guest rooms.'

'Oh, how *kind* you are, Papa!'

Angel observed Jason's look of surprise when Rose threw her arms around him and hugged him. She then gave Kenelm another shy smile before allowing herself to be taken off to bed.

Angel handed Rose over to the care of her maid and went

back to the morning room, where she found Jason alone and sitting on a sofa.

'Babberton is gone off to change his coat before we dine,' he explained, holding out her refilled wine glass. 'Do you mind my being here in all my dirt? I fear if I go upstairs I shall be too tired to come down again.'

'Not at all,' she said, sitting beside him. 'You have had a very wearing day.'

'Damnable.'

One question had been nagging away at her since his return. She said, 'I did not like to ask while Rose was present, but your cousin…?'

'We left him in Huntingdon with his post-chaise, free to go where the devil he wishes.' He hesitated. 'I saw the look on your face when we left. You were worried about what I might do.'

'I was afraid you would fight with him.'

'I was very tempted when we walked into the George and found him in a private parlour, trying to put his arm about Rose. Babberton saved me the trouble. Before I could stop him he pulled Knowsley to his feet and dealt him a crashing blow to the chin. Kenelm was all for calling him out, but I persuaded him against it.'

'You did?'

'Yes. You look astonished.'

'I am. I thought…'

'You thought I would run him through!' He shrugged. 'It didn't take me long to realise the fellow is not in his right mind. He began by talking of Rose's resemblance to her mother and saying he could not help himself. Then he began calling her Lavinia. He took great pleasure in telling me that they had been lovers since shortly after Nell was born, although I know very well he was not the only one.'

His mouth twisted. 'She cast her favours very wide, it seems. Including royalty.'

'Oh, heavens! And that did not make you lose your temper?'

He shook his head. 'I had suspected it already. What I did not know was that she had sold the Darvell jewels to pay Knowsley's gambling debts, as well as her own. The twisted logic being that the money would be his to spend one day.'

'Oh, that was very wrong of them!' exclaimed Angel. 'That makes me so angry. I think now that Mr Knowsley *should* be punished!'

'And so he will be—but not by me. He is already in debt again, and now I have remarried it is unlikely his creditors will consider his claims to be my heir are very strong. He will most likely have to fly the country.' He glanced at her. 'I thought you'd consider that a better solution than my fighting with him.'

'I do,' she told him. 'Not merely because duelling is against the law, Jason, but for your own peace of mind. I know you would regret it if you killed him.' She twisted her hands together for a moment before going on. 'It must have been difficult for you *not* to call him out. Knowing how he and Lavinia deceived you.'

'Do you know, it was not that hard at all? When I saw the fellow gibbering about losing his head over Rose, just because of her resemblance to her mother, all I felt was pity.' He took the glass from her and put it down with his own on the nearest table before pulling her into his arms. 'I was besotted with Lavinia once, Angel, but that was a very long time ago, and for the last few years of our marriage I hated her. I hated myself, too, for being such a fool. I was filled with loathing and regret, but now even that has faded to almost nothing.'

'Oh, has it?' she asked, intently studying his neckcloth.

'Yes. I realise now that what I felt for her was infatuation. Nothing like the deep and abiding love I feel for you, Angel mine.' His fingers gently pushed her chin up and he kissed her. 'It has taken me far too long to tell you that. I have struggled against admitting it, even to myself, but I am saying it now and I will continue to say it every day of my life if you will let me.' His arms tightened. 'Can you ever forgive me for being such a crass fool, my love?'

'Of course I can,' she said softly.

'And…one more thing,' he said, clearly determined there should be no more secrets. 'About the annulment. It is far more complicated than non-consummation and involves a very public investigation, which I would never put you through, Angel. I was quite wrong about it.'

'Now, that I can never forgive!' she exclaimed wrathfully. 'When I think of those weeks…the nights when I longed for you to take me to your bed—'

'You must not think that I did not suffer too,' he said, with feeling. 'Oh, Angel, what can I do to make it up to you? I do love you, you know. Quite desperately!'

'I think it is going to take a very long time,' she murmured, slipping her arms about his neck. 'But those words are a good start. I have been waiting my whole life for you to say them.'

He kissed her face, her eyes, her nose, her cheeks, whispering, 'I love you!' over and over, until she was sighing with happiness. Then, with a growl of triumph, he captured her lips and kissed her long and thoroughly.

Thus it was that Mr Babberton, coming into the room, saw the Duke and Duchess entwined in each other's arms and softly withdrew again.

Epilogue

April sunshine poured down upon Rotherton House, which was filled with family and friends staying for the wedding of Mr Kenelm Babberton and Miss Rose Haringey. The state rooms had been turned into one vast ballroom for the evening celebrations, but now everyone was driving off to the little church in Middlewych for the ceremony itself.

Everyone except the Duke and Duchess of Rotherton.

Angel went in search of Jason and found him in his dressing room, standing before the looking glass and wrestling with his cravat. The floor around him was littered with lengths of discarded muslin, mute witness to his failed attempts.

He met her eyes in the mirror. 'I cannot get the confounded knot right!'

'We have a few minutes yet. The last of the guests have only just left and I have sent Rose on ahead with Mama. They will meet us inside the church.' She hid a smile when another mauled cravat was thrown to the floor. 'Where is Adams? Can he not help?'

'I sent him away. Damme, I have never yet let my valet tie my neckcloth!'

She waited quietly while he arranged a fresh length of muslin about his neck and tied an intricate knot.

'There.' He gave one of the folds a final tweak and looked at himself critically in the glass. 'That will have to do, I suppose.'

She stepped closer and placed one hand on his chest while she inspected his efforts. 'That is very good, but will it stop you kissing me?'

In answer to her teasing, he dragged her into his arms.

'Well, madam,' he said, when he finally raised his head, 'how does it look now?'

'You have probably quite ruined it!' she said crossly, her cheeks burning.

He turned towards the looking glass.

'No,' he said, studying himself critically. 'In fact, I think it looks better. If anyone asks, I shall tell them it is called the Angel's Kiss. What think you?'

'I think you are being nonsensical,' she told him, trying to sound severe, although she knew there was a deep blush of pleasure on her cheeks. 'You have yet to fasten the diamond pin in place.'

'Will you do that for me?'

'Of course.'

Angel picked it up from the dressing table and when she turned back he was holding out one hand, observing its slight tremble.

'I have no idea why I am so nervous today.'

'Hush. Keep your chin up,' she admonished him. 'Your stepdaughter is getting married. It is no wonder you want it to go well. Be easy, my love, it is only a country wedding, like our own.'

He huffed out a sigh. 'I was never this anxious when we were married.'

He was silent as she inserted the pin carefully between the snowy folds of muslin at his throat, then he exclaimed, 'We should have been married in town, with all the pomp that a duchess deserves!'

She chuckled. 'That would have taken a whole year to organise. As it is we have been married for twelve months and thus we can concentrate upon Rose's nuptials.' The pin secure, she placed her hands against his chest again and smiled lovingly up at him. 'Believe me, Jason, I was very happy to be married from Goole Park, with all my family around me.'

'And now, Angel mine?' He covered her hands with his own, his grey eyes searching his face. 'Are you truly happy now?'

'Oh, can you doubt it, my love?' She stretched up to kiss him lightly, then tucked her hand in his. 'Come along, Your Grace. Everyone will be waiting for us. You must do your duty by your stepdaughter.'

'Duty, bah! You know I abhor all this fuss.'

She chuckled. 'You might as well get used to it, my love. Look upon it as practice for when Nell marries. And then, of course, there will be our own children.' She placed one hand on the swell of her belly, where their baby was growing within her. 'I hope this will be the first of many.'

Jason's face softened for a moment, then he said gruffly, 'That is another reason we should not be doing this. You should be resting.'

'Fustian! I am feeling very well.' She threw him a saucy glance from under her lashes. 'When we were in bed this morning you said I was blooming.'

He relented then, as she had known he would.

'And you are. You get more beautiful every day.'

He bent his head and kissed her again.

Angel felt the tug of desire as his lips captured hers, so strong it was a physical ache, and she gave a little sigh of disappointment when he stopped.

'It is my turn to remind you of our duty, madam,' he murmured, his eyes glinting.

He took her arm and escorted out to the waiting carriage.

They bowled through the spring sunshine to the little parish church, where they found the vicar waiting at the door.

'All the guests are inside and seated, Your Grace,' he greeted them. 'If you are ready to join them?'

Jason waved him on. 'Aye, aye, let us go in. Lead the way, sir.'

The vicar went ahead of them and disappeared into the shadowed interior of the church, but Jason held back. Angel glanced up and saw his face was grim, set. The look of a private man steeling himself for another public appearance.

Her fingers moved from his sleeve to his hand. 'Come along, my love. We can do this together.'

The tension eased, he gripped her hand. 'With you beside me, my angel, I can do anything.'

She returned his smile, tucked her hand back into his sleeve, and silently they went together into the church.

* * * * *

If you enjoyed this story, be sure to read
Sarah Mallory's other great reads

Snowbound with the Brooding Lord
The Major and the Scandalous Widow
The Night She Met the Duke
The Duke's Family for Christmas
Cinderella and the Scarred Viscount

And be sure to check out her
Lairds of Ardvarrick miniseries

Forbidden to the Highland Laird
Rescued by Her Highland Soldier
The Laird's Runaway Wife